Six Great Stories

The fight at the stockade

Six Great STORIES

Edited by

GERTRUDE MODEROW
MARY YOST SANDRUS
JOSEPHINE MITCHELL
ERNEST C. NOYES

Illustrated by

ALEXANDER KEY

SCOTT, FORESMAN AND COMPANY
CHICAGO·ATLANTA·DALLAS·NEW YORK

14,494

557

Table of Contents

Treasure Island

This is a boy's story told by a boy. It is about a one-legged sailor and his parrot, a desert island, pirates, buried treasure, and fights on land and sea.

"Look out for the seaman with one leg."

2

Treasure Island

*Written by Robert Louis
Stevenson, an English au-
thor, who lived from 1850
to 1894 . . . Published first
in 1883 . . . Still a best seller.*

PART I
THE OLD BUCCANEER

Chapter I

The Old Sea-Dog[1] at the "Admiral Benbow"

I AM telling this story
because Squire[2] Trelawney, Doctor Livesey,
and the rest of these gentlemen have asked
me to write it, and to tell everything except
where the island is. I shall not tell where it
is because there is still treasure hidden there,
but I shall tell the rest of the story from the

[1]**Sea-Dog**, an old sailor. [2]**Squire**, a country gentleman in
England.

3

time when my father kept the "Admiral Benbow Inn" and the brown old seaman with the sword cut first came to live there.

I can see him as if it were yesterday, as he came to the inn door with his sea-chest following behind him in a hand-cart. He was a tall, strong, heavy, nut-brown man. His pigtail fell over the shoulders of his soiled blue coat. His hands were big, with black, broken nails, and across one side of his face he had an ugly white scar. He looked around and whistled to himself, then broke out in that old sea-song that he sang so often:

"Fifteen men on the dead man's chest—
Yo-ho-ho and a bottle of rum!"[3]

Then he rapped on the door with a stick that he carried, and when my father came, called loudly for a glass of rum. This he took slowly, still looking about him at the high hills and up at our sign-board.

[3]**rum,** a strong drink.

"This is a handy place," he said at last, "and a pleasant place for a grog[4] shop. Do you have much company?"

My father told him no, very little company—he wished there were more.

"Well, then," he said, "this is the place for me. Here, you, bring up my chest!" he cried to the man who came with him.

"I'll stay here a bit," he told my father. "I'm a plain man; rum and bacon and eggs is what I want, and that head[5] up there for to watch ships off. What might you call me? You might call me captain. Oh, I see what you want—there," and he threw down three or four gold pieces. "You can tell me when I have eaten up all of that," he said, looking very fierce, indeed.

And bad as his clothes were, and roughly as he spoke, he did not look like a common sailor. He looked like a man who would make

[4]**grog**, a strong drink mixed with water. [5]**head**, a point of high land running into the water.

people obey him or would strike if they did not. The man with him told us the stage-coach had brought him down that morning to the "Royal George Inn" and that he had asked what inns there were along the coast. He heard that ours was good and had decided to live there. And that was all we could learn of the captain.

He was a man who talked very little. All day he stayed around the house or upon the hills with a spy-glass.[6] All evening he sat in a corner near the fire, and drank rum and water very strong. Often he would not speak when we spoke to him—he would look up sudden and cross and blow so loudly through his nose that we and the people who came to our house soon learned to let him be. Every day, when he came back from his walk, he would ask if any seaman had gone along the road. At first we thought he wanted company of his own

[6]**spy-glass,** a glass by which one can see things a long way off.

kind, but at last we saw that he wanted to keep away from them. When a seaman came to the "Admiral Benbow Inn," he would look in at him through the door before coming into the room, and at those times he was always as quiet as a mouse. For me there was no secret about the matter, for I, too, was afraid.

He had promised me one day that he would pay me four pennies on the first of every month if I would keep my "eye open for a seaman with one leg" and let him know if any came. Often enough, when the first of the month came around, and I asked him for my money, he would only blow through his nose and look very cross. But before the week was out, he was sure to think better of it, bring me my money, and tell me again to look out for "the seaman with one leg."

How much I feared that one-legged man, even in my dreams, I cannot tell you. On stormy nights, when the wind shook the whole house and the waves roared along the bay and up the rocks, I would dream of him in a thousand forms. Now the leg was off at the knee, now at the hip; and again he was a huge man who had never had but one leg, and that was in the middle of his body. To see him jump and follow me over fields and fences was the worst of dreams. And you may be sure I earned the money the captain paid me.

But though I was so afraid of the seaman with one leg, I was far less afraid of the captain himself than any other who knew him. There were nights when he took much more drink than his head would carry, and then he would sit and sing his wild old sea songs. Sometimes he would make all of the frightened company listen to his stories or sing with him. Often I have heard the house shake with his "Yo-ho-ho and a bottle of rum," all the others joining in for dear life and each in his fear singing louder than the other. For in these fits he would often strike his hand upon the table and grow very angry at a question. Sometimes he was angry because no question was asked, and so he thought we were not following his story. Nor would he let anyone leave the room till he had drunk himself sleepy and gone off to bed.

His stories were what frightened people most of all—stories about hanging, and walking the plank,[7] and storms at sea, and wild deeds, and places on the Spanish Main.[8] He must have lived his life among some of the most wicked men that God ever let go on the sea; and the words he used in these stories frightened our plain country people almost as much as the bad deeds of which he told. My father was always saying that people would stop coming to the inn because of their fear of him, but I believe his being there helped our business. People were afraid at the time,

[7]**walking the plank,** "being put to death by walking along and off a plank extending from a ship's side over the water." —Thorndike Dictionary. [8]**Spanish Main,** the northeast coast of South America and the sea near it.

but on looking back they really liked it. It was a fine bit of change in a quiet country life; and there was always a party of young men who seemed to look up to him. They called him a "true sea-dog" and a "real old salt," and such names, and said there was the kind of man that made England feared on the sea.

In one way he was about to ruin us, for he kept on staying week after week and month after month, so that all the money he had given us had been gone a long time, and still my father did not have the heart to ask him for more. If ever he spoke of it, the captain would blow through his nose so loudly that my poor father would creep out of the room, and I am sure that his death came sooner and was more unhappy because of the fear in which he lived.

All the time he lived with us, the captain made almost no change in his clothes. When part of the brim of his hat fell down, he let it hang from that day on, though it was often in his way. Before the end, his coat was nothing but patches which he himself had put on. He never wrote or received a letter. He never spoke except to the neighbors, and he spoke to them only when he was drunk. None of us had ever seen him open his great chest.

Only once did anyone cross him, and that was when my poor father had become very ill. Doctor Livesey came late one afternoon to see him, took a bit of dinner from my mother, and sat down to smoke until his horse came from the village. The doctor had hair as white as snow, and bright, black eyes, and pleasant manners. The captain was very dirty. Very drunk, he sat with his arms on the table. Suddenly he began to sing his old song:

"Fifteen men on the dead man's
chest—
Yo-ho-ho and a bottle of rum!
Drink and the devil have done
for the rest—
Yo-ho-ho and a bottle of rum!"

At first I had thought "the dead man's chest" to be that big box in his room. I had even dreamed of it along with the one-legged seaman.

But by this time we had almost stopped paying any notice to his song. That night it was new to only Dr. Livesey, who, I knew, did not like it. He looked up quite angry before he went on with his talk, but the captain sang on and at last struck the table in a way we all knew to mean—"Be quiet!" All but Dr. Livesey stopped talking. He went on, clear and kind, drawing at his pipe after every word or two.

The captain glared at him, struck his hand again, glared still harder, and then cried out with a curse, "Quiet, there!"

"Did you speak to me, sir?" asked the doctor.

When the captain told him, with another curse, that he had, the doctor replied, "I have only one thing to say to you, sir, that if you keep on drinking, the world will soon be free of a very dirty scoundrel!"

The old fellow's anger was terrible. He jumped to his feet, pulled out and opened a knife, and cried out that he would pin the doctor to the wall.

The doctor never so much as moved. He spoke to the captain over his shoulder as before, and in a rather high voice so that all in the room might hear, "If you do not put that knife up at once, I promise, upon my honor, you shall hang for it."

Then followed a battle of looks between them, but the captain put up his knife and went back to his seat like a beaten dog.

"And now, sir," continued the doctor, "since I know there is such a fellow here, you may be sure I shall have my eye on you day and night. I am not a doctor, only—I am an officer of the law; and if I hear another word against you, I shall see that you are driven out."

Soon after that the doctor's horse came to the door and he rode away, but the captain was quiet that evening and for many evenings to come.

Chapter II

Black Dog Appears and Disappears

Soon after this a strange thing happened—the first of a number of strange things which at last freed us of the captain. His affairs still troubled us, however, as you will see. It was a very cold winter with long, hard frosts and high winds; and we feared from the first that my poor father would not live to see the spring. Every day he grew weaker. My mother and I had to care for the inn alone and were kept busy enough without thinking much of our unpleasant guest.

It was one January morning, very early—a cold, frosty morning—the bay was all gray, the sun was still low, only touching the hill-top and shining far out on the sea. The captain was up earlier than usual and set out along the shore, his sword swinging under his old blue coat, his spy-glass under his arm, and his hat on the back of his head. His breath

15

looked like smoke as he walked away, and the last sound I heard of him, as he turned the big rock, was a cry of anger, as though he was still thinking of the doctor.

Mother was with Father, and I was setting the table for the captain's breakfast, when the door opened and in stepped a man whom I had never seen before. He was pale and fat and had lost two fingers of the left hand; and though he wore a sword, he did not look like a fighting man. I was always watching for seamen, with one leg or two, and this one looked strange to me. He did not look like a seaman, and yet he had the air of a seaman about him.

I asked him what he wanted, and he said he would take a drink; but as I was going out of the room to bring it, he sat down on a table and told me to come near. I stopped where I was.

"Come here, son," said he. "Come nearer here."

I took a step nearer.

16

"Is this table for my mate[1] Bill?" he asked, with a kind of sneer.[2]

I told him I did not know his mate Bill, and this was for a man who stayed at our house, whom we called the captain.

"Well," said he, "my mate Bill would be called the captain as like as not. He has a cut on one cheek, and a mighty pleasant way with him, especially in drink, has my mate Bill. We'll say that your captain has a cut on one cheek—and we'll say, if you like, that that cheek is the right one. Ah, well! I told you. Now, is my mate Bill in this here house?"

I told him he was out walking.

"Which way, son? Which way is he gone?"

I pointed out the rock, and told him the captain would return soon, and answered a few other questions. "Oh," said he, "this will be as good as drink to my mate Bill."

---

[1]mate, in this case, a shipmate, a fellow sailor on a ship.
[2]sneer, a look which shows that one person looks down upon another.

17

His face, as he said these words, was not at all pleasant, and I had my own reasons for thinking that the stranger was mistaken, even if he meant what he said. But it was no business of mine, I thought. Besides, I did not know what to do. The man kept hanging about just inside the door, peeping around the corner like a cat watching for a mouse. Once I stepped out into the road, but he immediately called me back. Then as I did not come quickly enough for his fancy, he ordered me in with a curse that made me jump.

As soon as I was back again, he returned to his former manner, patted me on the shoulder, and told me I was a good boy, and that he had taken quite a fancy to me. "I have a son of my own," said he, "much like you, and mighty proud I am of him. But the great thing for boys is training, son—training. Now if you had sailed along of Bill, you wouldn't have stood there to be spoke to twice. That was never his way, nor the way of such as sailed with him. And here, sure enough, is my mate Bill, with a spy-glass under his arm, bless his old heart, to be sure. You and me will just go back into the parlor, son, and get behind the door, and we will give Bill a little surprise—bless his heart, I say again."

So saying, the stranger backed along with me and put me behind him in the corner so that we were both out of sight. I was afraid, as you may fancy, and the more so because the man himself was afraid. He took hold of his sword, and all the time we were waiting, he swallowed as if he felt a lump in his throat.

At last in came the captain. He shut the door behind him without looking to the right or left and marched straight across the room to where his breakfast lay waiting for him.

"Bill," said the stranger in a voice I thought he tried to make brave and big.

The captain turned quickly and faced us. All the brown had gone out of his face, and even his nose was blue. He had the look of a man who sees a ghost or the Evil One,[3] and upon my word, I felt sorry to see him turn so old and sick.

"Come, now, you know me; you know your old shipmate, surely," said the stranger.

The captain started back.

"Black Dog!" said he.

"And who else?" returned the other. "Black Dog as ever was, come for to see his old shipmate, Billy, at the 'Admiral Benbow Inn.' Ah, Bill, Bill, we have seen a sight of times, us two, since I lost them two fingers," said he holding up his hand.

"Now, look here," said the captain, "you've run me down; here I am; well, then, what do you want?"

"That's you, Bill," returned Black Dog, "you're in the right of it. I want a glass of rum from this dear child here, as I've took such a liking to; and we will sit down, if you please, and talk square, like old shipmates."

[3] the Evil One, the devil.

When I returned with the drinks, they were already seated on either side of the captain's breakfast table—Black Dog next to the door and sitting sideways, so as to have one eye on the captain and one, as I thought, on the door.

He told me to go and leave the door wide open. "None of your keyholes for me, son," he said, as I left them together and went into the bar.[4]

For a long time, though I did my very best to listen, I could hear nothing but low talking; but at last the voices began to grow higher, and I could pick up a word or two, mostly curses, from the captain.

"No, no, no, no, and an end of it," he cried once. And again, "If it comes to hanging, hang all, say I."

Then all of a sudden there was a terrible noise of curses; the chair and table went over in a heap; a ringing of steel followed, and

[4]**bar,** room where drinks are served.

then a cry of pain. The next moment I saw Black Dog running wildly and the captain following close after him, both with swords in their hands and Black Dog streaming blood from the left shoulder. Just at the door the captain aimed at his enemy one last great cut, which would surely have killed him had it not struck our big sign-board instead. To this day you can see the mark on the frame.

Once out upon the road, Black Dog, wounded though he was, ran wonderfully fast and was gone over the edge of the hill in half a minute. The captain, for his part, only stood for a while looking at the sign-board. Then he passed his hand over his eyes several times and turned back into the house.

"Jim," says he, "rum," and as he spoke, he leaned against the wall, then caught himself with one hand on the door.

"Are you hurt?" cried I.

"Rum," he said again. "I must get away from here. Rum! Rum!"

I ran to bring it, but I was so frightened by all that had happened that I broke the glass and spilt the rum. While I was still getting in my own way, I heard a loud fall in the front room, and running in, found the captain lying full length upon the floor. At the same time my mother, hearing the cries and fighting, came running to help me. Between us we lifted his head. He was breathing very loud and hard, but his eyes were closed, and his face was a dreadful color.

"Dear, dear me!" cried my mother, "what a shame upon our house! And your poor father sick!"

We had no idea what to do to help the captain, nor any other thought but that he had been hurt in the fight with Black Dog. I got the rum, to be sure, and tried to put it down him, but his teeth were shut so tightly I could not. We were very glad indeed when the door opened and Doctor Livesey came in.

"Oh, doctor," we cried, "what shall we do?

Where is he hurt? What has happened?"

"Hurt?" said the doctor, "no more hurt than you or I. The man has had a stroke, as I told him. Now, Mrs. Hawkins, just run back to your husband and tell him nothing about this. For my part, I must do my best to save this fellow's good-for-nothing life; and Jim here will get me a basin."

When I got back with the basin, the doctor had already cut the captain's sleeve and laid bare his great strong arm. It was tattooed[5] in several places. "Here's luck," "A fair wind," and "Billy Bones, his fancy," were clearly done on his lower arm, and up near the shoulder there was a gallows[6] with a man hanging from it—done, as I thought, very well.

"The end he is expecting," said the doctor, touching this picture. "And now, Mr. Bones, if that be your name, we shall have a

---

[5]**tattooed**, marked with figures or pictures made by putting in colors through very small holes in the skin. [6]**gallows**, place where a person is hanged.

look at the color of your blood. Jim," he said,
"are you afraid of blood?"

"No, sir," said I.

"Well, then, you hold the basin," said he,
and with his knife he opened a vein.

A great deal of blood was taken before the
captain opened his eyes and looked about him
in a dreamy way. He saw the doctor and
looked angry; then he saw me and seemed
more at ease. But suddenly his color changed,
and he tried to raise himself, crying:

"Where is Black Dog?"

"There is no Black Dog here," said the
doctor, "except what you have on your back.
You have been drinking again; you have had
a stroke just as I told you; and I have, very
much against my own will, just pulled you
out of the grave. Now, Mr. Bones—"

"That's not my name," he broke in.

"Much I care," returned the doctor. "It
is the name of a pirate whom I know. Now
what I have to say to you is this: One glass of

557

rum will not kill you; but if you take one, you will take another and another; and if you do not break off, you will die. Do you understand that? Die and go to join others of your kind. Come, now, get up. I will help you to your bed for once."

Between us, with much trouble, we got him to his room and laid him on his bed, where his head fell back on the pillow as if he were completely tired out.

"Now, mind you," said the doctor, "I give up my care of you. The name of rum for you is death." And he went off to see my father, taking me with him.

"This is nothing," he said as soon as he had closed the door. "I have taken enough blood to keep him quiet for a time. He should stay where he is for a week—that is the best thing for him and for you, but another stroke would end him."

Chapter III

The Black Spot

About noon I stopped at the captain's door with some cooling drinks. He was lying much as we had left him and seemed very weak.

"Jim," he said, "you are the only one here worth anything, and very good I have been to you. Never a month but I gave you a bit of money for yourself. And now, you see, I'm pretty weak and all the rest have left me. Won't you bring me some rum?"

"The doctor—," I began.

Then he broke in, cursing the doctor as much as his weak voice would let him. "That there doctor," he said, "what do he know about seamen? I been in places hot as the sun, and men dropping around with Yellow Jack,[1] and I lived on rum, I tell you. It has been meat, drink, man, and wife to me, and if I am not to have it now, I'm done for. My

[1]Yellow Jack, yellow fever.

blood will be on you, and on that doctor," and he began again to curse.

"Look how my fingers shakes. I can't keep them still. I haven't had a drop this blessed day, and if I don't have some soon, I'll have the horrors.[2] I seen some already. I seen Flint in the corner there as plain as day, and if I get the horrors, I'll raise Cain.[3] Your doctor himself said one glass wouldn't hurt me. I'll pay you well for a drink."

He was growing more and more excited, and my father, who was very weak that day, needed quiet. Besides, I knew the doctor had said one glass would not kill him, but I did not like to have him offer me money.

"I want none of your money," said I, "except what you owe my father. I shall get you one glass and no more."

When I brought it, he seized it and quickly drank it out.

---

[2]**the horrors,** terrible dreams. [3]**raise Cain,** make trouble.

"There," said he, "that's some better, sure enough. And now, did the doctor say how long I was to lie in this old bed?"

"A week at least," said I.

"A week!" he cried. "I can't do that. They could have a black spot[4] on me by then. They are about to find me this blessed minute. They lost what they got, and now they want to get what is mine. Is that a seaman's way to act, I want to know? But I was a saving man. I never wasted good money of mine, or lost it neither. I am not afraid of them; and I can fool them. I did it once, and I can do it again."

As he was speaking, he slowly raised himself from his bed, catching my shoulder with a hold that almost made me cry out, and moving his legs like dead weights. His words were full of spirit, but his voice was weak.

---

[4]**black spot.** Pirates used this way of telling their captain they would no longer obey him. On a piece of black paper they would write what they wanted him to do.

"That doctor has done me," he said. "My ears is singing. Lay me back." But before I could do so, he had fallen back and lay quiet for a time.

"Jim," he said at length, "you saw that seaman today?"

"Black Dog?" I asked.

"Yes, Black Dog," said he. "He's a bad one, but there is worse that sent him on. Now if I can't get away, and they give me the black spot, mind you, it's my old sea-chest they want. You get a horse and go to—well, yes, I will!— go to that doctor fool and tell him to call all hands—officers and such, and get those fellows when they come here to the inn. He can get all old Flint's crew, all of them as is left. I was old Flint's first mate,[5] I was, and now I'm the only one as knows the place. He gave it to me just before he died. But you are not to tell until they get the black spot on me or until

[5] **first mate,** as used here, an officer on a ship, next to the captain in power.

you see that Black Dog again, or a seaman with one leg, Jim—him above all."

"But what is the black spot, captain?" I asked.

"That will be a call. I'll tell you if they get that. But you keep your eye open, and I'll divide with you equals, upon my honor, I will."

Soon after this I gave him his medicine, which he took like a child; then he fell into a heavy sleep, and I left him. What I should have done had all gone well, I do not know. Perhaps I should have told the whole story to the doctor, for I was in great fear that the captain would be sorry for what he had told me and make an end of me. But my poor father died quite suddenly that evening, which put all other matters to the side. Our sorrow, the visits of the neighbors, the funeral, and all of the work of the place kept me so busy that I had little time to think of the captain, far less to be afraid of him.

He came down next morning, to be sure, and had his meals as usual, though he ate little. However, I am afraid he had more than his usual supply of drink, for he helped himself, blowing through his nose so no one dared to cross him. On the night before the funeral he was as drunk as ever, and it was shocking at that time to hear him sing his wild old sea song. But he was so weak we were afraid he would die, and the doctor was suddenly called to a case many miles away and did not come to the house after my father's death.

I have said the captain was weak, and indeed he seemed to grow weaker rather than stronger. He moved about very slowly. Sometimes he put his head out of the door to look at the sea, holding to the door as he did so. He never spoke to me directly, and I believe he had forgotten what he had told me, but he was more quick-tempered than ever. He had an alarming way now, when he was drunk, of drawing his sword[6] and keeping it before him on the table. His mind did not seem clear. Once, to our great wonder, he sang a different song, a kind of country love song which he must have heard when he was a young man before he began to follow the sea.

So things passed until about three o'clock one very cold afternoon. I was standing at the door full of sad thoughts about my father when I saw a man coming very slowly up the road. He was plainly blind, for he tapped before him with a stick and had a great green shade over his eyes and nose. He was bent, as if with age, and wore a great old sea-cloak with a hood that made him the most dreadful-looking man I had ever seen. He stopped a little from the house and called in an odd sing-song voice.

"Will any kind friend tell a poor blind man, who has lost the sight of his eyes in the service of his country, England—God bless

[6]**drawing his sword,** pulling it out of its cover.

King George—in what part of the country he is now?"

"You are at the 'Admiral Benbow Inn,' my good man," said I.

"I hear a voice," said he, "a young voice. Will you give me your hand, my kind young friend, and lead me in?"

I gave him my hand, and he caught it so tightly I was afraid of him. I tried to pull back, but he pulled me close to him.

"Now, boy," he said, "take me to the captain."

"Sir," said I, "upon my word I dare not."

"Oh, is that it?" he cried angrily. "Take me in at once, or I'll break your arm."

"Sir," said I, "it is for yourself I mean. The captain is not what he used to be. He sits with a drawn sword. Another gentleman—"

"Come, now, march," he broke in, and I never before heard a voice so cruel. "Lead me straight up to him, and say, 'Here's a friend for you, Bill.' If you don't, I'll do this," and he gave my arm a wrench that nearly made me faint. I took him to where the poor old captain was sitting, far gone in drink, and cried out the words as he had told me. The captain raised his eyes, saw the blind man, and at once looked very sick. He started to rise but could not.

"Now, sit where you are," said the blind man. "Even if I can't see, I can hear a finger move. Business is business. Hold out your left hand. Boy, take his left hand and bring it near to my right."

Both of us did as we were told, and I saw something pass from the blind man's hand to the captain's.

"And now that's done," said the blind man. He let go my hand, quickly left the room, and went out into the road, where I heard his stick go tap-tap-tapping along.

It was some time before either the captain or I could think; but at length, and at almost the same time, I let go his hand and he looked into it.

"Ten o'clock!" he cried. "Six hours! We'll do them yet!"

He sprang to his feet, but even as he did so, he put his hand to his head and fell full length to the floor.

I ran to him, calling my mother, but the captain was dead. It was a strange thing. I certainly had never liked the man, though of late I had begun to feel sorry for him, but when I saw that he was dead, I gave way to a flood of tears. It was the second death I had known, and the sorrow of the first was still fresh in my heart.

Chapter IV

The Sea-Chest

I LOST no time in telling my mother all that I knew, and perhaps I should have told her long before. We saw at once that we were in danger. It was certain that some of the man's money—if he had any—should have been ours, but we knew his shipmates would never give us any of what they found. The captain had told me to ride at once for Dr. Livesey, but I could not do that because it would have left my mother alone. Indeed, it seemed that neither of us could stay in the house any longer, for every little noise we heard filled us with fright.

Every moment we seemed to hear men coming, and with the dead body of the captain on the floor and the thought of the hateful blind beggar near at hand and ready to return, I almost jumped out of my skin for fright. Something must be done quickly, and at last we thought of going together to ask for help in the village. Without waiting for hats or coats, we ran out at once into the gathering dark.

The village was near, but out of sight on the other side of the next bay. We were very glad, too, that it was not in the direction from which the blind man came and which we supposed he had taken when he left. We were not many minutes on the road, though we stopped at times to catch each other's hands and listen fearfully.

It was already dark when we reached the village, and I shall never forget how glad I was to see the lights in the windows; but that was the only help we could get, for not a man would return with us to the inn. The more we told of our troubles, the less they wanted to leave their own safe homes. The name of Captain Flint, though new to me, was well-known to some there and filled them with fear. Some of them had seen several strange men on the road, and for that matter they feared anyone who had sailed with the captain. They would go with us to call an officer, but not one would help us to defend our home.

Angry at them, my mother said, "If none of you dare, Jim and I dare. Back we will go the way we came, small thanks to you, big chicken-hearted[1] men! We will have that money if we die for it. And I would thank you for that bag, Mrs. Crossley, to bring back our just pay in."

Of course I said I would go with my mother, and of course they all cried out at our foolishness. They gave me a pistol, promised to have horses ready for us in case the robbers followed us as we returned, and one boy was to ride to Dr. Livesey's for help.

My heart beat wildly as we set out in the cold night on our dangerous trip. A full red

[1]chicken-hearted, afraid.

moon was beginning to rise and was already showing over the tops of the hills. This made it more necessary for us to hurry, for we knew it would soon be as bright as day and we could easily be seen by the robbers.

When we stepped into the house, we stopped for a moment, shaking, for we were alone in the dark with the dead captain's body. Then my mother lit a candle, and there lay the captain as we had left him, on his back with his eyes open and his arms spread out.

"Draw down the blind, Jim," said my mother; "they might come back and watch outside. And now," she said, when I had done so, "we have to get the key off of *that*, and who is to touch it, I should like to know?"

I went down on my knees at once. On the floor by his hand was a little round of paper, black on one side. I was sure that this was the black spot, and taking it up, I read on the other side, "You have till ten."

"We have till ten, mother," said I, and

just as I said it, the clock began to strike. This sudden noise frightened us, but the news was good, for it was only six.

"Now," she said, "that key."

I felt in his pockets, one after another, but it was not there. Instead I found only a few pieces of money, a knife, and several other small things of no value.

"Perhaps it's around his neck," said my mother.

Little as I wanted to do it, I opened his shirt at the neck, and there, sure enough, hanging to a bit of string, we found the key. I cut the string with his own knife, and together my mother and I hurried up to the little room where he had slept so long and where his box had stood ever since he came to us.

"Give the key to me," said my mother, and quickly she turned the lock and threw back the top.

Nothing did we see but a suit of very good

clothes, carefully brushed and folded. They had never been worn, my mother said.

Under these we found many little things but nothing of value. Next we found an old coat, white with sea-salt. My mother pulled it up, and there lay before us the last of his things—a bundle tied up in oilcloth[2] and looking like papers, and a bag which gave out a sound like the ring of gold.

"I'll show those fellows that I'm an honest woman," said my mother. "I'll have what is mine and not a bit more. Hold this bag." And she began to count out money from the captain's bag and put it into the one I was holding.

That was not easy, for the coins were of all countries and sizes. There was very little English money, and it was this that my mother could count most easily.

When we were about half-way through, I suddenly stopped, for I heard a sound which

[2]oilcloth, cloth covered with oil to keep out water.

brought my heart into my mouth—the tapping of the blind man's stick upon the hard road. It drew nearer and nearer; then he struck on the door. We heard the handle being turned and the bolt rattling as he tried to enter. Then for a long time all was quiet, and at last we heard the tapping again; but this time the beggar was going slowly back down the road.

"Mother," said I, "take all of it and let's go," for I was sure the man knew we were there and would soon come with the others.

But my mother would not take more than was hers, nor would she take less. It was not yet seven, she said; she knew her rights and would have them, and she was still sorting money when we heard a low whistle away off on the hill. That was enough for both of us.

"I'll take what I have," she said, jumping to her feet.

"And I'll take this to make up for the rest," said I, picking up the oilcloth bag.

In a moment we were both feeling our way down the steps, leaving the candle in the captain's room. The next moment we had opened the door and were running away. Nor had we started a moment too soon. The fog was rapidly rising, already the moon was shining on the hill, and soon we should both be in the clear moonlight. And this was not all, for soon we heard men running toward our house and saw that one was carrying a light.

"My dear," said my mother suddenly, "take the money and run on. I am going to faint."

This was certainly the end for both of us, I thought. But we were just at a little bridge, and I helped her to the edge of the bank, where, sure enough, she fell on my shoulder. How I found strength to do it, I do not know, but I pulled her down the bank, and there we stayed, still within hearing distance of our home.

Chapter V

The Last of the Blind Man

So eager was I to know what the men were doing that I went back up the bank again, stood behind a tree, and from there watched the road before our door. They soon came, eight or ten of them, running hard, the man with the light in front of the others. Three men ran together, hand in hand, and I could see that the middle one was the blind man.

"Down with the door!" he cried.

"Aye, aye, sir!" answered two or three, and they rushed at the door. Surprised to find it open, they stopped to talk together, but the blind man again shouted at them.

"In, in, in!" he cried, and swore at them for being so slow.

Four or five of them went in at once, while two stayed on the road with the blind man. Soon there was a cry of surprise, and a voice calling:

"Bill's dead!"

But the blind man only shouted, "Search him, some of you, and the rest of you go up and get the chest."

I could hear them running up our old stairs so that the house must have shaken with their steps. Then there were more shouts of surprise, and the window of the captain's room was thrown open with a slam and a ring of broken glass. A man leaned out and spoke to the blind man, who was waiting on the road below.

"Pew!" he cried, "they've been here before us. Someone has already robbed the chest."

"Is it there?" shouted the blind man.

"The money is."

"Flint's fist,[1] I mean, and hang the money!" he returned.

"We don't see it," answered the man.

---

[1] **Flint's fist,** Flint's handwriting. They wanted a paper Flint had written.

"Here, you below here, is it on Bill?" cried Pew.

At that another man came to the door. "Bill has been searched already," said he; "nothing left."

"It was those people at the inn—that boy. I wish I had put his eyes out," cried Pew. "They were here no time ago—they had the door locked when I tried it. Look around, men, and find them."

"Sure enough, they left a light here," said the man at the window.

"Find them! Find them!" cried Pew, again, striking with his stick on the road.

Then there followed a great noise all through our old house, heavy feet running about, chairs thrown over, doors broken in, until the very rocks rang. Then the men came out on the road, one after another, and said we were nowhere to be found. Just then we heard the same whistle which had put such fear into my mother and me while we were counting the dead captain's money, but this time it was nearer and came again and again. It was plainly a signal to warn the pirates of danger.

"There's Dirk again," said one, "twice! Run!"

"Run, you coward!" cried the blind man. "Dirk was a coward from the first—why should you mind him? They must be close by; they can't be far; you have your hands on it. Find them, you dogs! Oh, if I had eyes!"

Two of the men began to look here and there, but not very carefully, and each one, I thought, kept one eye on the road.

"You have your hands on thousands, you fools! You'd be as rich as kings if you could find it, and you know it's here, and you stand there doing nothing. Not one of you dared face Bill, and I did it—a blind man! And I have to lose my chance for you. I have to beg for my drinks when I might be rolling in a coach! If you had the courage of a bug in a bread-bag, you would catch them even yet!"

"Hang it, Pew, we have the money," said one.

"They might have hid the blessed thing," said another. "Take the money, Pew, and don't stand there squalling."

Squalling was the word for it, for he was so angry that at last he struck at them right and left. They in turn cursed back, threatened him in dreadful words, and tried to catch the stick and take it away from him.

The quarrel saved us, for before it was over, another sound came from the top of the hill on the side of the town—the sound of horses running. Almost at the same time there was a shot from the trees beside the road. The robbers turned at once and ran in every direction, one along the bay, one across the hill, and so on, so that in half a minute no one was left but the blind man. He ran up and down the road, calling wildly for the others.

"Johnny," he called, "Black Dog, Dirk, you won't leave old Pew, mates—not old Pew!"

Just then the noise of horses sounded at the top of the hill. Four or five men came in sight, racing toward us.

The blind man lost his head and ran right in front of the nearest horse. The rider tried to save him, but down he went with a wild cry. He fell on his side, then rolled over on his face, and moved no more.

I jumped to my feet and called the men, who were already stopping because of the accident. I soon saw who they were. One was the boy who had gone from the village to call the doctor; the rest were officers whom he had met on the road and brought back to us.

The blind man was dead, stone dead. As for my mother, we carried her to the village, gave her a little cold water and smelling-salts, and found she was soon as well as ever; but the robbers had escaped.

"They got off clean, and there is an end," said Mr. Dance, one of the officers; "only I am glad I stepped on Mr. Pew's corns."

He went back with me to the inn, and such a sight as it was! Even the clock had been thrown down in the hunt for my mother and myself. Nothing had been taken away except the captain's money bag and a little silver from our money box; but everything in the house was broken, and I could see at once that we were ruined. Mr. Dance could not understand the reason.

"They got the money, you say? Well, then, what did they want? More money?"

"No, sir; not money," said I. "In fact, sir, I think I have the thing they wanted in my coat, and to tell you the truth, I should like to get it put away safe."

"To be sure, boy, quite right," said he. "I can take it, if you like."

"I thought perhaps Doctor Livesey—" I began.

"Right," said he, "quite right. Doctor Livesey is a gentleman and an officer of the law. I should like to talk to him about this myself, and, if you like, I can take you along."

We walked back to the village where the horses were, got on them, and soon were at the doctor's house.

Chapter VI

The Captain's Papers

WE RODE hard all the way to the doctor's house, but when I knocked at the door, the maid told me the doctor was not in. He had gone up to the Hall,[1] she said, to have dinner and pass the evening with Squire Trelawney.

"So there we go," said Mr. Dance.

At the Hall a maid opened the door for us and led us into a great room where the squire and the doctor sat, pipe in hand, on either side of the bright fire.

Squire Trelawney was over six feet tall, and broad. He had a rough and ready face, all browned and lined by his long travels. His eyebrows were very black and moved quickly, and this gave him a look of having a quick, high temper.

"Come in, Mr. Dance," said he.

"Good evening, Dance," said the doctor,

[1]the Hall, the big fine home owned by the Squire.

with a nod. "And good evening to you, friend Jim. What good wind brings you here?"

Mr. Dance stood up straight and tall and told his story like a lesson. The two gentlemen sat forward and looked at each other, so interested they forgot to smoke. When they heard how my mother went back to the inn, the doctor struck his knee and the squire cried, "Brave woman," and broke his long pipe against the arm of his chair. The squire got up from his seat and walked up and down the room, and the doctor, as if to hear better, took off his white wig and sat there looking very strange with his own close-cut black hair.

"Mr. Dance," said the squire, "you are a very fine fellow. And as for riding down that mean black rascal, I think that was an act as good as killing a snake. This boy Hawkins is certainly brave. Hawkins, will you ring that bell? Mr. Dance must have a drink."

"And so, Jim," said the doctor, "you have the thing they were after, have you?"

"Here it is, sir," said I, and gave him the package.

The doctor looked at it as if he could hardly wait to open it, but he put it in the pocket of his coat.

"Squire," said he, "when Dance has had his drink, he must, of course, return to his duties, but I mean to keep Jim Hawkins here to sleep at my house, and I think we should get the cold pie and let him eat."

"As you will," said the squire, "but Hawkins has earned better than cold pie."

So a big meat pie was brought in and put on a side table, and I had a good supper while Mr. Dance was praised again, and then he left.

"And now," said Doctor Livesey.

"And now," said Squire Trelawney.

"One at a time, one at a time," laughed the doctor. "You have heard of this Flint, I suppose?"

"Heard of him!" cried the other. "Heard of him, you say! He was the most bloodthirsty pirate that ever sailed. The Spaniards were so afraid of him that, I tell you, sir, I was proud that he was English. I've seen his sails with my own eyes, and the coward captain I sailed with went back to land."

"Well, I've heard of him myself," said the doctor. "But the point is, did he have money?"

"Money!" cried the squire. "Did you hear the story this boy just told? What were those men after but money?"

"That we shall soon see," replied the doctor, "but you are talking so much I can't get a word in. What I want to know is this: Suppose we do find out where Flint buried his treasure. Will it amount to much?"

"Amount, sir!" cried the squire. "It will amount to this: I shall fit out a ship, take you and the boy along, and we'll have that money if we hunt a year."

"Very well," said the doctor. "Now, if Jim is ready, let us open the package."

He laid it on the table, cut it open, and found two things—a book and a sealed paper.

"First let us try the book," said the doctor.

The squire and I both looked over his shoulder. On the first page we found only a few bits of writing—"Billy Bones, his fancy," "Mr. W. Bones, mate," "No more rum," "Off Palm Key he got it." I could not help wondering who it was that had "got it" and what "it" was that he got. A knife in his back, like as not. "Not much help there," said the doctor and passed on.

The next ten or twelve pages were filled with strange notes. There was a date at one end of the line and at the other was an amount of money as in common account books, but instead of writing, only crosses between the two. On June 12, 1745, the amount of seventy pounds was due to some person, and there was nothing but six crosses to show why. In only a few cases the name of a place would be added.

The notes covered more than twenty years, and the amounts grew larger as time went on. At the end the whole amount was given with the words, "Bones, his pile."

"I cannot make head or tail of this," said the doctor.

"The thing is as clear as day," cried the squire. "This is the fellow's account book. These crosses stand for the names of ships they sank. These figures show his share, and when he was afraid he might forget, he added something to make it clear. 'Off Caraccas,'² now here was some poor ship sunk off that coast. Poor men that sailed there—dead long ago."

"Right," cried the doctor. "See what it is to be a traveler. Right! And the amounts kept growing larger."

There was little else in the book except the names of the other ships he had robbed and a table giving the value of the French,

²**Caraccas,** a city in South America. The word should be spelled Caracas.

English, and Spanish money he had taken.

"A careful man!" cried the doctor. "He wasn't one to be fooled by others."

"And now," said the squire, "for the paper."

The doctor opened the paper with great care and found the map of an island. On it were marked the latitude and longitude, hills, bays, and everything that would be needed to bring a ship to a safe landing on its shores. It was about nine miles long and five across and had two fine harbors and a hill about halfway down the west coast marked "The Spy-Glass." There were several things added at a later date, but, above all, three crosses in red —two at the north end of the island and one in the southwest. Beside the last, in the same red ink but in writing very different from the captain's, these words: "Most of treasure here."

Over on the back the same hand had written:

"Tall tree, Spy-Glass shoulder, bear-ing[3] a point to the N. of N.N.E."[4]

"Skeleton Island E.S.E.[5] and by E."

"Ten feet."

"The bar silver is in the north cache;[6] you can find it by the trend[7] of the East hummock,[8] ten fathoms[9] south of the black crag with the face on it."

"The arms are easy found in the sand hill N. point of North inlet cape, bearing E. and a quarter N."   "J. F."

That was all, but little as it was, it filled the two men with joy.

"Doctor," cried the squire, "give up your practice at once. Tomorrow I start for Bristol. In three weeks' time we will have the best ship and the best crew in England. Hawkins shall come as cabin-boy. You will make a fine

---

[3]**bearing**, in the direction of. [4]**a point to the N. of N.N.E.,** a direction on a map a little east of north. **N.N.E.,** north northeast. [5]**E.S.E.,** east southeast, a direction a little south of east. [6]**cache**, hiding place (pronounced *cash*). [7]**trend**, direction. [8]**hummock**, a low hill. [9]**fathoms**. A fathom is a measure of six feet.

one, Hawkins. You, Livesey, are ship's doctor, and I am admiral. We can take Redruth, Joyce, and Hunter. We'll have good winds and a quick trip, and no trouble finding the spot, and then money to eat—to roll in!"

"Trelawney," said the doctor, "I'll go with you, and so will Jim. There's only one man I'm afraid of."

"And who is that?" cried the squire. "Name the dog, sir!"

"You," replied the doctor, "for you cannot hold your tongue. We are not the only ones who know about this paper. Those fellows who broke into the inn this evening, and more, I am sure, are after that money. We must none of us go alone till we get to sea. Jim and I must stick together for a time. You take Hunter with you when you ride to Bristol, and from first to last not one of us must say a word of what we have found."

"Livesey," returned the squire, "you are right. I promise you I shall not say a word."

"Mr. Silver, sir?" I asked.

62

PART II – THE SEA COOK

Chapter VII

I Go to Bristol

It was longer than we had thought before we were ready for the sea, for we had to make many changes in our first plans. The doctor had to go to the city for a man to take charge of his practice. I lived on at the Hall under the care of old Redruth, the gamekeeper,[1] full of the happiest dreams of the sea and strange islands.

I looked at the map for hours and hours until I knew well every little part of it. Sitting there before the fire, I dreamed of landing on the island at every possible point; I walked over every foot of it. I climbed many times to the top of that tall hill they had marked the Spy-Glass, and from the top saw

[1]**gamekeeper,** a man employed to watch birds and animals and see that they are not stolen or killed by hunters.

the most wonderful sights. Sometimes the island was thick with savages with whom we would fight; sometimes it was full of wild animals that hunted us, but in all my dreams there was nothing half so wonderful as the things we really did later.

So the weeks passed, till one day there came a letter for the doctor with this note on the outside: "To be opened, if Dr. Livesey is not there, by young Hawkins." I read it and found this wonderful news which I could hardly believe:

> Old Anchor Inn, Bristol
> March 1, 17—
> "My dear friend: As I do not know whether you are at the Hall or still in the city, I send this to both places.
> "The ship is bought and ready, and you never saw a sweeter one—a child might sail her. Her name is *Hispaniola*.
> "I got her through an old friend, Blandy, who has helped me in every pos-

sible way. And so, I may say, did all the men here as soon as they learned we were looking for treasure."

"The doctor will not like that," said I. "The squire has been talking after all."

Then I read on farther and found these words:

"Blandy himself found the *Hispaniola* and got her at a very low price. So far everything is going well. The workmen, to be sure, were very slow, but time changed that. It was the crew that troubled me.

"I wished twenty men—in case of savages or pirates—and I had a hard time to find half that many, till one day, quite by chance, I found just the man I needed.

"I happened to be standing beside him near the shore one day and fell in talk with him. I found he was an old sailor, knew all the seamen here, had lost his health on shore, and wanted to go back to sea again as a cook. He had come down that morning, he said, to get a smell of salt.

"I was greatly touched—so would you have been—and took him on at once to be ship's cook. Long John Silver, he is called, and has lost a leg; but I think that speaks well for him, since he lost it in the service of his king. Our government is paying him nothing. What thanks for such fine service!

"Well, sir, I thought I had found only a cook, but I had found a whole crew. Silver and I got together in a few days some of the toughest old salts you could find—not pretty to look at, but none the less brave. I know we could fight a warship.

"Long John even let go two out of the six or seven I had already taken on. He showed me clearly that they were very poor sailors whom we could never trust with such important business as this.

"I am in the best of health and spirits,

eating like a pig and sleeping like a tree, but I shall not enjoy a moment till I see my own sailors on the ship. Now for the sea! Hang the treasure! It is the sea that has turned my head. So now, come quickly, if you trust me.

"Let the boy go at once to see his mother, with Redruth for a guard, and then come on as soon as possible.

John Trelawney.

"P.S.—I did not tell you that Blandy is to send a party to look for us if we don't turn up by the end of six months. He has found a fine fellow for sailing master—a stiff man, I am sorry to say, but in every other way a real find. Long John also found a very able man for a mate—a man named Arrow. I have a boatswain with pipes,[2] so things will be in good order on board our good ship.

[2]**boatswain with pipes,** an officer on a ship who gives orders to the sailors by means of a pipe or whistle. Sailors call him the "bos'n."

"I forgot to tell you that Silver is a man of means; he always keeps a nice account in the bank. He leaves his wife to take care of his business; and as she is a woman of color, an old bachelor like you or me might well guess that it is his wife, as much as his health, that sends him back to sea.

J. T.

"P.P.S. The boy may stay one night with his mother.

J. T."

As you may fancy, I was half beside myself with joy, and if ever I hated a man, it was old Redruth because he did nothing but complain about the trip. Anyone else would have been glad to go in his place if he only had the chance.

The next morning he and I set out on foot for my home, and there I found my mother in good health and spirits. The captain was gone where he could no longer trouble us. The squire had had everything set to rights and the sign newly painted. He had even bought some new chairs and tables—above all, a beautiful arm-chair for my mother. He had also found a boy to do my work so that she would not want help while I was gone to sea on the *Hispaniola* to hunt for treasure.

Until then I had thought only of the wonderful time I was going to have, but when I saw that boy, I began to think of the home I was leaving, and I gave way to tears. I am afraid I led the boy a dog's life, for he was new to the work and slow, and at every possible chance I set him right and put him down.

The night passed, and the next day, after dinner, we were again on the road. I said good-by to mother, and the bay where I was born, and the dear old "Admiral Benbow"— since the sign-board had been newly painted, not quite so dear. One of my last thoughts was of the captain, who had walked along the shore with his turned-up hat, his sword-cut face, and his old spy-glass. Soon we turned the corner, and my home was out of sight.

The stage-coach picked us up at the "Royal George Inn" that evening. I was crowded in between a fat old gentleman and Redruth, but even so, I must have gone to sleep at the very first and then slept all the way. When I woke up the next morning, we were standing before a large building in a city street, and I saw that day had already come.

"Where are we?" I asked.

"Bristol," said Redruth. "Get down."

Mr. Trelawney was staying at a place far down near the shore to watch over the work on the ship. There we went, and to my delight our way led us past ships of all sizes and kinds and from many countries. In one, the men were singing at their work; in another, there were men high over my head hanging to ropes that looked no thicker than threads.

Though I had lived by the shore all my life, I seemed never to have been near the sea till then. The smell of salt seemed something new. I saw the most wonderful figureheads[3] that had been far over the ocean. I saw, too, many old sailors with rings in their ears, and pig-tails, and a rolling sea-walk. If I had seen as many kings, I could not have been more delighted.

And I was going to sea myself—to sea in a ship with a piping boatswain and pig-tailed, singing seamen. I was going to sea, bound for a strange island and to hunt for buried treasure.

While I was still in this happy dream, we came suddenly to a large inn and met Mr. Trelawney, all dressed up like a sea captain. He came out of the door, smiling and trying hard to walk like a sailor.

"Here you are!" he cried; "and the doc-

---

[3]**figureheads,** statues on the front of ships.

tor came last night. Good!—the ship's company is complete."

"Oh, sir," cried I, "when do we sail?"

"Sail!" said he. "We sail tomorrow."

Chapter VIII

At the Sign of the "Spy-Glass"

W HEN I had eaten my breakfast, the squire gave me a note addressed to John Silver, at the "Spy-Glass." He told me I would find the place by following the shore and watching for a little place with a large spy-glass for a sign. I set off, glad to be able to see more of the ships and seamen, and picked my way among boxes, carts, and people, for this was the busiest time of day at the water-front.

The inn was a bright little place. The sign was newly painted, the windows had neat red curtains, and the floor was cleanly sanded. There was a street on either side and an open door on both sides, which made the little room pretty clear, even though there was a great deal of tobacco smoke in it.

The men there were mostly seamen who talked so loudly that I hung at the door almost afraid to enter.

As I was waiting, a man came out of a side room, and at once I was sure he was Long John. His left leg was cut off near the hip, but under his left arm he carried a crutch with which he moved about as quickly as any man with his own two legs. He was tall and strong, with a large face which was plain but bright and smiling. Indeed, he seemed in the best of spirits, whistling as he moved about among the tables with a merry word or a slap on the shoulder for his guests sitting there in the "Spy-Glass."

From the first time I had read of Long John in Mr. Trelawney's letter, I was afraid he might be the very one-legged man I had watched for so long at the old Benbow Inn. But one look at this man was enough. I had seen the captain, and Black Dog, and the blind man Pew, and I thought I knew what a pirate was like—a very different person from this clean and pleasant gentleman.

I lost my fear at once, went through the

door, and walked right up to the man where he stood leaning on his crutch and talking to a seaman.

"Mr. Silver, sir?" I asked, holding out the note.

"Yes, my boy," said he; "such is my name, to be sure. And who may you be?" When he saw the letter I had brought, he said quite brightly, "Oh, I see. You are our new cabin-boy, and glad I am to see you." And he shook my hand warmly.

Just then a man at the far side of the room rose and ran for the door. It was close by him, and he was gone in a minute; but I saw who he was. He was the yellow-faced man wanting two fingers who had come to the "Admiral Benbow."

"Oh," I cried, "stop him! It's Black Dog!"

"I don't care who he is," cried Silver, "but he hasn't paid his bill. Harry, run and catch him!"

75

One of the others who was near the door jumped up and ran after him.

"If he is the king himself, he must pay his bill," cried Silver, and then dropping my hand, he asked, "Who did you say he was? Black what?"

"Dog, sir," said I. "Has not Mr. Trelawney told you of the pirates? He was one of them."

"So," cried Silver. "In my house! Ben, run and help catch him. One of those fellows, was he? Was that you drinking with him, Morgan? Step up here!"

An old gray-haired, brown-faced man came up, hanging his head.

"Now, Morgan," said Long John, "you never saw that Black—Black Dog before, did you?"

"Not I, sir," said the other.

"Did you know his name?"

"No, sir."

"By the powers, it's good for you!" cried

Silver. "If you had ever been with the like of that, you would never put another foot in my house, you may lay to that![1] And what was he saying to you?"

"I don't know, sir," said Morgan.

"Do you call that a head on your shoulders?" cried Long John. "Don't know, don't you? Come now, what was he talking about —seas, captains, ships? Speak up. What was it?"

"We was talking of sailing," said Morgan.

"Sailing, was you? And a very fine thing, too, you may lay to that. Get back to your place, you fool."

And then, as Morgan rolled back to his seat, Long John spoke to me in a low voice, which pleased me very much.

"He is quite an honest man, Morgan is, only a fool. And now," he ran on in a louder voice, "let me see—Black Dog—no, I don't know the name. Not I. But, I think I have—

[1]**you may lay to that,** you may be sure of that.

yes, I have seen him. He used to come here with a blind man, he did."

"That he did, you may be sure," said I. "I knew that blind man, too. His name was Pew."

"It was!" cried Silver. "Pew! That was his name. Yes, it was. Oh, he was a bad one, he was! If we run down this Black Dog now, there will be news for our captain. Ben can run fast. Few men can run faster than him. He should run him down, by the powers! He talked sailing, did he? Well, I'll just sail him, I will!"

All the time he was shouting these things, he was bumping along on his crutch, striking tables with his hand, and acting so excited that any judge in the land would have believed him. Seeing Black Dog right here, I was afraid again, and I watched the cook closely, but he was too smart for me. When the two men came back, tired, and said they had lost Black Dog in the crowd, he seemed so angry about it that I was sure of the innocence of Long John.

"See here, my boy," said he, "here is a hard thing on a man like me. There is Captain Trelawney—what will he think? Here I have this scoundrel sitting in my own house, drinking at my own table. Here you comes and tells me of it, and here I let him get away right before my eyes. Now, Hawkins, you help me out with the captain. You're just a boy, you are, but you're smart as paint. I see that when you first came in. Now, here it is— what could I do with this old wooden leg of mine? When I was an A B seaman,[2] I could have run after him and caught him easy, I could; and now—"

Then he stopped, and he looked surprised as if he had just remembered something.

"The bill," he cried. "Three drinks of rum! Well, bless me, if I didn't forget my

[2]**A B seaman**, able-bodied seaman. Long John was able-bodied before he lost his leg.

bill," and falling on a chair, he laughed until he cried. I could not help joining, and we laughed together until the place rang again.

"Why, what an old fool I am," he said at last, wiping his eyes. "You and me should get on well, my boy. I declare, I should be just ship's boy. But come now, this will never do. I'll put on my old hat and step along of you to the captain and tell him all about this. For I tell you, boy, this is bad! Neither you nor me has come out of it very well. But, bless me, that was a good one about my bill!"

And he began to laugh again so loudly that, though I did not know why, I again had to join him.

On our little walk along the shore, he told me about all the ships that we passed by and about the work that was going on. One was loading, another one unloading, and another making ready for the sea. Every now and then

he told me some little story of ships or seamen or repeated some saying of the sea until
I had learned it well. I began to think he was
a very good friend.

When we got to the inn, the squire and
the doctor were sitting together, finishing a
drink before they should go to visit the ship.

Long John told the story from first to last.

"That was how it was, now wasn't it?" he
would say to me now and again. And he told
it just as it was.

The two gentlemen were sorry that Black
Dog got away, but we all felt there was nothing to be done now; and Long John took up
his crutch and left.

"All hands on board by four this afternoon!" called the squire after him.

"Aye, aye, sir," cried the cook.

"Well, squire," said the doctor, "I don't
think much of some of your men, but I will
say this: John Silver suits me."

"That man is fine," said the squire.

"And now," said the doctor, "Jim may come on board with us, may he not?"

"To be sure, he may," said the squire. "Take your hat, Hawkins, and we'll see the ship."

Chapter IX

Powder and Arms

THE *Hispaniola* lay some way out, and we rowed about among other ships before we reached her, but at last we were on board and were met by the mate, Mr. Arrow. He was a brown old sailor with rings in his ears and cross-eyed. He and Mr. Trelawney were very friendly, but soon I saw that Mr. Trelawney and the captain were not.

The captain was a sharp-looking man who seemed angry with everything on the ship and soon told us so, for as soon as we reached the cabin, he came in.

"Well, sir," he said, "better speak plain, I think. I don't like this trip; I don't like the men, and I don't like my officer. That is short and sweet."

"Perhaps, sir, you don't like the ship?" asked the squire, in a very cool way.

"I cannot say to that, sir; I have not yet

tried her. She seems good, but more I can't say."

"Perhaps, sir, you may not like me, either?" said the squire.

But here the doctor cut in.

"Wait a bit, wait a bit," said he, "no use of such questions now. The captain has said too much or too little, and for my part I want him to tell us what he means. You say you don't like this trip. Now, why?"

"I was hired, sir, on what we call sealed orders[1] to sail this ship for that gentleman where he might tell me," said the captain. "So far, so good. But now I find that every man on board knows more than I do. I don't call that fair, do you?"

"No," said the doctor, "I don't."

"Next," said the captain, "I learn we are going after treasure—hear it from my own

[1]**sealed orders.** Usually the captain of a ship knows the whole plan of his trip. But if he sails under sealed orders, he does not know where he is going until the orders are opened after the boat is at sea.

men! Now that is dangerous work. I don't like money hunts at all; and I don't like them, above all, when they are secret and when the secret has been told to the parrot."

"Silver's parrot?" asked the doctor.

"That is a way of speaking," said the captain. "Told to everybody, I mean. I think neither of you gentlemen knows what you are about, but I can tell you. This is life or death and a dangerous trip."

"That is all clear and, I think, true enough," said the doctor. "We are taking a big chance, but we know more about it than you think. Next, you say, you don't like the men. Are they not good seamen?"

"I don't like them, sir," returned the captain. "And I think I should have had the choosing of my own hands, if you go to that."

"Perhaps you should," returned the doctor. "My friend should, perhaps, have taken you along with him, but he did not mean to slight you. And you don't like Mr. Arrow?"

"I don't, sir. I think he's a good seaman, but he's too free with the crew to be a good officer. A mate should keep to himself— should not drink with the men."

"Do you mean he drinks?" cried the squire.

"No, sir, only he talks too freely with the men."

"Well, now, the long and short of it, captain?" asked the doctor. "Tell us what you want."

"Well, gentlemen, are you set on making this trip?"

"Like iron," answered the squire.

"Very good," said the captain. "Then, here is another thing. They are putting the powder and arms in the fore-hold.[2] Now you have a good place under the cabin. Why not

---

[2]**fore-hold.** The hold is the part of the ship below the decks. The fore-hold is the front part of the hold. The sailors on a ship sleep in the front part. The captain's plan was to move the arms back away from the men whom they did not know well and to put next to the arms the men whom they trusted most.

put them there? Then you are bringing four of your own people with you, and they tell me some of them are to have berths forward. Why not put them here beside the cabin?"

"Any more?" asked Mr. Trelawney.

"One more," said the captain. "There's been too much talking already."

"Far too much," answered the doctor.

"I shall tell you what I have heard myself," continued Captain Smollett; "that you have a map of an island; that there are crosses on the map to show where treasure is; and that the island lies—" And he named the exact place.

"I never told that to a soul," cried the squire.

"The hands know it, sir," returned the captain.

"Doctor, that must have been you or Hawkins," cried the squire.

"It matters little who it was," replied the

doctor. And I could see that neither he nor the captain believed Mr. Trelawney. Nor did I, for he talked too freely; yet this time I believe he was right and that no one had told just where the island was.

"Well, gentlemen," said the captain, "I don't know who has this map, but I want it kept secret even from Mr. Arrow and me. If not, I will not go."

"I see," said the doctor. "You wish to keep this matter dark and to arm the stern part of the ship with my friend's own people and all the arms and powder on board. In other words, you fear trouble with the crew of the *Hispaniola*."

"Begging your pardon, sir," said Captain Smollett, "you have no right to tell what I am going to say. No captain has the right to go to sea at all if he fears trouble from his men. As for Mr. Arrow, I believe him honest; some of the men are the same; all of them may be, for what I know. But it is my duty to look after the ship and every man on her. I see things going, as I think, not quite right, and I ask you to be careful or let me go. That is all."

"Captain Smollett," began the doctor with a smile, "did you ever hear the story of the mountain and the mouse? You make me think of that story. When you came in here, you were thinking of more than this, were you not?"

"Doctor," said the captain, "you are smart. When I came in here, I thought I should get fired. I had no thought that Mr. Trelawney would hear a word."

"No more would I," cried the squire. "Had Livesey not been here, I should have let you go. As it is, I have heard you. I will do as you wish, but I think the less of you."

"That's as you please, sir," said the captain. "You'll find I do my duty." And with that he left.

"Well," said the doctor, "I believe you have at least two honest men on board with you—that man and John Silver."

"Silver, if you like," was the answer, "but as for that captain, I care very little for him. He is not a man for England to be proud of."

"Well," said the doctor, "we shall see."

When we came up again, the men had already begun to take out the arms and powder, singing at their work, while the captain and Mr. Arrow stood by watching.

The new plan was quite to my liking. The whole ship had been put in good condition, and six berths³ had been made in the stern.⁴ At first Mr. Trelawney had planned that he, Mr. Arrow, Hunter, Joyce, the doctor, and the captain were to use these. Now two more berths had been made ready in the stern, and I was to get one of them.

We were all hard at work changing things

---

³**berths,** sleeping-places on a ship. ⁴**stern,** the rear of the ship.

about when the last man or two, and Long John along with them, came aboard.

The cook came up the side of the ship like a monkey. When he saw what was going on, he cried, "What does this mean?"

"Orders to change the powder, Jack," answered one.

"Why, by the powers," cried Long John, "if we do, we'll miss the morning tide."

"My orders!" cried the captain shortly. "You may go below, my man. The men will want supper."

"Aye, aye, sir," answered the cook, and touching his cap, he went below at once.

"That is a good man, captain," said the doctor.

"Perhaps, sir," replied the captain. "Easy with that, men—easy," he went on to say to the men. Then, suddenly, as he saw me looking at the ship's gun, he cried, "Here, you ship's boy, out of that! Off to the cook and go to work!"

And as I hurried off, I heard him say to the doctor, "I will have no favorites on my ship." And at once I felt just as the squire did and hated the captain deeply.

Chapter X

The Voyage

ALL that night we were in a great hurry getting things in place. We had never had a night at the "Admiral Benbow" when I did half as much work, and I was tired as a dog, when, just before day, the whistle blew for the ship to start. I might have been far more tired, but nothing could have made me leave the deck then; all was so new and interesting to me—the short commands, the loud notes of the whistle, the men running here and there in the soft lights of the ship.

"Now give us a song," cried one.

"The old one," cried another.

"Aye, aye," said Long John who was standing by, and at once he began with the song I knew so well:

"Fifteen men on the dead man's chest—"

And then all the men joined in with:

"Yo-ho-ho and a bottle of rum!" And at the third "ho" they pulled with a will.

Even my great interest in the ship could not keep that song from carrying me back to my old home, and I seemed to hear the captain shouting as if he were right with us. But soon the anchor was up; there it hung dripping at the bows; soon the sails began to draw,[1] and then the land began to slip by on either side. And before I could lie down for an hour's sleep, the *Hispaniola* had begun her trip for the Island of Treasure.

I shall not tell in full all that happened, but the trip was fairly pleasant. The ship was a good one, the men were good sailors, and it was certain the captain knew his business. But before long two or three things happened which must be told.

Mr. Arrow, first of all, was even worse than the captain had feared. He could not

---

[1]**the sails began to draw.** They began to fill with the wind; they would then move the ship.

command the men, and they did what they pleased with him. Then he began to go about the ship day after day, showing sure signs that he had been drinking. Sometimes he fell and cut himself; sometimes he lay in a deep sleep all day; and sometimes for a day or two he would not drink but would do his work well.

We could never make out where he got the drink, no matter how closely we watched him. When we asked him to his face, he would only laugh if he was drunk; or if he was not, he would say that he had had nothing but water. He was not only a poor officer, but he had a bad influence on the men.

It was plain that in this way he would soon kill himself; so we were not much surprised or very sorry when one dark night we missed him and never saw him again.

"Overboard!" said the captain. "Well, gentlemen, that saves the trouble of putting him in irons."[2]

²irons, chains.

But there we were without a mate, and it was necessary, of course, for one of the men to take his place. The boatswain, Job Anderson, seemed the best man on board and served in Arrow's place from that time on. Mr. Trelawney had followed the sea and often took a watch[3] himself in good weather. And the coxswain,[4] Hands, was a careful old seaman, who could be trusted with almost any kind of duty.

He was a great friend of Long John Silver. "John is no common man," said Hands to me. "He had good training in his young days and can speak like a book when he wants to. And brave—a lion is nothing by the side of Long John! I see him fight four and knock their heads together—him all alone and without a gun."

Every man on the ship liked Silver and

---

[3]**took a watch,** took his turn on duty as guard. [4]**coxswain,** an officer who has charge of a rowboat and its men. Sailors call him the "cox'n."

even did just as he said. He had a way of talking to each and doing some service for all of
them. To me he was always kind and always
glad to see me in the galley,[5] which he kept as
clean as a new pin. The dishes were always
in their places shining, and his parrot was in
a cage in the corner.

"Come away, Hawkins," he would say,
"come and have a talk with John. Nobody
I'm more glad to see than you, my son. Sit
down and hear the news. Here's Captain
Flint—my parrot, named after the famous
pirate—here's Captain Flint saying we'll have
good sailing on our voyage. Wasn't you,
captain?"

And the bird would say, "Pieces of eight![6]
Pieces of eight! Pieces of eight!" till I wondered why it was not out of breath or till John
put a cover over the cage.

[5]**galley,** the kitchen on a ship. [6]**Pieces of eight,** Spanish
money. Each piece was marked with an "8" to show that it
was worth eight smaller pieces of money. Pieces of eight
are not used now.

"Now that bird," he would say, "is maybe two hundred years old, Hawkins, and if anybody has seen more sin, it must be the devil himself. She sailed with that pirate, the great Captain England. She's been all over the world. In Spain was where she learned 'pieces of eight.' To look at her you would think she was a baby, but you've seen a lot, haven't you, captain?"

"Stand by to go about,"[7] the bird would cry out. "And a fine one she is," the cook would say, and give her a bit of sugar. Then the bird would swear on, bad as any pirate. "There," John would say, "you can't touch mud and still keep clean. This poor old bird of mine is cursing blue fire and none the wiser. She would do it just the same in Sunday School."

And then John would bow his head

---

[7]**Stand by to go about,** a command on ship meaning to make ready to change the ship's course.

in the solemn way he had that made me believe that he was the very best of men.

All this time Squire Trelawney and the captain had not made friends with each other. The squire showed plainly that he did not like the captain. The captain, on his part, never spoke but when he was spoken to, and then sharp and short and dry. When driven to it, he said that the crew seemed to be good and that all had worked fairly well. As for the ship, he had taken a great fancy to her. "But," he would say, "all I say is, we are not home yet, and I don't like the trip."

The squire, at this, would turn away and march up and down, holding his head high.

"A little more of that man," he would say, "and I should fly to pieces."

We had some bad weather which only proved the strength of the *Hispaniola*. Every man on board seemed happy, and well he should, for I am sure there never was a company so spoiled since Noah[8] put to sea. There was rum for everybody; there were cakes on special days, such as birthdays, and always a barrel of apples open for anyone to help himself.

"Never knew good to come of it yet," said the captain to the doctor. "Spoil the hands entirely."

But good did come of the apple barrel, as you shall hear, for without it we should not have known of our danger and might all have been killed.

This is how it came about. It was about the last day of our trip out. Sometime that night or at least before noon of the next day we expected to come in sight of the Treasure Island. The *Hispaniola* was sailing bravely, and all were in the best of spirits because we

[8]**Noah.** Noah built an ark and saved himself and his family from the flood described in the Bible.

were so near the end of the first part of our voyage.

Just after the sun went down, when my work was all done and I was on my way to bed, I thought I should like an apple. I ran up on deck. All the men were in the bow[9] watching for the island. One of them was singing softly to himself, and that was the only sound to be heard except the sound of the sea against the bow and around the side of the ship.

I had to get down into the barrel, for there were very few apples left. With the soft sound of the water and the rocking of the ship, I had almost fallen asleep when a heavy man sat down close by. The barrel shook as he leaned against it, and I was about to get out when he began to speak. It was Silver, and before he had said ten words, I would not have shown myself for the world. In-

[9]**bow,** the front of the ship.

stead I lay there shaking and listening, for his very first words showed me that I alone must save the lives of all the honest men on board.

Chapter XI

What I Heard in the Apple Barrel

No, NOT I," said Silver. "Flint was captain. I was quartermaster.[1] The same time I
lost my leg, old Pew lost his eyes. It was a
smart doctor that took care of us, but he was
hanged like a dog and dried in the sun like
the rest. That was Roberts' men, and that was
what came of changing names to their ships.
Now what a ship was named, so let her stay,
I says. So they did with the one that brought
us back safe after one of our best catches. So
it was with the old *Walrus*, Flint's old ship,
that I've seen covered with red blood and
ready to sink with gold."

"Ah!" cried another voice, that of the
youngest man on board. "Flint was a fine
man, he was!"

---

[1]**quartermaster,** an officer who has some of the smaller
duties on a ship, such as helping with the steering and taking charge of the lights.

"Davis was a man, too, by all accounts," said Silver. "I never sailed along of him; first with England,[2] then with Flint, that's my story, and now here on my own account. I got nine hundred from England and two thousand from Flint, and I have it all safe in a bank. Not bad for a common sailor, is it? Where's all England's men now? I don't know. Where's Flint's? Why, most of them right here on this ship and glad to get their food—begging before that—some of them. Old Pew, as had got rich, where is he now? Dead, but for two years before that, that man was starving. He begged, and he stole, and he cut throats, and then he starved at last, by the powers!"

"Well, it ain't much use, after all," said the young seaman.

"'Tain't much use for fools, you may lay to it," cried Silver. "But now, you look here,

---

[2]**England.** Here Long John is speaking of Captain England, the captain of a pirate ship.

young man, you are young, but as smart as they come. I see that when I set my eyes on you, and I'll talk to you like a man."

You can guess how I felt when I heard this old scoundrel speaking to another in the very same words of praise as he had used to myself.

I think, if I could, I would have killed him at once. But he went on, little thinking that I heard him.

"Here it is about gentlemen of fortune.[3] They live hard, and they take a chance at hanging, but they eat and drink like kings. Then when a trip is done, they have hundreds of pounds[4] instead of hundreds of pennies in their pockets. Now most of it goes for drink and a good time, but not so with me. I puts it all away, some here, some there. It never is safe to put your money all in one

---

[3]**gentlemen of fortune.** Instead of calling themselves by their true name, pirates, these men called themselves "gentlemen of fortune." [4]**pounds,** English money. A pound is worth about $4.86.

place. I'm getting old, and once back from this trip, I'll set up like a real gentleman. And how did I begin? Before the mast,[5] like you!

"Gentlemen of fortune," he went on, "do not trust each other, but I have a way with me, I have. I get along. There was some that was afraid of Flint, but he himself was afraid of me. His men was the toughest on the sea, but when I was on his ship, they was more quiet than lambs with me. You may be sure of yourself on old John's ship."

"Well, I tell you now," said the boy, "I never half liked this job till I had this talk with you, John, but there's my hand on it."

"And a brave one you are, and smart, too," answered Silver, shaking the boy's hand, "and a fine gentleman of fortune you will make."

By this time I had begun to understand

---

[5]**mast,** the high pole which holds up the sails. **Before the mast.** The common sailors slept in the front part of the ship, or before the mast. Silver, then, began as a common sailor.

their words. By a "gentleman of fortune" they meant no more nor less than a common pirate. The talk I had just heard was the last act in the ruin of one of the honest men—perhaps the last one left on the ship. Just then Silver gave a low whistle, and another man came to join the party.

"Dick's square," said Silver.

"Oh, I knew he was square," returned the voice of the other. It was Hands. "He's no fool, is Dick. But, look here," he went on, "here's what I want to know—how much longer are we going to wait? I've had about enough of the captain, I have! I want to go into that cabin, I do. I want their food and their wines and that."

"Hands," said Silver, "your head never was much good. But you can hear, I guess; anyway, your ears is big enough. Now, here is what I say—you are to live hard, and you are to speak soft, and you are to let drink alone till I give the word, and you may lay to that."

"Well, I don't say no, do I?" growled Hands. "What I says is, when? Tell me that."

"When! by the powers!" cried Silver. "Well, now, if you want to know, I can tell you. The very last possible minute, and that's when. Here is a fine seaman, this captain, sails the ship for us. Here is this squire and doctor with a map. I don't know where it is, do I? No more do you. Well, then, I want these two to find the money and help us get it on board. Then we'll see. If I was sure of you all, that captain would sail us half-way back again before I struck."

"Why, we are all seamen on board here, I should think," said Dick.

"All ship's hands, you mean," snapped Silver. "We can sail a boat, but who can tell which way to go? If I had my way, this captain would take us back most of the way; then we wouldn't get off our course and run out of food. But I know the kind you are. I'll finish them at the island, as soon as the money is on board, and that is too soon. It makes me sick to sail with the likes of you!"

"Easy, Long John," cried Hands. "Who was crossing you?"

"Why, how many ships, think you, have I seen captured, and how many brave lads have I seen drying in the sun?" cried Silver, "and all for this same hurry and hurry and hurry. You hear me? I seen a thing or two at sea, I have. If you would just stick to your work and let me plan this, you would live high, you would. But not you! You want your drink tomorrow, and go hang."

"There is others could handle a sail and steer as well as you, John," said Hands. "They just liked a good time, they did. They wasn't so high and dry."

"So?" said Silver. "Well, where are they now? Pew was that kind, and how did he die? Flint was, and he died of drink. They was a fine lot, they was; only where are they now?"

"But," asked Dick, "when we do lay them away, what are we going to do with them?"

"Just the man for me, you are!" cried the cook. "That's what I call business! Well, what do you think? Put them on some island with no food or nothing? That was the way of England. Or cut them down? Flint or Bill Bones would take that way."

"Bill was the man for that," cried Hands. " 'Dead men never bite,' says he."

"Right you are," said Silver. "An easy man I am, but this is important. Duty is duty, and I say, 'Kill them.' When I get back home and am living like the king himself, I don't want one of them coming to see me. Wait is what I say, but when the time comes, kill them!"

"John," cried Hands, "what a man you are!"

"You will say that when you see me with Trelawney," said Silver. "I mean to break his head off with these two hands. Dick," he added, "you go like a good boy and get me an apple."

You may fancy what fear this put into me! I would have jumped and run, but I had not strength enough to do it. I heard Dick rise, and then Hands stopped him and cried:

"Oh, stop that! Don't go eating apples. Bring us a drink of rum."

"Dick," said Silver, "I trust you. There is the key. Fill a can and bring it up."

Afraid though I was, I could not help thinking that this must be how Mr. Arrow got the strong waters that killed him.

Dick was gone but a few minutes. While he was away, Hands went on talking in a voice so low I heard only a few words, but this much was clear, "Not another man of them will join us." I knew then that there were still some faithful men on board.

When Dick returned, each of the three took a drink—one "To luck," another with a "Here's to old Flint," and Silver himself sang,

"Here's to ourselves and hold your luff,[6] plenty of prizes and plenty of duff."[7]

Just then I noticed that the moon was up, and almost at the same moment the voice of the lookout shouted, "Land!"

[6]**luff,** a part of the sail. **hold your luff,** hold the sails in such a way that the ship will not move. Here Silver means to tell his men to wait quietly until the best time to strike. [7]**duff,** pudding.

SIX GREAT STORIES

Chapter XII

Council of War

FROM every part of the ship men came running up on deck. I climbed carefully out of the barrel, hid for a minute behind a sail, then ran to join Hunter and Doctor Livesey. All of the hands were there already.

Just as the moon came up, the fog had lifted, and to the south and west we saw two low hills, then a third and higher one. All this seemed like a dream to me, for I was still very much afraid. Then I heard the captain giving orders, and the ship turned so that it would just clear the island on the east.

"And now, men," said the captain, "has any one of you ever seen that land there?"

"I have, sir," said Silver. "I've gone there with a trading ship that I was cook in."

"The best place to land is on the south behind a little island, I fancy?" asked the captain.

"Yes, sir. That was a great place for pirates once, and a hand on our ship knew all the names for it. There are three hills in a row. The big one, the last one to the south, they call the Spy-Glass because they always kept someone on the watch there when they were cleaning in the bay, for that is where they cleaned the ships, sir, asking your pardon."

"I have a map here," said the captain. "See if that is the place."

Long John's eyes burned in his head as he took the map, but by the fresh look of the paper I knew it was not the one he wanted, for it was not the one we had found in Billy Bones's chest. It was an exact copy, though, with names, heights, and everything except the red crosses and the written notes. Silver must have been very angry at this, but he had the strength of mind not to show it.

"Yes, sir," said he, "this is the spot, to be sure, and very well done. Who might have made this, I wonder? The pirates didn't know enough. Oh, here it is: Captain Kidd's[1] bay—just what my shipmate called it. There is a strong current runs along the south and up the west coast, too. Right you were, sir, to keep to the east side."

"Thank you, my man," said the captain. "I'll ask you, later on, to give us some help. You may go."

I was surprised to see how boldly Silver told all this about the island, and I must say I was afraid again when I saw him coming nearer to me. He did not know, to be sure, that I had heard him from the apple barrel, but I knew by this time that he was a very dangerous fellow, and I could hardly help jumping away when he put his hand on my arm.

"This here is a sweet spot," said he, "—a sweet spot for a boy to get ashore on. You can swim and climb trees and hunt goats and

[1]**Captain Kidd,** a famous pirate.

115

go up on those big hills like a goat yourself. Why, it makes me young again. I was going to forget my wooden leg, I was. A fine thing it is to be young and have ten toes, and you may lay to that. When you want to go on shore, just ask Old John, and he'll put you up a bite to take along." And smiling at me as if we were the best of friends, he went below.

The captain, Mr. Trelawney, and Doctor Livesey were talking together, and much as I wanted to tell my story, I dared not openly break in upon them. While I was still trying to think of some way, the doctor called me. He had left his pipe below and wanted me to bring it, but as soon as I was near enough to speak without being heard by the men, I said, "Doctor, let me speak. Get Mr. Trelawney and the captain down to the cabin, then call me. I have terrible news."

The doctor's face changed ever so little, but in a minute he was master of himself.

"Thank you, Jim," said he, quite loudly; "that was all I wanted to know," as if he had asked me a question.

The three men spoke together for a little, and though none of them started or raised his voice, I knew that the doctor had told them what I said. Soon I heard the captain giving an order, and all hands were called on deck.

"My men," said the captain, "I have a word to say to you. This island is the place we have been sailing to. Every man on board has done his duty—I shall never ask to see it done better. We are going below to drink to your health, and you will have drinks brought to you to drink to our health. And now, my men, a cheer for the gentleman that does it."

The cheer followed—that was a matter of course—but it was given with such a will that it was hard to believe that these same men were planning to kill us.

"One more for the captain!" cried Long John. And this also rang out loudly.

The three gentlemen went below, and soon word was sent that I, too, was wanted. I found them seated around the table saying little, but looking troubled.

"Now," said Mr. Trelawney, "you have something to say. Speak up."

As short as I could make it, I told what Silver had said. None of them spoke till I was done, and none of them moved, but all kept their eyes upon me from first to last.

Then they made me sit down and drank to my health.

"Well, captain," said Mr. Trelawney, "you were right, and I was wrong. I was a fool."

"No more than I, sir," said the captain. "I never heard of a crew that planned trouble but what showed signs so any man with an eye in his head could see and take such steps as were needed. But this crew beats me!"

"Captain," said the doctor, "that is Silver —a very bright man."

"He would look very well hanging, sir," returned the captain. "But this is talk; it don't lead to anything. Now, I see three or four points: First, we must go on because we can't turn back. If I gave the word to turn around, they would rise at once. Second, we have time before us—at least until this treasure is found. Third, there are some hands here who are honest. Now, sir, it will have to come to blows sooner or later. Let us surprise them and come to blows some fine day when they least expect it. We can count, I take it, on your own home servants, Mr. Trelawney?"

"As upon myself," returned Mr. Trelawney.

"Three," said the captain; "and we four make seven. Now, about the honest hands?"

"Most likely Trelawney's own men that he picked up before he met Silver."

"No," replied Mr. Trelawney. "Hands was one of mine."

"I did think I could trust Hands," added the captain.

"And to think they are all English!" cried Mr. Trelawney. "Sir, I could find it in my heart to blow up the ship!"

"Well, gentlemen," said the captain, "the best I can say is not much. We must keep quiet and watch. That will be hard, I know. I would rather come to blows at once, but there is no help for it till we know our men. Keep quiet and watch."

"Jim, here," said the doctor, "can help us most of all. The men like him, and he notices everything."

"Jim, I have the greatest faith in you," added Mr. Trelawney.

This troubled me a good deal. How was I to help? And yet, strangely enough, it was through me that we did come out safe. But just then there were only seven whom we

knew we could trust, and one of them was a
boy; so of the grown men there were only six
on our side to nineteen on theirs.

The man of the island

PART III
MY SHORE ADVENTURE

Chapter XIII

How I Began My Shore Adventure

WHEN I came on deck the next morning, the island looked very different. Although there was no wind, we had gone quite a distance during the night and now lay about a mile from the low east coast.

Gray woods covered most of the land. Their dark color was broken by spots of yellow sand along the coast and by many tall pine trees on the hills, but the general coloring was even and sad. The hills ran high above the trees in sharp points of bare rock. All were of strange shapes, but the Spy-Glass, the tallest hill on the island, was the strangest of all. It was steep on every side, then was cut off suddenly and flat at the top.

The *Hispaniola* was rolling and tearing at her anchor as if she would break away. I had to hold fast to the rails, for though I was a good enough sailor when the ship was moving forward, this standing still and being rolled about like a bottle was a thing I had never learned to stand without getting sick at my stomach.

Perhaps it was this, perhaps it was the look of the island with its gray, sad woods and wild, stone peaks and the ocean roaring up the shore—at least, I hated the very thought of Treasure Island. The sun was bright and hot, and the shore birds were fishing and crying about us, and you would have thought any boy would be glad to get on land after being so long at sea, but instead my heart sank into my shoes, as the saying is.

We had a hard morning's work before us, for there was still no wind, and the boats had to be got out and the ship pulled three or four miles around the corner of the island and up into the little bay. I went into one of the boats, where, of course, I had no business. It

124

was very hot, and the men complained a great deal over their work. Anderson was in command, and instead of keeping the others in order, he complained as much as they.

"Well," he said with a curse, "this won't last always."

I thought this a bad sign, for, up to that day, the men had gone about their work willingly. Now the very sight of the island seemed to make them rebel against any command.

All the way in, Long John stood in the bow and watched the ship closely. He knew the way perfectly, and though the man sounding[1] the depth found the water deeper than we had expected, John was perfectly sure of his course.

"The tide is strong," he said, "and the current has dug out this here bay, in a manner of speaking, like a spade."

---

[1]**sounding,** measuring the depth of the water by letting down a weight on the end of a line.

We stopped about a third of a mile from the shore with the mainland on one side and a little island on the other. The bottom was clean sand. The sound of the anchor as it fell into the water sent clouds of birds wheeling and crying over the woods, but in less than a minute they were down again, and all was once more quiet.

The place was covered with woods, the trees came right down to the high-water mark, and the shores were flat; the hills some distance away formed a great half-circle around the tiny bay. Two little rivers emptied into the bay; the leaves had the bright look of poison, and the air was heavy with the smell of rotten trees.

"I don't know about treasure," said the doctor, "but we are sure to find fever here."

When the men came back on the ship, they became harder and harder to control. They lay about complaining, and even the ones we had trusted carried out orders most carelessly. Plainly, the strike was coming soon.

Long John, too, saw the danger and was busy going from one group to another, advising the men. He was all smiles and far more than willing to work. If an order was given, John would be up at once with a happy "Aye, aye, sir!" and when he had nothing else to do, he kept up one song after another as if to hide from the men his own uneasiness.

Even Long John had a hard time keeping his men in order. Of all the bad signs that troubled us that day, this was the worst, and we went below to talk it over.

"If I give another order," said the captain, "the whole ship will come down over our ears all at once. You see, when I speak, they talk back. If I speak again, they will start to fight; if I do not, they will think we are all afraid of them, and that would never do. Now, we have only one man who can help us."

"And who is that?" asked the doctor.

"Silver, sir," returned the captain. "He

wants just as much as we do to keep things quiet. He will soon talk them out of this if he has a chance, and I want to give him that chance. Let us allow the men to go on shore this afternoon. If they go, you mark my words, sir, Silver will bring them back again as gentle as lambs."

This was decided upon, and loaded pistols were given to all of the sure men. Hunter, Joyce, and Redruth were told the whole story and seemed less surprised than we had expected. Then the captain went above to talk to the crew.

"My men," said he, "we have had a hot day, and all are tired. A turn on shore will harm no one. The boats are still in the water. You may take them, and as many as want may go on shore for the afternoon. I'll fire a gun half an hour before the sun sets."

I believe they must have thought they would step on the treasure as soon as they stepped on land, for they gave a cry of joy that sounded to the hills and sent the birds once more flying over the bay.

The captain was too bright to be in the way. He left Silver to plan the party, and I am sure it was well that he did so, for if he had been with them, they would have known full well that he could not help discovering their plans. Silver was the captain, and a hard time he had with his band. Some doubted his promises, for they knew if he was not true to us, he probably would not be true to them. Some were really good men at heart and could not be led to take the ship and kill innocent men.

At last, however, the party was made up. Six men were to stay on board, and the others, among them Silver, were to go on shore.

Then it was that there came into my head the first of the wild plans that helped so much to save our lives. I got into one of the boats, and almost at the same moment it started.

None in that boat seemed to mind me,

but Silver called to ask if that were I, and I began at once to wish myself back on the ship. The boats raced for the shore, but the one I was in had some start; she was lighter and had the better men; so she went far ahead of the other. As soon as her bow struck the shore, I jumped out and ran in among the trees while the others were still far behind.

I heard them calling me, but you may be sure I paid no heed. I jumped, broke through, and ran straight ahead until I could run no longer.

Chapter XIV

The First Blow

I WAS so pleased at having escaped Long John that I began to enjoy myself and look around me with some interest on the strange land I was in. I had crossed a swampy place covered with low trees and had now come out upon the edge of an open, sandy space about a mile long. On it were a few pines and many trees that looked like oaks but had lighter leaves. These, I learned later, were called live oaks. On the far side stood more low hills.

What a joy it would be to explore, I thought. No one lived on the island, I had left the others behind, and I should find no living thing here except birds and wild animals.

I walked here and there among the trees. I saw flowers different from any I had ever seen before. Here and there I saw snakes, and one raised its head and made a sound like the

131

spinning of a top. Little did I know what an enemy he was and that the sound he made was the famous rattle. Then came more of the oaks reaching from the top of one of the low, sandy hills to the edge of another low place, which was steaming in the sun and through which another little river found its way to the sea.

Suddenly a wild bird flew up with a cry, another followed, and soon a cloud of birds was circling and screaming in the air. I thought at once that some of the men must be coming near, and I was right, for soon I heard a voice which came nearer. I crawled under one of the oaks and stayed there as quiet as I could be.

Another voice answered; then the first, which I now knew to be Silver's, took up the story. Silver's voice ran on for quite a while. The other spoke only a few words now and then. They were talking earnestly and almost fiercely, but I could not understand what they said. Then they seemed to have stopped and perhaps to have sat down, for the birds began to grow more quiet and then to light again.

And now I began to feel that there was new work for me to do. Since I had been so foolish as to go on shore with these pirates, the least I could do was to listen and learn as much as possible about their plans.

Crawling on all fours, I slowly went toward them till at last, raising my head to an opening in the leaves, I could see Long John Silver and his companion. The sun beat full upon them. Silver had thrown his hat on the ground beside him, and his face, shining with the heat, was lifted to the other's. He seemed to be begging for something.

"Tom," he was saying, "this is because I think so much of you, and you may lay to that! If I hadn't took to you like I did, do you think I'd be here warning you? It's all up, and there's nothing to do about it. Just to save your neck I tell you this, and if one of them wild ones knew, where would I be? Now, tell me, where would I be?"

"Silver," said the other—and his face was red and his voice was shaking—"Silver," said he, "you are old and honest, or have the name of it; and you have money, more than a lot of us; and you are brave, or I miss my guess. And will you let that kind of mess lead you away? Not you! As sure as God sees me, I'd rather lose my hand. And if I turn against my duty—"

Just then I heard a loud cry. It was like a cry of anger, then there was a second, and then a terrible scream. The rocks on the hills sent it back many times; the birds rose again so thick they darkened the sky; then all was quiet again, and nothing could be heard except the sound of the waves, but that terrible cry was still ringing in my head.

Tom jumped high at the sound, but Silver did not move. He stood where he was, watching closely like a snake about to strike.

"John," cried the other, reaching out his hand. "Hands off!" cried Silver, jumping back as if deadly afraid.

"Hands off, if you like, John Silver," returned the other. "You're afraid of everything because you know you're doing wrong. But in heaven's name, what was that?"

"That?" said Silver, smiling, but watching more closely than ever. "That? Oh, I suppose that was Alan."

"Alan!" cried Tom. "Then may his soul rest in peace, for he was a true seaman! As for you, John Silver, you've been my mate a long time, but you can be that no more. If I die like a dog, I'll die doing my duty. You've killed him, have you? Then kill me, too, if you can."

With that the brave fellow turned his back on the cook and started for the shore. But he did not go far. John caught a branch of a tree, held himself up by it, and threw his crutch at Tom. The point of it struck the poor fellow right between the shoulders. His hands flew up, and, with a low cry, he fell.

↓ Like enough, his back was broken, but even if he had not been badly hurt, he had no time to get up. Silver was on top of him in a moment and twice ran a long knife deep into his poor body. From my hiding-place I could hear his heavy breathing as he struck the blows.

I do not know what it is to faint, but I do know that for a while after that everything looked black to me. Silver and the birds and the tall top of the Spy-Glass went round and round before my eyes, bells rang, and voices shouted in my ears.

When I came to myself, Silver had pulled himself together, had his crutch under his arm and his hat on his head. Tom lay still on the ground, but Silver minded him not one bit. He was coolly cleaning his knife on the grass.

Everything else was as before, and I could

hardly believe that just a minute before a man had been so cruelly killed right there before my eyes.

Now John put his hand into his pocket, brought out a whistle, and blew upon it several times. Just why he did this I did not know, but I was afraid again. More men would be coming. I might be discovered. They had already killed two; might not I be next?

I began at once to crawl back again as quickly and quietly as I could to the more open part of the wood. I could hear calls coming and going between the pirates, and this sound gave me wings. I ran as I never ran before, not thinking what way I was going as long as it took me farther from them. As I ran, I grew more and more afraid.

Indeed, who could be more entirely lost than I? When the gun was fired, how should I dare go down to the boats with those murderers? Would not the first one who saw me run a knife through me? Would not the very fact that I had run away from them show them clearly that I was afraid of them and therefore knew of their plot? It was all over, I thought. Never again should I see the ship, the squire, the doctor, and the captain. There was nothing left for me but to starve or be killed by the pirates.

All this while I was still running, and without taking notice I had got into a part of the island where there were not so many wild oaks; the trees were larger and seemed more like forest trees. Among them were a few great pine trees. The air, too, was more fresh than down near the shore.

And here a new fear brought me to a stop with my heart in my mouth.

Chapter XV

The Man of the Island

SOME stones fell from the side of the hill and rattled through the trees. Looking that way, I saw something jump behind a tree. What it was, I could not tell. I saw only that it looked large and dark, but I was none the less afraid of it.

Now I was cut off on both sides. Behind me were the pirates; before me I knew not what. Even Silver seemed less terrible. I turned and, looking quickly over my shoulder, started back toward the boats.

The thing appeared again and, making a wide circle, began to head me off. I was tired, but I felt that even if I had been as fresh as I was in the morning, I could not have escaped. From tree to tree the thing ran, going on two legs like a man, but bending almost double. However, a man it was; I could no longer doubt that.

I remembered stories I had heard of wild men and was on the point of calling for help, but the very fact that it was a man made me feel more nearly safe, and my fear of Silver rose again. I stood still, looking about me for some way to escape. Then I remembered the pistol which I carried but had forgotten in my great fear. With my hand on it I turned and walked toward the man.

He must have been watching me closely, for as soon as I started toward him, he appeared again, took a step toward me, stopped, and stepped back. Then, to my surprise, he fell on his knees and held up his hands to me.

"Who are you?" I asked.

"Ben Gunn," he answered, and his voice sounded harsh like a rusty lock. "Poor Ben Gunn, I am, and you are the first man I have seen in three years."

I could see that he was a white man like myself, but his skin was badly burned by the sun. Even his lips were black, and his light blue eyes looked wild in so dark a face. His clothes were bits of old sea cloth held together by all kinds of queer fastenings—buttons, little sticks, and pieces of grass.

"Three years!" I cried. "How did that happen?"

"I was marooned,"[1] said he. "They just left me here, they did. Three years now, and I had to live on just what I could find here on the island. And many a time have I wished for home food. Do you have a piece of cheese with you? No? Many a night have I dreamed I was eating some, and then in the morning, here I were."

"If I ever get back to the ship again," said I, "you shall have all you want of it."

All this time he had been feeling my coat, rubbing my hands, looking at my shoes, and seeming as pleased as a child at seeing another person.

"If you ever get back to the ship, says

[1]**marooned,** put on shore and left alone.

you?" he repeated. "Why, now, what would stop you?"

"Not you, I know," I answered.

"And right you was," he cried; "now you—what do you call yourself, mate?"

"Jim," I told him.

He repeated the name several times, quite pleased.

"Well," said he, "I have lived that rough as you never heard of, but the Lord put me here, and I have thought it all out, and not a drop of rum will I ever take again—except just a drop now and then for luck. I'll be good, and," he added looking around and speaking in a very low voice, "I'm rich."

I now felt sure that the poor fellow had lost his mind during those three years, and I must have shown this in my face, for he repeated hotly, "Rich! rich! I says, and let me tell you this. I can make a rich man of you, and you will thank your stars, you will, that you was the first to find me."

Then a troubled look came over his face. He tightened his hold on my hand and shook his finger in my face.

"Now, tell me true. Is that Flint's ship?" he asked.

At this a happy thought came to me. I began to believe that here was a friend, and I answered him at once.

"No, it is not," I said, "and Flint is dead, but there are some of his men with us, which is very bad for the rest of us."

"Not a man—with one—leg?" he cried.

"Silver?" I asked.

"Yes, Silver!" said he. "That were his name."

"Silver is our cook and the leader of their band," I told him.

"If you were sent by Long John," said he, "I am as good as dead right now. But were you?"

I made up my mind in a moment and told him the whole story of our journey and

143

of the trouble we were having. He heard me with the greatest interest, and when I had done, he patted my head.

"A good boy you are," he said, "and in a bad way. Well, you just trust Ben Gunn. Do you think, now, that your Mr. Trelawney would be good enough to help me if I help him—him being in such a bad way?"

I told him Mr. Trelawney was the kindest of men.

"But, you see," returned Gunn, "I don't want just to be a servant to open a gate and have some nice clothes to wear. What I want is money—say a thousand pounds of what is as good as mine already."

"I am sure he would," said I. "As it was, we were to divide with all hands."

"And will he take me home?" he added.

"Why," I cried, "he is a gentleman. And besides, if we get away from the others, we shall need you to help work the ship home."

"So you would," said he, and he seemed satisfied with that.

"Now, I'll tell you this," he said, "this much and no more. I were in Flint's ship when he hid the treasure—he and six other men. They were on shore almost a week and us on the ship. One fine day Flint come back by himself in a little boat. How he done it not a man of us could make out, but there he was and the six of them dead. Billy Bones was the mate, and Long John was the quartermaster, and they asked him where the treasure was. 'You can go on shore and stay if you like,' he says, 'but as for the ship, she'll hunt for more, by thunder.' "

"Well, I was in another ship three years back, and we sighted this island. 'Boys,' said I, 'here is Flint's treasure; let's land and find it.' The captain didn't like it, but the men were all of one mind, and we landed. Twelve days we looked, and every day they had harder words for me, till one fine morning all hands went back to the ship. 'As for you,' says they, 'take this spade, and find the money for yourself.'

"Well, three years have I been here, and not a taste of English food from that day to this. Just you say them words to Mr. Trelawney," he went on. " 'Three years he were the man of the island. Sometimes, maybe, he would say a prayer; sometimes, maybe, he would think of his old mother; but most of his time were took up in another way.' And then you pinch him, just as I do!" And he looked at me in the most trusting way and pinched my arm hard.

"Then," he went on, "then you say this: 'Gunn is a good man, and he puts a lot more trust in a gentleman that was born a gentleman than in a gentleman of fortune.' "

"Well," I said, "I don't understand one word of what you are saying, but no matter. How can I get back to the ship?"

"Now," said he, "that is a question. Well,

I have a boat that I made with my two hands. I keep her under the white rock. If we have to, we might try her after dark. Hi," he broke out, "what was that?"

Just then, although the sun was still an hour or two high, there was the roar of a cannon.

"They have begun to fight!" I cried. "Follow me!"

I began to run toward the bay, while close behind me Gunn followed easily.

"Left, left," said he; "keep to your left hand! Keep under the trees! There's where I killed my first goat. They don't come here any more—afraid of me they are. And here is where I come to pray when I think maybe Sunday is come."

So he kept talking as I ran. He neither expected nor received any answer.

The shooting began again, then stopped, and then, not a quarter of a mile from me, I saw our flag flying above a wood.

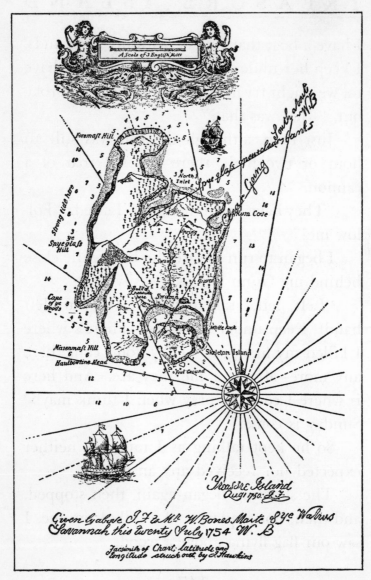

A Scale of 3 English Miles

Foremast Hill

North Inlet

Spye glass sh...ldes South bank · W.B

Skeleton Island

Strong tide here

ye Spyeglass Hill

Haulbowline Head

Mizenmast Hill

Cape of ye Woods

Spring

Swamp

Graves

Swamp

Bulk of Treasure here

White Rock

Foul Ground

Rum Cove

Haul Gang

Treasure Island
Aug¹ 1750. J.F.

Given by above J.F & Mr. W. Bones Maite of ye Walrus
Savannah this twenty July 1754 W. B

Facsimile of Chart, latitude and
longitude struck out by J. Hawkins

PART IV—THE STOCKADE[1]

Chapter XVI

Narrative Continued by the Doctor — How the Ship Was Abandoned

It was about half-past one—three bells, as the seaman says—when the two boats went ashore from the *Hispaniola*. The captain, Mr. Trelawney, and I were below talking things over. Had there been a wind, we should have attacked the six pirates who were left with us, pulled in the anchor, and sailed away to sea. But there was no wind at all, and to make matters more trying, we found that Jim, too, had gone ashore.

We did not in the least doubt him, but we were afraid for his life. It seemed an even chance that we should never see him again.

The air seemed heavy, and the day was

---

[1]**Stockade,** a high fence of thick posts stuck closely together in the ground. See the first picture in the book.

hot. The six pirates sat together complaining. At the shore we could see the two boats made fast, a man sitting on each.

Waiting was hard, and it was decided that Hunter and I should go on shore to get what information we could.

The other boats had gone a little to the right, but Hunter and I pulled straight in where we expected to find a house shown on the map. The two guarding the boats seemed uneasy at seeing us. They stopped the sea song which they had been singing, and I could see they were talking over what they ought to do. Had they gone and told Silver, all might have turned out differently; but they had their orders, I suppose, and decided to stay where they were and continue their song.

There was a little bend in the coast. I steered so as to put it between us; so even before we landed, we were out of sight of the two. As soon as our boat stopped, I jumped out and ran toward where I thought to find the house. Before I had gone a hundred yards, I came upon it.

At the top of a low hill was a spring of clear water, and over the spring had been built a log house large enough to hold about forty people. On each side of the house were holes through which one might shoot. All around this a wide space had been cleared, and then around it had been built a fence six feet high with no gate or opening. It was too strong to pull down without much time and work and too open to shelter anyone who might attack; so the people in the house had everything their own way. They could stay safe within and shoot the others down like birds. All they needed were good guards and food.

What I liked most was the spring. For though we had a good place on the *Hispaniola*, with enough arms and food, we did not have water. I was thinking this over when there came ringing over the island the cry of a man at the point of death. My heart almost stopped. "Jim is gone," I thought.

It is one thing to have been an old soldier, but still more to have been a doctor. I knew we had no time to waste. Making up my mind at once, I returned to the shore and jumped into the boat.

Hunter rowed well. We made the boat fly, and soon we were back again on the ship.

I found them all shaken, as was natural. Mr. Trelawney was sitting, his face very white, thinking what danger he had led us into, the good soul! and one of the six hands was little better.

"That man," said the captain, "is new to this work. He came near to fainting when he heard the cry. Another like that, and he would join us."

I told my plan to the captain, and he agreed.

Hunter brought the boat close against the ship, and Joyce and I set to work loading her with arms, food, and medicine. Old Redruth, with several loaded guns, stood near to protect us. Mr. Trelawney and the captain stayed above, and the captain called Mr. Hands, the principal man of the six.

"Mr. Hands," he said, "here are two of us, each with two guns. If any one of you six gives a signal of any kind, that man is dead."

They were a good deal surprised, and after talking a little, started below, thinking, no doubt, to surprise us from behind. But when they saw Redruth waiting for them there, they went about the ship again, and a head came up on deck.

"Down, dog!" cried the captain.

The head went down, and we heard no more of them.

By this time we had loaded the boat as much as we dared. Joyce and I made for shore as fast as our oars would take us.

This second trip troubled the guards in the other boats more than our first one. They again stopped their song, and one of them jumped on shore and ran up into the woods. I had half a mind to destroy their boats, but I was afraid Silver and the others might be near, and all might be lost if I tried too much.

We soon touched land in the same place as before and carried our supplies to the house. Then Joyce and Hunter remained behind as guards, while I returned to the ship.

That we should have even tried to get a second boat load seems more daring than it really was. There were more of them, but we were better armed and felt sure that if they attacked us we could defend ourselves.

Mr. Trelawney was waiting for me, all faintness gone from him now. He caught the boat and tied it, and we fell to loading again for our very lives. We could not take everything even in this second load, and we dared not risk a third; so we had to drop some of the arms into the water. But how we should have liked to take them with us!

By this time the tide was going down, and the ship was beginning to pull at her anchor. Voices were heard in the direction of the two boats at the shore. We felt, then, that Joyce and Hunter were safe, for they were some distance to the east. Still we knew it was time for us to be off.

Redruth ran down and got into the boat, and the captain spoke to the men.

"Now, men," said he, "do you hear me?"

There was no answer.

"Gray, I am speaking to you."

Still no answer.

"Gray," he said, a little louder, "I am leaving this ship, and I order you to follow your captain. I know you are a good man at heart, and I dare say not one of you is as bad as he makes out. I have my watch in my hand, and I give you half a minute to join me." Then, after a moment, "Come, my fine fellow, I'm risking my life and the lives of these good gentlemen every second."

155

There was a sound of blows, and out came
Gray with a knife-cut on the side of his face.
He came running to the captain.

"I'm with you, sir," he said.

And the next moment he and the captain
were in the boat, and we had pushed off. We
were clear of the ship but were not yet in our
log house.

Chapter XVII

Narrative Continued by the Doctor — The Jolly-Boat's[1] Last Trip

THIS last trip was quite different from the others. In the first place, the little boat was gravely overloaded. Five grown men, and three of them over six feet high, were already more than she should have carried. With the weight of the arms and food she almost went under water.

Several times the water came in, and the tails of my coat were wet before we had fairly started. The captain made us move things about a little, and we got her to lie more evenly. All the same, we were afraid to breathe.

In the second place, we were pulling against a strong current which was taking us out of our true course. If it had its way, we should come to shore beside the other boats, where the pirates might appear at any moment.

[1] Jolly-Boat, a small boat belonging to a ship.

"I cannot keep her headed for the stock-ade, sir," said I to the captain. "The tide keeps carrying her down. Could you pull a little stronger?"

"Not without turning her over," said he. "You must keep up, sir, if you please—keep up till you see you are gaining."

I tried, and found that when I headed straight east instead of north we could more nearly keep our course. "We shall never get on shore at this rate," said I.

"If this is the only course we can take, we must take it," returned the captain. "You see, sir, we cannot take a chance of being boarded by the pirates. Besides, the way we are going, the current must get weaker soon, and then we can turn back along the shore."

"It is less already, sir," said Gray; "you can turn her a bit now."

"Thank you, my man," said I, quite as if nothing had happened, for we had all quietly made up our minds to treat him like one of our own party. Suddenly the captain spoke again, and I thought his voice was a little changed.

"The gun!" said he.

"I have thought of that," said I, sure that he was thinking of an attack on the stockade. "They could never get it on shore; if they did, they could never get it through the woods."

"Look behind you," replied the captain.

We had entirely forgotten the cannon on the ship, and there, to our horror, we saw the five men busy about her, getting off the heavy cover which was kept over her while we were sailing. At that same moment I remembered that we had left on board the shot and the powder for the cannon. "Hands was Flint's best shot," said Gray, his face white.

"Who is the best shot here?" asked the captain.

"Mr. Trelawney," said I.

The captain turned toward him and said, "Will you please pick off one of those men for me? Hands, if possible."

Mr. Trelawney pointed his gun and coolly fired at Hands, who by this time was loading the cannon. But just at that moment Hands stepped to one side, the ball passed over him, and one of the other four fell.

The cry he gave was returned not only by the others on the ship but also by a number of voices from the shore. Looking that way, I saw the other pirates running from the trees and jumping to their places in the boats.

"Row, now," said the captain. "We must get on shore, or all is lost."

"Only one of their boats is being manned, sir," I said; "perhaps the others are going around by shore to cut us off."

"They'll have a hot run, sir," returned the captain.

During this time we had covered a good distance and had taken in only a little water. We were now close to shore. A few moments more and we could land. We were no longer afraid of the pirates' boat, for the tide which had held us back was now holding them back. The little point of land lay between us; so they could not fire at us. The one danger was the gun on the ship.

"Tell us when they're ready to fire, and we'll hold the boat back with the oars," said the captain. "If I dared, I'd stop and pick off another man." But we dared not stop, for we could see that Hands was about to fire.

"Ready!" cried Mr. Trelawney.

"Hold!" cried the captain.

And he and Redruth backed[2] with a great pull that sent the end of the boat under water. At the same moment we heard the report of the cannon. The ball must have gone over our heads, and the wind from it may have helped to put our boat under water.

The boat did sink, quite gently, in three feet of water, leaving the captain and me still on our feet. The other three fell head first into the water and came up wet to the skin.

[2]**backed,** rowed the boat backward.

So far there was no great harm. No lives were lost, and we could wade in to the shore without any trouble. But all of our stores and three of our five guns had gone down with the boat. Without even thinking what I did, I had caught mine up and held it up over my head. The captain, like the wise man he was, had carried his over his shoulder. To add to our troubles, we heard voices coming toward us along the shore, and we had two things to fear. First, we might be cut off from the stockade; second, Hunter and Joyce might be attacked by a number of men, and we doubted if they could defend themselves. Hunter could fight, we knew; but Joyce was a pleasant man for a house-man and to care for one's clothes, but not entirely fitted for a man of war. With all this in our minds we waded to shore as fast as we could, leaving behind us the poor little boat and a good half of our powder and food.

Chapter XVIII

Narrative Continued by the Doctor—
End of the First Day's Fighting

As FAST as possible, we ran across the wood between us and the stockade, and at every step we heard the voices of the pirates coming nearer. Soon we could hear their feet striking the ground and the breaking of branches as they ran through the trees.

I began to see that we must fire before we even reached the fence.

"Captain," said I, "Trelawney is the best shot. Give him your gun; he cannot use his own."

Trelawney took it and, cool as he had been from the start, he stopped a moment to look it over. At the same time I remembered that Gray had no arms at all and handed him my sword. It did all our hearts good to see him spit on his hand and make the blade sing through the air. It was plain that our new hand was well worth having with us.

A few steps farther we came to the edge of the wood and saw the fence in front of us. We came to the middle of the south side, and almost at the same moment seven of the pirates reached the southwest corner.

They stopped as if surprised, and before they could start again, not only we but also the two men from the house had time to fire. Even though we did not fire together, the shots did their business. One of the enemy fell, and the rest turned and ran into the woods. We loaded again and then walked around the outside of the fence to see the fallen man. He was stone dead—a ball through the heart.

Just at that moment another shot rang out, a ball whistled past my ear, and poor Redruth fell his length on the ground. Both Mr. Trelawney and I returned fire, then loaded again and turned to look after poor Redruth. We could see with half an eye that all was over.

Our fire, returning upon them so quickly, must have scattered the pirates once more, for we were allowed without any more trouble to get poor Redruth over the fence and into the house.

Poor old man! He had not said one word of surprise or of fear from the very first of our troubles till now when we laid him down to die. He had carried out every order silently and well; he was the oldest one in our party, and now it was he who was to die.

The squire went down on his knees beside him and kissed his hands, crying like a child.

"Be I going, doctor?" he asked.

"My man," said I, "you are going home."

"I wish I had had a cut at them first," he replied.

"Redruth," said the squire, "say you don't hold this against me, please!"

"Would that be respectful like, from me to you?" he asked. "However, so be it!"

After a little while he said he thought one

of us might read a prayer. "It is often done, sir," he said. And not long after, without another word, he passed away.

By this time the captain had found a tall pine tree, which had fallen near the house. With the help of Hunter he had set it up at a corner of the house. Then he had climbed upon the roof and with his own hands had run up our colors.[1]

He seemed very glad to have this done. He came back into the house and set about counting the stores as if nothing had happened. But he had an eye on Redruth all this time, and as soon as all was over, he came with another flag and spread it over the poor fellow.

"Don't take on so, sir," he said, holding the squire's hand. "All is well with him; no fear for a hand that has lost his life in his duty." Then he took me to one side.

"Doctor," he said, "in how many weeks

[1]colors, flag.

do you expect your friends to start looking for us?"

I told him it was not a question of weeks but of months; that if we were not back by the end of August, they would send for us, but not before that. "You can count it up," I said.

"Well," said he, looking troubled, "allowing for all good gifts from heaven, I should say we were in a pretty bad way."

"How do you mean?" I asked.

"I mean, sir," he replied, "it is too bad we lost that second load. As for powder and shot, we are all right. But the food is short— so short, doctor, that perhaps we are as well without that extra mouth." And he pointed to the dead man on the floor.

Just then, with a whistle, a ball passed high over the roof of the house and fell in the woods behind us.

"Well," said the captain, "fire away! You have little enough powder already, my boys."

167

The next shot was a better one, and the ball fell inside the fence, throwing up a cloud of sand.

"Captain," said Mr. Trelawney, "the house cannot be seen from the ship. It must be the flag they are firing at. Would it not be wiser to take it in?"

"Strike my colors!"[2] cried the captain. "No, sir, not I." And I think we were all glad that he felt so.

All through the evening they kept firing away. Ball after ball flew over or fell short or threw up sand near the stockade, but none hurt us.

"There is one good thing about all this," said the captain. "They are firing right across the woods in front of us; so none of them will be there. The tide has gone down; our stores should be above the water now. Who will go down and bring up the meat?"

Gray and Hunter came forward. Well

[2]**Strike my colors,** take down my flag.

armed, they stole down toward the shore, but it was no use. The pirates were there before them and were already carrying away our things. Silver was in command, and every man now carried a gun. Silver must have brought his own stores on board without the squire's knowing anything about it.

The captain sat down to his log[3] and wrote:

"Alexander Smollett, master; David Livesey, ship's doctor; Abraham Gray, carpenter's mate; John Trelawney, owner; John Hunter and Richard Joyce, owner's servants, landsmen—being all that is left faithful of the ship's company—with stores for ten days on short rations, came to shore this day and flew British colors[4] on the log house in Treasure Island. Thomas Redruth, owner's servant, landsman, shot by mutineers;[5] James Hawkins, cabin-boy—"

[3]log, a book in which a ship's daily records are kept. [4]flew . . . colors, raised a flag. [5]mutineers, persons who refuse to obey their officers or leaders.

I, too, was wondering where the boy might be when we heard a call from the land side.

"Doctor! Squire! Captain! Hunter, is that you?"

I ran to the door to see Hawkins, safe and sound, climbing over the stockade.

Chapter XIX

Narrative Resumed by Jim Hawkins ~ The Garrison[1] at the Stockade

As soon as Ben Gunn saw the colors, he stopped and sat down.

"Now," said he, "there is your friends, sure enough."

"Perhaps it is the pirates," I answered.

"That!" he cried. "Why, in a place like this where none comes but gentlemen of fortune, Silver would fly the Jolly Roger[2] and don't you think he wouldn't. No, there is your friends. There has been blows, too, and I guess your friends has had the best of it; and there they are in the old stockade that was made years ago by Flint. He was a man with a head, was he! Except for drink, his like never was seen. He was afraid of none, not he; only Silver."

"Well," said I, "that may be so; but all the

[1]**Garrison,** soldiers defending a fort. [2]**Jolly Roger,** a pirate's flag, black with a skull and two bones crossed in white on it.

more reason that I should hurry and join them."

"No, mate," he returned, "not you. You are a good boy, I know it; but you are only a boy. Now Ben Gunn is smart. Rum wouldn't bring me there where you are going, not till I see your captain and gets it on his word of honor. And you must not forget my words: 'A great sight,' you must say, 'a great sight more confidence'—and then you pinches him."

And he pinched *me* the third time with the same air of brightness.

"And when you want Ben Gunn, you know where to find him. Just where you found him today. And him that comes is to have a white thing in his hand, and he's to come alone. Oh! and you say this: 'Ben Gunn,' says you, 'has reasons of his own.'"

"Well," said I, "I think I understand. You have a plan, and you want to see the squire or the doctor, and you will be where I found you. Is that all?"

"And when?" he added. "Why, from about noon to about six bells."[3]

"Good," said I, "and now may I go?"

"You won't forget?" he asked. " 'A great sight, and reasons of his own,' says you. Reasons of his own, that is the main thing! Well, then, I guess you can go. And if you was to see Silver, you wouldn't go and sell me, would you? 'No,' says you, and if the pirates come ashore, there will be men killed before morning."

Just then there was a loud report, and a cannon ball came tearing through the trees and fell in the sand near where we were talking. The next moment each of us had run in a different direction.

All through the next hour reports shook the island, and balls kept tearing through the woods. I moved from one hiding-place to another while those terrible balls kept fol-

---

[3]six bells. Time on a ship is told by bells. Six bells means three o'clock.

lowing us. At last, though I still dared not go to the stockade, where the balls fell thickest, I began to gain heart and crept down to the trees along the shore.

The sun had just set. The tide was far out, so much of the sand was dry; and the air, after the heat of the day, seemed very cold.

The *Hispaniola* lay where we had left her, but sure enough, there was the Jolly Roger waving from her top. As I looked, there was another report, and one more round of shot whistled through the air. It was the last round fired.

I lay for some time watching the men. They were breaking up something on the shore—the rowboat. There was a great fire burning near the mouth of the river, and between that point and the ship one of the boats kept going and coming.

The men were shouting like children, but their voices sounded as if they had had too much to drink.

At last I thought I might return to the stockade, which was pretty far down along the shore. As I rose to my feet, I saw, rising from among the low trees, a high, white rock. This, I thought, might be the white rock of which Gunn had spoken. Some day we might need a boat, and now we should know where to find one.

Then I walked carefully along the edge of the woods to the back of the stockade and was soon with my own party.

I told my story and then began to look about me. The house was made of pine logs— roof, walls, and floor. Of course this made the floor very uneven. There was a porch at the door, and beside this a little spring flowed into a basin made of a great iron ship's kettle with the bottom broken out and sunk to the top in the sand.

The sides of the hill and all inside of the stockade had been cleared of trees to build the house. Most of the soil had been washed away after the trees had been cut down, but where the little stream ran down from the kettle, the grass was still green. Trees still grew very close around the stockade—so close that if the pirates had come up to attack us, we could not have seen them until they were upon us.

The cold evening wind blew through the cracks in the house and brought with it a rain of fine sand. There was sand in our eyes, sand in our mouths, sand in our food, and sand dancing in the spring. Our chimney was a hole in the roof. Only a little of the smoke found its way out, and the rest blew about the house, burned our noses, and kept us wiping our eyes.

Gray, the new man, had his face tied up in bandages because of the cut which he got in breaking away from the pirates. Poor old Redruth lay along the wall stiff and cold under the Union Jack.[4]

[4]Union Jack, the British flag.

If we had not been busy, we should all have felt very blue, but the captain was never a man for that. All hands were called up before him, and he divided us into watches.[5]

The doctor, Gray, and I made one watch; the squire, Hunter, and Joyce made the other. Tired as we were, two were sent out to get wood for the fire, two were sent to dig a grave for Redruth, the doctor was named cook, and I was put at the door to watch. The captain himself went from one to another, keeping up our spirits and helping in every way he was able.

From time to time the doctor came to the door for a little air and to rest his eyes, which were almost smoked out of his head. When he came, he always had a word for me.

"That man, the captain," he said once, "is a better man than I am. And when I say that, it means a lot, Jim."

[5]**divided us into watches,** divided us into groups to act as guards.

Another time he came, put his head on one side, and looked at me.

"What kind of man is this Gunn?" he asked.

"I don't know, sir," I said. "I am not sure his mind is right."

"If there is any doubt about it, it is," said the doctor. "He could not help seeming a little bit strange after living alone on this island for three years. Was it cheese you said he wanted?"

"Yes, sir," I answered.

"Well," said he, "you have seen my snuff-box,[6] I am sure. And you never saw me take snuff. In that box I have a piece of cheese which came from Italy—very good. Well, that will go to our friend Gunn!"

Before we ate, we buried old Redruth and stood around sadly for a time. Then the doctor, the squire, and the captain, after they had

---

[6]snuff-box, box holding powdered tobacco, which it was once the fashion to breathe into the nose.

had a drink, got together to talk over their plans.

Our stores were so low we should soon have to give up; so the best thing to do was to kill off as many pirates as we could until they pulled down their flag or ran away with the ship. Four of them had already been killed, two were hurt—one at least was badly hurt or perhaps dead.

They had rum in the ship, and we knew they would drink so much they would forget to keep watch. Besides, it was hot; they had camped in a very wet place, and they had no medicines; so the doctor was sure they would all be ill before a week.

"Then," said the doctor, "they will try to shoot all of us down; but if they cannot do that, soon they will be glad to leave."

"First ship I ever lost," said the captain.

I was dead tired, and when I got to sleep, I slept soundly. The rest were up and had had breakfast when I heard a cry of "Flag of truce!"[7] Then another voice cried, "Silver himself!" At that I jumped up, rubbing my eyes, and ran to a hole in the wall.

[7]**flag of truce,** a white flag which means that the persons carrying it want to stop fighting for a while.

Chapter XX

Silver's Embassy[1]

Sure enough, there were two men, one of them waving a white cloth and the other, Silver himself, standing by.

It was still quite early and cold. The sky was bright and clear, but a heavy mist lay low over the land and showed that the island was a damp, unhealthy place.

"Keep out of sight, men," said the captain. "Ten to one this is a trick.

"Who goes? Stand, or we fire!"

"Flag of truce!" cried Silver.

The captain kept himself out of the way of a shot, should any be fired. He turned and spoke to us.

"Dr. Livesey, watch the north side, please; Jim the east; Gray the west. All hands to their arms, and be careful." And then he turned to Silver.

"And what do you want?" he cried.

[1]**Embassy,** an errand to a ruler or leader.

The other man answered, "Captain Silver, sir, to come up and make terms."

"Captain Silver! I don't know him. Who is he?" cried the captain. And we could hear him saying to himself, "Captain, is it? Captain, indeed."

Long John answered for himself.

"Me, sir. These poor fellows chose me captain after you ran away—ran away and left them. We'll join you again if we can come to terms. All I ask is your word, Cap'n Smollett, to let me out of here safe and give me one minute to get away before your men fire at me."

"My man," said the captain, "I do not wish to talk to you. If you wish to talk to me, you may come; that is all. If there is any shooting done, it will be on your side, and may the Lord help you."

"A word from you is enough," cried Long John gayly. "I know a gentleman when I see one, and you may lay to that."

The man who carried the flag tried to hold Silver back, but Silver laughed and walked up to the stockade. Then he threw his crutch over, climbed up, and dropped safely to the other side.

I must say I was far too taken up with what was going on to be of any use as a guard. Indeed, I had left the opening where I had been told to stand and had slipped over behind the captain.

Silver had hard work getting up the hill, for it was steep, it was covered with tree stumps, and the sand was so soft that his crutch sank into it. But at last he stood before the captain and touched his hat just as any good soldier might have done.

"Here you are, my man," said the captain. "You had better sit down."

"Can I come into the house, captain?" asked Long John. "This is a cold morning to sit outside on the sand."

"Why, Silver," said the captain, "if you

had pleased to be an honest man, you might have been in your own place on the ship right now. This is your own doing. You are my ship's cook—and then you were treated right— or you are Cap'n Silver, a common pirate, and then you can go hang!"

"Well, well, cap'n," returned the sea cook, sitting down on the sand as he was told, "just give me a hand up again, that's all. A sweet, pretty place you have here. And there is Jim! The top of the morning to you, Jim. Why, there you all are together like a happy family."

"If you have anything to say, my man, better say it," said the captain.

"Right you are, Cap'n Smollett," replied Silver. "Duty is duty, to be sure. Well, now you look here, that was a good lay of yours[2] last night. Yes, indeed, it was a good lay, and some of my men was afraid—maybe all of them was, and maybe I was; maybe that's why I came here. But you mind, cap'n, that will

[2] **a good lay of yours,** a good trick you played.

never happen again, no indeed. My men will just have to slow up a little on the drink. Maybe you think we had all been drinking, but not I. I was only dog tired, and if I hadn't gone to sleep just that minute, I'd have caught you in the act, I would. He was still living when I got to him."

"Well," said the captain, as cool as he could be.

Little did he understand of what Silver said, but you could not have guessed it from his manner. As for me, I began to understand. Ben Gunn's words came back to me. I began to think gladly that he had paid the pirates a visit while they lay around the fire drunk and that now we had one less to fight.

"Well, here it is," said Silver; "we want that treasure, and we are going to get it—that's our point. And I reckon your point is you would just as soon not be killed. Now you have that map."

"And what if I have?" asked the captain.

"Oh, well, you have, I know that," returned Long John, "and we want it. Now I don't want to hurt any of you."

"Well," said the captain, "we know just what you expect to do, and we don't care, for you can never do it." And the captain coolly filled his pipe.

"If Gray—" Silver broke out.

"Stop there!" cried the captain. "Gray told me nothing, and I asked him nothing; and I would see you and him and this whole island blown to pieces first. That's what I think of you, my man."

This bit of temper seemed to cool Silver down. "Like enough," said he, "and seeing as how you are about to take a pipe, I'll just take one myself."

He filled his pipe and lighted it, and the two men sat smoking for quite a time, now looking each other in the face, now looking away, now leaning over to spit. It was as good as a play to see them.

"Now," said Silver, "here it is. You give us the map, and stop shooting poor seamen, and breaking their heads in while they are sleeping. Then you can choose. You can come along with us once we get that money, and, upon my honor, we'll put you on shore in some safe place. Or if you don't want that, you can stay here, you can. We'll divide stores with you, and I tell you, on my honor, as before, the first ship I see I'll send here to pick you up. Now that's talking. Better you could never get. And I hope"—speaking more loudly—"that all hands here will think this over, for what is said to one is said to all."

The captain rose from his seat. "Is that all?" he asked.

"Every last word," answered John.

"Very good," said the captain. "Now you hear me. If you will come up, one by one, I'll put you all in irons and take you home for a fair trial. If not, as my name is Smollett, I'll stand by the king's colors and see you all in the bottom of the ocean. You will never find that money. You can't sail the ship—not a man among you could. You can't fight us— Gray got away from five of you. These are the last good words you get from me; for, upon my word, I'll kill you the next time I see you. Now go, and be quick."

Silver's face was a picture. His eyes flashed with anger. "Give me a hand up!" he cried.

"Not I," returned the captain.

"Who will give me a hand up?" he roared.

Not one of us moved. With a fierce curse he crawled to the corner of the house, pulled himself up on his crutch, and spat into the spring.

"There!" he cried, "see what I think of you. Before an hour I'll tear down this old house. Laugh now, but before an hour you will laugh on the other side."

With another curse he walked to the fence, was helped over, and was soon lost among the trees.

Chapter XXI

The Attack

As soon as Silver disappeared, the captain, who had been watching him, turned toward the house and found not a man of us at his post but Gray. It was the first time we had seen him angry.

"Quarters!"[1] he shouted. And then, as we got back to our places, "Gray," he said, "your name will go in the log; you have stood by your duty like a man. Mr. Trelawney, I am surprised at you, sir. Doctor, I thought you had been in the army! If that was how you served, sir, you would have been better at home."

The doctor's men were all back at their places, the rest were busy loading the spare guns, and everyone with a red face, you may be certain.

[1]**Quarters,** go to your places.

189

The captain looked on for a while in silence. Then he spoke.

"My men," said he, "I have given Silver a red-hot word on purpose; and before the hour is out, as he said, they will be upon us. They have numbers—I need not tell you that—but we fight under cover. A minute ago I should have said we were fighting under command. I have no doubt that we can beat them if you choose."

Then he went the rounds and saw that all was clear.

On the two short sides of the house, east and west, there were only two holes; on the south side where the porch was, two again; and on the north side, five. There were twelve guns for the seven of us. The firewood had been built into four piles, tables you might say, one about the middle of each side. On each of these tables some ammunition and four loaded guns were laid ready to be used. The swords were placed in the middle.

"Put out the fire," said the captain; "we don't need the heat, and we must not have smoke in our eyes." Mr. Trelawney carried out the captain's command.

"Hawkins hasn't had his breakfast. Hawkins, help yourself, and back to your post to eat it," continued Captain Smollett. "Hurry now, my boy, you'll want it before you are done. Hunter, serve out drinks to all hands."

And while this was going on, the captain finished, in his own mind, the plan of the defense.

"Doctor, you will take the door," he continued. "Watch, and don't let them see you; keep within, and fire through the porch. Hunter, take the east side, there. Joyce, you stand by the west, my man. Mr. Trelawney, you are the best with a gun—you and Gray will take this long north side with the five holes. It is there the danger is. If they can get up to it and fire in upon us through those holes, things would begin to look bad. Hawkins, neither you nor I are much good with the guns; so we will stand by to load and bear a hand."[2]

As the captain had said, the cold air had passed. As soon as the sun rose above the trees, it fell with all its force, and the sand was baking. The men took off their coats and rolled up their sleeves. We stood there in the heat, waiting. An hour passed away.

"Hang them!" said the captain. "This is as dull as a dark day."

Just at that moment came the first sound of the attack.

"If you please, sir," said Joyce, "if I see anyone, am I to fire?"

"I told you so!" cried the captain.

"Thank you, sir," returned Joyce.

Nothing followed for a time; but we were all ready, the men at their places, the captain out in the middle of the house with his mouth shut and a frown on his face.

[2]**bear a hand,** help.

Suddenly Joyce seized his gun and fired. The report had not died away until another was heard and another from without. Then one after another, from every side of the house, reports were heard. Several bullets struck the house, but not one entered. As the smoke cleared away, the woods around us looked as quiet as before. Nothing moved; the enemy were nowhere in sight.

"Did you get your man?" asked the captain.

"No, sir," replied Joyce. "I believe not, sir."

"Next best thing to tell the truth," said the captain. "Load his gun, Hawkins. How many should you say there were on your side, doctor?"

"Three shots were fired on this side, two close together, one a little to the west."

"Three!" repeated the captain. "And how many on yours, Mr. Trelawney?"

But it was not easy to answer this. There

had come many from the north—seven, Squire
Trelawney thought; eight or nine, Gray said.
From the east and west only one fire had come.
It was plain that the attack would come from
the north, and on the other three sides they
were making a show. But Captain Smollett
made no change in his plans. If the enemy
had a chance at any of the holes, they would
kill us like rats in our own stronghold.

Nor had we much time left for thought.
Suddenly, with a loud cry, a little cloud of
men came from the woods on the north side
and ran straight on our stronghold. At the
same moment, fire was opened from the
woods, and a rifle ball sang through the opening, breaking the doctor's gun into bits.

Then they came over the fence like mon-
keys. Squire and Gray fired again and again.
Three men fell, but of these one was not
hurt, for he jumped up and ran back into the
woods.

Two had been killed, one had fled, four

had made good their hold inside our fence; while from the woods seven or eight men kept up a hot fire on the house.

The four who were on the inside made straight for our building, shouting as they ran, and the men among the trees shouted back to encourage them. Our men fired several times, but such was their hurry that not one appeared to have hit his mark. In a moment the four were upon us.

The head of Job Anderson appeared at the middle hole.

"At 'em, all hands, all hands!" he shouted.

At the same moment another took hold of Hunter's gun, wrenched it from his hands, got it through the hole, and with one blow, laid the poor fellow senseless on the floor. At the same time a third, running all round the house, appeared suddenly in the door and attacked the doctor with his sword.

A moment ago we were firing, under cover, at an enemy on the outside; now it was we who lay without cover and could not return a blow.

The house was full of smoke, and this made us feel a bit more safe. Cries and shouts, firing of guns, and one loud groan sounded in my ears.

"Out, boys, out, and fight 'em in the open! Swords!" cried the captain. I took a sword from the pile, and someone, at the same time, getting another, gave me a cut across the hand which I hardly felt. I ran out of the door. Someone was close behind, I knew not whom. Right in front, the doctor was running down the hill after one of the pirates, and just as my eyes fell upon him, beat down his guard and sent him falling on his back with a great cut across his face.

"Round the house, boys! Round the house!" the captain cried; and even in the noise I could tell a change in his voice.

I followed his command, and with my sword raised, ran round the corner of the

196

house. Next moment I was face to face with Anderson. He roared out, holding his sword high above his head. I had not time to be afraid, but before the blow landed, leaped to one side and, falling in the soft sand, rolled down the hill.

When I first went out of the door, the other pirates had been all ready to make an end of us. One man in a red cap, with his knife in his mouth, was even upon the top of the fence and had one leg across. Well, so short had been the time that when I found my feet again, the fellow with the red cap was still half-way over, another still just showing his head above the top. And yet, in this short time, the fight was over, and the victory was ours.

Gray, following close behind me, had cut down big Anderson before he had time to get over his last blow. Another had been killed in the very act of firing into the house. A third, as I had seen, the doctor had ended with one blow. Of the four who had come up over the top, only one was left, and he was now climbing out again with the fear of death upon him.

"Fire, fire from the house!" cried the doctor. "And you, boys, back under cover."

But his words were lost, and the last pirate got away and escaped into the woods. In three seconds nothing was left of the enemy but the five who had fallen.

The doctor and Gray and I ran fast for cover. The others would soon be back where they had left their guns, and at any moment fire might begin again.

By this time the house was cleared of smoke, and we saw with one look the price we had paid for victory. Hunter lay stunned; Joyce, shot through the head, would never move again. Right in the center Squire Trelawney was holding the captain, one as pale as the other.

"The captain is hurt," said the squire.

"Have they run?" asked the captain.

"All that could, you may be sure," returned the doctor, "but five of them will never run again."

"Five!" cried the captain. "Come, that's better. Five against three leaves us four to nine. The odds are better than we had at starting. We were seven to nineteen then, or thought we were, which is as bad to bear."

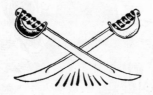

"By your leave, I'll strike these colors."

PART V – MY SEA ADVENTURE

Chapter XXII

How My Sea Adventure Began

THERE was no return of the pirates, and we had the place to ourselves and a quiet time to help the wounded and get dinner. Squire and I cooked outside, in spite of the danger, and even there we could hear the loud cries of the men the doctor was trying to help. Out of the eight who had fallen in battle only three were still living —one of the pirates, Hunter, and the captain. The first two of these were as good as dead. The pirate died under the doctor's care. Hunter lived all day, but some of his bones were broken, and his head was hurt badly. He died, without making a sound, sometime in the night.

As for the captain, though his wounds were painful, he was not so badly hurt. He was sure to get well, the doctor said, but for weeks to come he must not walk or move his arm, nor so much as speak when he could help it.

My own small cut on the hand was nothing. The doctor fixed it up, and just for fun pulled my ears for me.

After dinner Squire Trelawney and the doctor sat by the captain's side and talked a long time. Then the doctor took up his hat and guns, put on his sword, took the map, and set out toward the north through the trees.

Gray and I were sitting together at the far end of the house to be out of hearing of our officers, who were talking together. Gray took his pipe out of his mouth and almost forgot to put it back again so great was his surprise at seeing the doctor starting out alone.

"Why, in the name of Davy Jones![1] Is the doctor mad?" he said.

"Why, no," said I. "He is about the last of this crew for that, I take it."

"Well, shipmate," said Gray, "mad he may not be; but if *he's* not, then *I* am."

"I take it," replied I, "the doctor has his plan; and if I am right, he's going now to see Ben Gunn."

I was right, as appeared later; but, at the same time, the house being so hot, and the sand on the outside shining in the bright sun, I began to get another thought into my head, which was by no means right. I began to think about the doctor walking in the cool woods with the birds about him and the pleasant smell of the pines. As I sat cooking, with my clothes sticking to me, and so much blood about me, and so many poor dead bodies lying around, I had a feeling of hate for the place that was almost as strong as fear.

[1]**Davy Jones,** the spirit of the sea.

All the time I was washing out the house and then washing up the things from dinner, this feeling kept growing stronger and stronger. At last, being near a bread-bag and no one there looking at me, I took the first step toward my escape, and filled both pockets of my coat with bread.

I was a fool, if you like, and it was certain I was going to do a foolish thing; but I made up my mind to do it with all the care in my power. This bread, should anything happen to me, would keep me from starving, at least till far on in the next day.

The next thing I laid hold of was a pair of pistols, and as I already had some powder and bullets, I felt myself well supplied with arms.

As for the plan I had in my head, it was not a bad one in itself. It was to go down the point that divides the little bay from the open sea, find the white rock I had seen last evening, and see if it was there or not that Ben

Gunn had hidden his boat; a thing quite worth doing, as I still believe. But as I was certain I should not be allowed to leave the stockade, my only plan was to slip out when no one was looking; and that was so bad a way of doing it that it made the thing itself wrong. But I was only a boy, and I had made my mind up.

Well, as things at last fell out, I found a fine opportunity. Squire Trelawney and Gray were busy helping the captain with his bandages; the way was clear; I started for the thickest of the trees, and before I was missed, I was out of reach of my friends.

This was the second time I did a foolish thing in leaving my friends without saying a word. It was far worse than my first wild act when I left the ship in the pirates' boat, for now I left only two sound men to guard the house; but like the first, it was a help toward saving all of us.

I took my way straight for the east coast

of the island, for I wanted to go down the sea side of the point to keep from being seen from the bay. It was already late in the afternoon, although still warm and sunny. As I went on through the tall woods, I could hear from far before me not only the thunder of the waves but the blowing of the trees, which showed me the sea breeze was higher than usual. Soon the air began to feel cool, and a few steps farther on, I came into the open and saw the sea lying blue in the sun and the waves tossing along the shore.

I have never seen the sea quiet around Treasure Island. The sun might blaze above, the air be without a stir, the sea blue, but still these great waves would be beating along all the outside coast day and night. I don't believe there is anywhere a spot on the island where a man would be out of the sound of their noise.

I walked along beside the waves with great pleasure, till, thinking I was now far enough to the south, I went behind some thick bushes and moved carefully up the middle of the point.

Behind me was the sea, in front the bay. The high sea wind was already at an end. It had been followed by light winds from the south bringing great banks of fog. The bay lay still as when we had entered it. The *Hispaniola*, in that clear mirror, was showing plainly from the top of the masts to the water line, the pirate's flag hanging high.

Along the side of the ship lay one of the small boats—Silver in it, while two of the men leaned over the edge of the ship, one of them with a red cap—the very one I had seen some hours before with one leg over the fence. They appeared to be talking and laughing, though from where I was, as much as a mile away, I could, of course, hear no word of what was said.

All at once there began the wildest screaming, which at first gave me a bad start. But

I soon remembered the voice of Captain Flint and even thought I could make out the bird by her bright feathers as she sat upon her master's hand.

Soon after, the little boat pulled off for shore, and the man with the red cap and his companion went below the deck of the *Hispaniola*.

Just about the same time the sun had gone down, and as the fog was fast coming in, it began to grow dark. I saw I must lose no time if I were to find the boat that evening.

The white rock, easy enough to see, was still a good way down the point, and it took me quite a while to get up to it, crawling on all fours most of the way. Night had almost come when I laid my hands on its rough sides. Right below it there was a small hollow of green grass, hidden by banks and thick bushes about knee-deep. In the center, sure enough, was a little tent, like those the gypsies carry about with them in England.

I made my way to the tent, lifted a side, and there was the boat I was looking for. It was very small and light—made of wood and covered with skins—and so it was very easy to carry.

Well, now that I had found the boat, you would have thought I should be content; but I had already thought of another plan. This was to slip out under cover of night, cut the ship adrift, and let her go ashore where she might. I had made up my mind that the pirates, having lost so many men, would go back to the ship and put out to sea. This, I thought, would be a bad thing for us, and now that I had seen how they left their men without a boat to watch the *Hispaniola,* I thought it might be done with little risk.

While I sat and waited for night to come, I ate my bread. It was a fine night for my plan. The fog was heavy, and the island was covered when, at last, I put the little boat on my shoulders and got it down to the water.

Through the fog I could see the light from the cabin of the ship. I pointed my boat toward it and started off.

Chapter XXIII

The Ebb-Tide[1] Turns

THE BOAT, as I soon learned, was very safe for a person of my height and weight, but by no means easy to guide. Do as you pleased, she would not go straight, and turning round and round seemed to be her best move. Even Ben Gunn himself had said that she was hard to guide until you knew her way.

It was certain I did not know her way. She turned every way but the one I wanted to go, and I should never have reached the ship at all but for the tide. It was well for me that I was being carried down, and there lay the *Hispaniola*, right before me. At first in the dark she looked like a large black mass, but my eyes soon found her shape, and the next moment, it seemed, I was next to her rope and had my hand on it.

The rope was tight, and the ship was pull-

[1] **Ebb-Tide,** low tide.

ing so hard at her anchor that I knew it would not be safe for me and my little boat if I cut it too quickly. This brought me to a full stop, and while I was trying to think of a way to carry out my plan, a puff of wind from the southwest made the ship swing a little to one side, and I felt the rope ease up in my hand.

With that I made up my mind, took out my knife, opened it with my teeth, and cut one thread after another till only two were left. Then I lay quiet, waiting for another breath of wind to change the ship again.

All this time I heard the sound of loud voices on the ship, but to tell the truth, my mind had been so taken up with other thoughts that I had hardly listened. Now that I had nothing else to do, I began to listen to their loud talk.

One, I could tell, was Hands, that had been Flint's gunner. The other, of course, was my friend of the red cap. Both men had been drinking, and they were also angry.

Curses flew between them, and every now and then there was such a burst as I thought would end with blows. But after a time the voices got lower and at last were quiet.

On shore, I could see the light from the camp fire of the pirates, which was burning through the trees. Someone was singing an old sea song, which I had heard more than once on the ship.

At last the wind came; the ship drew nearer in the dark. I felt the rope ease up once more and, with a good hard try, cut it through.

The wind was so light that it moved my boat very little, but I was almost thrown against the ship's side as she turned slowly across the current. I had to fight hard to keep from going under, and just as I made my way clear of the danger, my hands came across a light cord that was falling over the side of the *Hispaniola*. Without thinking, I took hold of it.

213

Why I should have done so, I cannot say, but once I had it in my hands and found it was fast, I decided to pull myself up and have a look through the cabin window. I pulled in, hand over hand, until I could see the roof and a part of the inside of the cabin.

By this time the ship and my little boat were gliding through the water pretty fast. We were already about on a line with the camp fire. The ship was "talking," as sailors say, for she was hitting the waves with a splash, and until I got my eye to the window, I could not understand why the men who were left on watch had taken no notice. It took only one look for me to see why. The two men were in a fight, each trying to kill the other.

I dropped back into my boat again, and none too soon, for I was near overboard. For a moment I could see nothing but those two red faces under the smoking light. I closed my eyes to let them get used to the dark again.

The men on the shore were about the fire singing that old song I had heard so often:

"Fifteen men on the dead man's chest—
Yo-ho-ho, and a bottle of rum!
Drink and the devil had done for the rest—
Yo-ho-ho, and a bottle of rum!"

I was just thinking about the words of that song and the two men on the ship when my little boat gave a sudden turn. At the same moment she seemed to change her course and to be moving much faster.

I opened my eyes at once. All round me the water was stirring, and the waves made a cutting sound. The ship herself, a few yards away, seemed to stagger in her course, and I saw her bow a little against the black sky. As I looked longer, I was sure she, too, was moving toward the south.

I looked over my shoulder, and my heart jumped into my mouth. There right behind me was the light of the fire on the shore. The current had changed and taken with it both the ship and my dancing little boat. We were now rushing toward the open sea.

Suddenly the ship in front of me turned from her straight course about as much as twenty degrees; and almost at the same moment one shout followed another from on board. I could hear feet pounding on the ladder. I knew then that the two men had come to their senses and were seeing their danger.

I lay down flat in the bottom of the boat, expecting every moment that the high waves would throw me into the deep sea, where all my troubles would end. I was not afraid to die, but I could not bear to look at the danger as it came.

So I must have stayed for hours, the waves beating me back and forth and sometimes covering me with flying spray. Every minute I thought would be my last. After a time I became so tired that sleep fell upon me, and in my rolling boat I lay and dreamed of home.

Chapter XXIV

The Cruise of the Coracle[1]

It was broad day when I opened my eyes and found myself rolling at the southwest end of Treasure Island. The sun was up but was still behind the hills which on this side came down to the sea in great high walls.

Haulbowline Head and Mizzenmast Hill were right by me—the hill bare and dark. The head stood out above walls almost fifty feet high, and all around it was much fallen rock. I was such a little way from the shore that my first thought was to land.

However, I soon gave up that plan. Among the rocks the waves beat high; loud pounding and heavy sprays, flying and falling, followed one after another. I saw myself, if I tried to go nearer the shore, beaten to death; or if I should land, I should never be able to make my way to the top of those high walls of rock.

[1]Coracle, a small light boat.

Nor was that all; I could see on top of the rocks and hear, falling into the sea with loud splashes, large slimy-looking sea animals, half a hundred of them together, it seemed. They made the rocks ring with their barkings.

I have learned since that they were sea-lions and would not have hurt me. But the look of them, added to the waves and the rocks on the shore, was more than enough to change my plan of landing in that place.

I felt certain that I should have a better chance somewhere before me. To the north the land runs in a long way, leaving, at low tide, a long stretch of yellow sand. To the north of that, again, there comes another point of land, Cape of the Woods, as it was marked upon the map, covered with tall green pines which came down to the edge of the sea.

I remembered what Silver had said about the current that sets to the north along the whole west coast of the island, and seeing that

I was now being pulled into it, I decided to leave this place and save my strength for landing upon the Cape of the Woods.

There were great, smooth, long waves upon the sea. The wind was blowing quietly from the south; the waves rose and fell unbroken. Had it been different, I must have been destroyed long ago; but as it was, my little boat was moving gently with the wind. I still lay upon the bottom.

I began after a little to grow very bold and sat up to try my hand at paddling. But even the smallest move in a boat as light as this one will change its course, and with a sudden turn she ran straight down a slope of water and struck her nose deep into the side of the next wave.

I was wet all over and cold with fear, and fell back into the bottom of the boat. Then she seemed to find her head again and led me as softly as before among the waves. It was plain she was to have her own way, and if I could not change her course, how was I ever to reach land?

In spite of my feeling of fear, I kept my head, for all that. First, moving with all care, I got the water out of my boat with my sea cap; then getting my eye once more above the edge, I set myself to study how it was she was able to slip so quietly through the waters.

I found each wave, instead of being big and smooth as it looks from shore, was for all the world like any range of hills on the dry land, full of peaks and valleys. The boat, left to herself, turning from side to side, found her way through these low places.

"Well, now," I thought to myself, "it is plain that I must stay where I am to keep the boat in balance; but it is plain, also, that I can put the paddle over the side, and from time to time in smooth places, give her a push toward land." No sooner thought upon than done. There I lay on my hands and knees with little use of my strength, and every now and then made a weak stroke or two to turn her head to shore.

It was very tiring and slow work, yet I could see I was drawing nearer to the Cape of the Woods. Though I was sure I could not make the landing at that point, I had still made some hundred yards to the east. I was, indeed, close to the shore. I could see the cool, green tops of the trees moving together in the breeze, and I felt sure I could make the next point of land.

It was high time, for I now began to feel the pain of thirst. The sun shining on the waves, and the sea water that fell and dried upon me, caking my very lips with salt, together made my throat burn and my head ache. The sight of trees so near at hand had almost made me sick with longing, but the current had soon taken me past the point; and as the next reach of sea opened out, what I saw changed my thoughts completely.

Right in front of me, not half a mile away,

was the *Hispaniola* under sail. I was sure, of course, that I should be caught; but I wanted water so badly that I hardly knew whether to be glad or sorry at the thought. Long before I could make up my mind, I was so taken by surprise that I could do nothing but look and wonder.

The *Hispaniola* was beautiful with her white sails shining in the sun like silver. When I first sighted her, all her sails were drawing;[2] she was following a course about northwest; and I supposed the men on board were going round the island on their way back where the ship had been anchored. Soon she began to turn more and more to the west, so that I thought they had seen me and were turning in chase. At last, however, she turned right toward the wind, and was held dead still, and stood there a while helpless, her sails shaking.

"What fools," said I; "they must still be

---

[2]**were drawing,** were pulling the ship along.

drunk as pigs." And I thought how Captain Smollett would have set them straight.

In the meantime, the ship, little by little, turned so that the sails filled again, and sailed for a minute or two, then brought up once more dead against the wind. This happened again and again. Back and forth, up and down, north, south, east, west, the *Hispaniola* sailed by leaps and bounds, each time ending as she had begun. It became plain to me that no one was steering her. If that were so, where were the men? They must be drunk or had left the ship, I thought, and perhaps if I could get on board, I might return her to her captain.

The current was carrying both my boat and the ship toward the south at an equal rate. The way the ship was sailing, she gained nothing on me, if she did not even lose. If only I might sit up in my boat and paddle, I was sure that I could gain upon her. The idea gave me new courage.

Up I got and was met by a cloud of spray, but this time I stayed with my purpose and set myself with all my strength to paddle after the *Hispaniola*. After I got into the way of the thing, I kept my boat between the waves, with only now and then a blow upon her bows and a dash of foam in my face.

I was now gaining rapidly upon the ship; I could see the brass shining, and still no one appeared upon the deck. I could not help but suppose she was deserted. If not, the men were lying drunk below, where I might tie them down, perhaps, and do as I pleased with the ship.

She still kept running away from me. At times not only was she carried by the current, but because of her size, she could drift faster than I could paddle.

But now, at last, I had my chance. The breeze fell, for a time, very low, and the ship turned slowly until her stern was toward me. I could see the cabin window still open and the light over the table still burning on into the day. She was standing still except for the current.

For the last little while I had even lost, but now with all my strength I set out to gain upon her. I was not a hundred yards behind when the wind came again with a sudden noise, and she was off again.

My first thought was one of despair, but my second was of joy. Round she came until her side was toward me—round still till she had covered a half, then more of the distance between us. I could see the waves rolling white under her. Big and tall she looked to me from my low place in the boat.

And then, of a sudden, I began to understand. I had no time to think—only time to act and save myself. I was on the top of one large wave when the ship came moving over the next. The bowsprit³ was over my head. I sprang to my feet and leaped, sending my

³bowsprit, a pole sticking out from the front of a ship.

boat under water. With one hand, I caught hold and pulled myself up, and, as I still held on panting, a dull blow told me that my boat was struck, and that I was left on the *Hispaniola* with no way of escape.

Chapter XXV

I Strike the Jolly Roger[1]

JUST as I pulled myself up, the wind came with a force that made one sail strike against another until the whole ship trembled. This nearly threw me off into the sea, and, losing no time, I crawled back along the bowsprit till I reached the deck.

Nothing there seemed to be in order; nothing was clean; not a man was to be seen, until suddenly the wind blew the sails to the other side, and there, sure enough, were the two watchmen.

Red Cap lay on his back, stiff as a stick, with his arms straight out from his sides, his teeth showing between his open lips. Hands sat leaning against the side of the ship, his head falling forward, his hands lying open beside him, his face white.

[1]**Strike the Jolly Roger,** lower the pirates' flag.

For a while the ship kept bucking like a wild horse. One sail filled, then another. Clouds of spray fell over us. Red Cap rolled from side to side, but always his teeth showed in that ugly grin. At every jump Hands seemed still more to fall into himself, his whole body bent farther from me until I could see none of his face, and at last only one of his ears could be seen above his shoulder.

At the same time, I saw, around each of them, spots of dark blood, and began to feel sure they had killed each other. But as I was looking and wondering, Hands turned part way around with a low cry, which told of pain and great weakness. This cry and the way his mouth hung open went right to my heart until I remembered the talk I had heard from the apple barrel.

I walked toward him.

"Come on board, Mr. Hands," I said, and none too pleasantly at that.

228

He opened his eyes slowly, but all he could do was to say the one word, "rum."

I knew there was no time to lose and hurried down the stairs into the cabin.

This looked worse than the deck. Nearly everything had been broken open in the hunt for the map. The floor was thick with mud where the men had sat down to drink after being out on shore. The white walls were covered with marks of dirty hands. Empty bottles rang as the rolling ship rolled one against another.

In the middle of the table a light was still burning.

I went into the cellar. All of the barrels were gone, and many of the bottles lay about, empty. However, I found one half full of rum, for Hands. For myself I found some food and water; then I went back to Hands.

"By the powers," he said, after he had taken a good drink, "but I did want some of that!"

229

I sat down in my own corner and began to eat.

"Much hurt?" I asked him.

"If that doctor was on board," he returned, "I could be right enough in no time; but no good never comes to me. As for that one," he said, pointing to Red Cap, "good and dead he is. He never was no seaman, anyway. And where might you have come from?"

"Well," said I, "I have come on board to take the ship, Mr. Hands, and for the present you will please look upon me as your captain."

He said nothing. Some of the color had come back to his face, though he still looked very sick and weak.

"By the way, Mr. Hands," I continued, "I cannot have these colors, and by your leave I'll strike them. Better none than these." And I ran to the color lines, pulled down that cursed black flag, and threw it into the sea.

"God save the king!" I cried, waving

my cap, "and there is an end to Captain Silver."

Hands watched me closely.

"I guess," he said at last, "I guess, captain, you want to get on shore now. Suppose we talks."

"Why, yes," said I, "with all my heart, Mr. Hands. Say on." And I went back to my eating.

"This man," he began, pointing weakly to the dead man, "—O'Brien were his name—this man and me was meaning to sail her back. But he's dead now, and who is to sail this ship, I don't see. Without I helps, you can't, as far as I can tell. Now look here. You gives me food and drink and something to tie up my cut with, you do; and I tells you how to sail her. That's square all around, I take it."

"I'll tell you one thing," said I. "I am not going back to where we were. I mean to get into North Inlet and ground her there."

"To be sure you do," he cried. "Am I

such a fool after all, now am I? And don't you think I can't see? I had my try at it, and I lost, and now you has the better of me. North, you say? North she goes. We sails this ship now any place you says."

This seemed to me good reasoning, and I went to work at once. In three minutes we had the ship sailing along with the wind around the coast of the island. We had good hopes of turning the north point before noon and of coming down as far as the bay on the other side of the island before high water. Then we might ground her safely and wait till low tide allowed us to land there.

Next I tied the tiller so as to hold the ship to her course for a time and went below for a cloth for Hands. With this and with my help he tied up the great cut he had received in his leg. Then, after he had eaten a little and had had another drink, he began to feel much better. He sat up, spoke more loudly and clearly, and looked in every way another man.

The wind served us beautifully. We sailed before it like a bird, with the view along the coast changing every minute. Soon we were past the high lands, then past a low sandy country covered with only small trees, and then we turned the corner of the hill that ends the island on the north.

I was very proud of my new command and pleased with the fine weather and the different views along the shore. I was now well supplied with water and good things to eat, and, though I knew I had done wrong in leaving the captain without asking him, I felt that he would be very glad when I brought back the ship.

I think I should have had nothing left to desire but for the way Hands followed my every move with his eyes. Though he looked old and tired and weak, always there was that strange smile on his face—

a smile which I could by no means trust—as he watched, and watched, and watched me at my work.

Chapter XXVI

Israel Hands

THE WIND, serving us just as we wished, now changed into the west. We found it easy to run from the northwest corner of the island to the mouth of North Inlet.

As we had no power to anchor and dared not ground her till the tide had flowed a good deal higher, we had nothing to do but wait. Hands told me how to keep the ship still. After trying a good many times, I learned how to do it, and we both sat without talking, over another meal.

"Captain," said he, after a while, with that same strange smile, "here is my old shipmate, O'Brien; suppose you was to throw him over. I ain't hard to please, as a rule, and I don't care if I did lay him out; but I don't judge him a very pretty sight now, do you?"

"I am not strong enough, and I don't like the job; there he lies, for all of me," said I.

"This here is one unlucky ship, Jim," he went on. "There has been a power of men killed in this here ship—a sight of poor men dead and gone since you and me set sail at Bristol. I never seen nothing like it, not I. There was this here O'Brien. Now, he's dead, ain't he? Well, now, I got no learning, and you be a boy as can read and figure; and to put it straight, do you take it that a dead man is dead for good, or do he come to life again?"

"You can kill the body, Mr. Hands, but not the spirit," I replied. "O'Brien is in another world and may be watching us this minute."

"Well," said he, "that's too bad—appears as if killing people is a waste of time. However, spirits don't count for much, by what I see. I'll take a chance with the spirits, Jim. And now, you have spoke up free, and I'll take it kind if you would step down into that cabin and get me a—well, a—I don't know the name for it. Well, you get me a bottle of wine, Jim—this here rum's too strong for me."

Now, Hands seemed to have something on his mind which made him hunt for words; and as for wanting me to go below for a drink of wine, I did not believe a word of it. He wanted me to leave him—so much was plain; but with what purpose I could not guess. His eyes never met mine; they kept moving up and down, back and forth, now with a look to the sky, now with a look at the dead man.

All the time he kept smiling, putting his tongue out in the most guilty manner, so that a child could have told that he was working some plan he did not want me to know about. I was quick with my answer, for I knew that he must not discover my thoughts.

"Some wine?" I said. "Far better. Will you have white or red?"

"Well, I guess it is all about the same to me, Jim," he replied; "just so it's strong and plenty of it."

"All right," I answered. "I'll bring you wine, Mr. Hands. But I'll have to hunt for it."

With that I hurried down the steps with all the noise I could make, took off my shoes, ran quietly along the gallery, then mounted the ladder where I could see him. I knew he would not expect to see me there, yet I took every care, and all that I feared was true.

He had got up on his hands and knees; and, though his leg must have hurt him badly when he moved, yet he pulled himself across the deck pretty fast. In half a minute he had reached a coil of rope, and pulled from it a long knife. I could see there was blood on it. He looked at it for a moment and tried the point with his hand. Then, quickly hiding it in his coat, he pulled himself back again to the place where I had left him.

This was all I wanted to know. Hands could move about; he was now armed; and if he had been at so much trouble to get me away from him, it was plain I was the one he expected to kill. What he would do afterwards—try to cross the island to the pirates, or fire the cannon, trusting that they might come first to help him—was, of course, more than I could say.

Yet I felt sure that I could trust him in one point, since our interests were the same; and that was in what to do with the ship. We both wanted her run on ground safe enough in a place where she could be got off again easily when the time came. Until then, I felt that Hands would not try to kill me.

While I was thinking about all this, I had not been sitting still. I had quietly run back to the cabin, put on my shoes, and reached for a bottle of wine. Now, with this in my hand, I came back to Hands.

He lay as I had left him, and his eyes were almost closed, as though he were too weak to bear the light. He looked up, however, at my coming, knocked the neck off the bottle like a man who had done the same thing often, and took a good drink, saying as he did, "Here's luck!" He lay quiet for a little and then, pulling out a stick of tobacco, asked me to cut him a piece.

"Cut me a bit of that," said he, "for I got no knife and not strength enough if I had. Cut me a bit, Jim; like as not it will be the last; for I'm not long for this world, I know."

"Well," said I, "I'll cut you some tobacco; but if I were you and thought myself so nearly dead, I would go to my prayers, like a Christian man."

"Why?" said he. "Now you tell me why."

"Why?" I cried. "You were asking me just now about the dead. You have broken your trust; you have lived in lies and blood; there is a man you have killed lying at your feet this moment; and you ask me why! For God's mercy, Mr. Hands, that is why."

I spoke with a little heat, thinking of the bloody knife that he was planning to end me with. He, for his part, took a drink of the wine I had brought him and spoke in a most solemn manner.

"For years and years," he said, "I have sailed the seas, and seen good and bad, all kinds of weather, food giving out, knives going, and what not. Well, now, I tell you, I never seen good come of being good yet. Him as strikes first is to my liking; dead men don't bite; them is my views—and so be it.

"And now, you look here," he added, suddenly changing his voice, "we've had enough of this. The tide is good enough by now. You just take my orders, Captain Hawkins, and we can sail right in and be done with it."

All told, we had only about two miles to run; the north bay was narrow and lay east and west; so the ship must be nicely handled to be got in. I think I steered well, and I am sure Hands was a very fine pilot.[1] We turned and turned in and out between the rocks so nicely that it was a pleasure to see.

The shores of North Inlet were covered with woods like those where we had landed

[1]**pilot,** a guide on the water who steers the boat.

on the south side; but the space was longer and narrower and more like the mouth of a river. Right before us we saw the wreck of a ship that was almost destroyed with age. It had been a great ship of three masts, but had been there so long that it was covered with plants and flowers that were growing on it. It was a sad sight, but it showed us that the bay was calm.

"Now," said Hands, "look there; there is a fine place for to ground a ship in. Nice flat sand, trees all around us, never a person about, and flowers growing like a garden on that old ship."

"And once on ground," I asked, "how shall we get her off again?"

"Why, so," he replied: "you take a line on shore there on the other side at low water; take a turn about one of them big trees; bring it back, take a turn round the capstan,[2] and wait for the tide. When high water comes,

[2]capstan, a machine sailors use for pulling.

all hands take a pull on the line, and off she comes as sweet as nature. And now, boy, you be ready. We are near the place now, and she is going too fast. Pull this way a little, watch there—easy now—hold fast!"

So he kept me working at his command, till, all of a sudden, he cried, "Now, my friend, turn to the wind!" And I moved the tiller[3] as far over as I could, and she turned round rapidly and ran straight on for the low, wooded shore.

The hard work of the last moves had kept me so busy that I had eased my close watch upon Hands. Even then, I was still so much interested, waiting for the ship to touch bottom, that I quite forgot the danger that was hanging over me. I was standing with my eyes on the water below spreading wide before the bows, when something made me turn my head. Perhaps I had heard a sound, or had seen him out of the corner of my eye; but,

[3]**tiller,** a bar used to steer or guide a boat.

sure enough, when I looked round, there was Hands, coming toward me with the knife in his right hand.

We must have both cried out when our eyes met; but while mine was the sharp cry of fear, his was a roar of fury. At the same time he threw himself forward, and I leaped to one side. As I did so, I let go of the tiller, which gave a quick turn. This, I think, saved my life, for it struck Hands and stopped him, for the moment, still.

Before he could pull himself together, I was safe out of the corner where he had me penned. Then I stopped, pulled a pistol from my pocket, took a cool aim, though he had already turned and was coming straight toward me, and pulled the trigger.

But no sound followed! The sea water had got into it, and it was of no use. Why had I not taken care to look after my pistols before, when I had discovered that Hands was armed? Now I was without help of any kind.

Hurt as he was, it was wonderful how fast he could move, his hair falling all over his face, which was as red as a red flag. I saw plainly that I must keep in the open and not simply retreat before him, or he would have me boxed in the bows. Once he got me there, he would run that knife deep into my body. I stood facing him and waited.

Seeing that I was going to jump, he stopped. A moment or two passed in quick moves on his part and answering moves from me. It was the kind of game I had often played at home about the rocks of Black Hill Cove; but never before with such wild heart-beats as now.

Still, as I say, it was a boy's game, and I thought I could hold my own at it against an older man who was wounded. Indeed, my courage began to rise so high that I thought of what might be the end of the game. While I saw that I could hold out for a long time, I saw no hope of any escape in the end.

Well, while things stood thus, suddenly the ship struck the bottom, staggered, ground for a moment in the sand, and then, quick as a blow, turned over to one side, till it stood at a sharp angle.

Both of us fell in a second, and both of us rolled, almost together, to the lower edge of the deck; the dead Red Cap, with his arms still spread out, rolled down after us. So near were we, indeed, that my head came against Hands's foot with a blow so hard it made my teeth rattle. But with all that, I was the first on my feet again. With the ship in this position, the deck was no place for running. I must find another way of escape.

I had no time to lose, for Hands was almost upon me. Quick as a thought, I sprang into the mizzen-shrouds,[4] went up hand over hand, and did not lose a second until I was seated on the crosstrees.[5]

[4]**mizzen-shrouds,** ropes running from the mast nearest the stern to the side of the ship. [5]**crosstrees,** pieces of wood placed across the mast near the top to extend the shrouds.

I had been saved by being quick. His knife had struck not half a foot below me, as I went toward the top. And there stood Hands with his mouth open and his face turned up to mine, with a look of the greatest surprise and disappointment.

Now that I had a moment to myself, I lost no time in loading my pistols to have them ready for service. After a moment Hands put the knife between his teeth and began to pull himself up toward me. Hurt as he was, he moved very slowly, and I had quietly finished my task before he was more than a third of the way up. Then, with a pistol in each hand, I said to him, "One more step, Mr. Hands, and I'll blow your head off! Dead men don't bite, you know."

He stopped suddenly. I could see by the workings of his face that he was trying to think, and this seemed to be so hard for him to do that, in my safe place, I laughed out loud. At last, and slowly, he spoke. In order to speak he had to take the knife from his mouth, but in no other way did he move the least bit.

"Jim," says he, "I guess we are both done, me and you, and all we can do is quit. I'd have had you but for that there fall, but I don't have no luck, not I. I guess I'll have to give up, which comes hard, you see, for a master seaman to a ship's young one like you, Jim."

I was listening to his words, and smiling away without a fear when, all in a breath, back went his right hand over his shoulder. Something sang through the air. I felt a blow and then a sharp pain, and there I was pinned by the shoulder to the mast.

In the sudden pain and surprise of the moment—I cannot say it was my own will to act, and I am sure it was without aim—both my pistols went off, and fell from my hands, but they did not fall alone. With a loud cry, Hands rolled head first into the water.

SIX GREAT STORIES

Chapter XXVII

"Pieces of Eight"

BECAUSE of the angle of the ship, the masts hung far out over the water, and from where I sat I had nothing below me but the waves of the bay. Hands, who had not been so far up the mast, fell near the ship. He rose once to the surface of the water and then sank again for good. As the water settled, I could see him lying in a heap on the clean, bright sand in the shadow of the ship's sides. A fish or two swam past his body. Sometimes, by the moving of the water, he appeared to move a little, as if trying to rise. But he was dead enough, for all that, being both shot and drowned, and was food for the fish in the very place he had wanted to have me lie.

I was no sooner certain of this than I began to feel sick, faint, and terrified. The hot blood was running over my back and down my arm. The knife, where it held my shoulder fast, seemed to burn like a hot iron. Yet it was not so much these real pains that troubled me, for these, it seemed, I could bear. It was the fear I had upon my mind of falling from the crosstrees into that still, green water, beside the body of Hands.

I held on with both hands till my nails were blue and shut my eyes as if to cover up the chance of harm. Little by little my mind came back again, my heart beat to a slower time, and I was once more master of myself.

It was my first thought to pull the knife out; but either it was in too hard or my nerve left me, and I stopped while I trembled. Strangely enough, this was all that was needed to free me. The knife had come the nearest in the world to missing me and was holding me by a very small piece of skin, and this the trembling tore away. The blood ran down the faster, to be sure, but I was my own master again and was only held by my coat and shirt.

These last I broke through with a sudden pull, and then I got myself down to the deck with all the care I could use. I went below and did what I could for my wound. It pained me a good deal, but it was not a deep cut and did not keep me from using my arm. Then I looked around me, and as the ship was now in a sense my own, I began to think of how I might clear it of the dead body of Red Cap.

He had rolled, as I have said, against the side of the ship and looked awful as he lay there with his face up. In that position I could easily have my way with him, and so many dreadful things had happened that I no longer had any fear of the dead. So I took him by the waist, and with one good lift rolled him over into the water. He went in with a heavy splash. The red cap came off and stayed on top of the water; and as soon as the waves had quieted, I could see him and Hands lying side by side, both seeming to move with the motion of the water. O'Brien, though still a young man, was very bald. There he lay, with his head shining, across the knees of the man who had killed him, and the fishes playing over both of them.

I was now alone upon the ship. The tide had just turned; the sun was so low in the sky that shadows of the trees upon the west shore of the bay fell in patterns on the ship. The evening breeze began to blow, and the sails were rattling back and forth.

I began to see a danger to the ship. I tried hard to bring all of the sails down, but it was not easy to do this alone. When the ship had grounded and turned on her side, some of the mainsail was hanging a foot or more in the water. This made it seem more dangerous, and I was afraid to try to pull that in. At last I got my knife and cut the ropes, and the sail dropped and fell out upon the water. This was all that I could do. For the rest, the *Hispaniola*, like myself, must trust to chance.

TREASURE ISLAND

By this time the whole bay was hid from the sun. The air began to feel cold; the tide was fast moving out to sea, the ship settling more and more on her beam-ends.[1]

I pulled myself forward and looked over into the water. It did not look too deep; so holding the cut rope in both hands, I let myself drop softly overboard. The water came just to my waist; the sand was firm, and I waded to the shore, leaving the ship on her side with her sails trailing wide upon the water. About the same time the sun went down, and the breeze whistled low among the tall, moving trees.

At last I was off the sea! Nor had I returned empty-handed. There lay the ship, clear at last of pirates and ready for our own men to board and get to sea again. So happy was I about taking the ship alone I could

[1] **on her beam-ends.** A ship is on her beam-ends when she leans over to one side so that the beams of wood running across the ship are standing on end or almost straight up in the air.

not get back to my friends soon enough, to boast of all I had done. I might be blamed a bit for running away, but getting back our ship was a good answer, and I hoped that even Captain Smollett would say that I had not lost my time.

So thinking, and in high spirits, I began to set my face toward the stockade and my friends. I remembered that the river to the east, which runs into Captain Kidd's bay, came from the two-topped hill upon my left. I set my course in that direction, so I could cross the stream where it was small. The wood was pretty open, and keeping along the lower points, I had soon turned the corner of that hill and not long after crossed the water where it was below my knees.

This brought me near to the place where I had first come upon Ben Gunn, and I walked with more care, keeping an eye on every side. Dark was coming on fast, and as I walked out between the two peaks, I saw a

red light against the sky, where, as I supposed, the man of the island was cooking his
supper before a great fire. And yet I wondered why he would not be more careful. If
I could see the fire, might it not reach the eyes
of Silver himself, where he camped upon the
shore?

Little by little the night fell blacker. It
was all I could do to see my way. The double
hill behind me and the Spy-Glass on my right
hand grew fainter, the stars were few, and in
the low ground where I was finding my way,
I kept falling among bushes and rolling into
sandy places. Suddenly a bright light fell
about me. I looked up and saw the moon rising behind the trees.

With this to help me, I was quick to cover
what was left of the space, sometimes walking, sometimes running as I drew near to the
stockade. Yet as I drew near the wood that
lies before it, I began to take my steps with
care. It would have been a poor end of my

adventures to get shot down by my own party by mistake.

The moon was higher in the sky, and its light began to fall here and there through the more open parts of the wood. Right in front of me a light of a different color appeared among the trees. It was red and hot, and now and again it was a little dark—as if it were dying out. For the life of me, I could not think what it might be.

At last I came right down to the edge of the clearing. The moon was covering it with a bright light. The house itself was still in a black shadow, with little streams of light playing over it. On the other side of the house a large fire had burned itself low and left a red glow which was very different from the silver light of the moon. There was not a sound anywhere.

I stopped with much wonder in my heart, and perhaps a little fear, also. It had not been our way to build great fires. The captain had been very careful with the use of the firewood, and I began to fear that something had gone wrong while I was away.

I stole round by the east end, keeping close in the shadow, and found a place where I could cross the fence. To make myself as safe as possible, I got down upon my hands and knees and crawled, without a sound, toward the corner of the house.

As I came nearer, my heart was suddenly and greatly lightened. I heard what was not a pleasant sound in itself, and I have not liked it at all at other times; but just now it was music to hear my friends snoring together so loud and peaceful in their sleep. The sea cry of the man on watch, "All's well," never sounded finer to my ear.

At the same time, I knew one thing; they were not keeping a good watch. If it had been Silver and his men that were now closing in on them, not a one of them would ever see the light of day. That was what it was, I thought, to have the captain wounded; and again I blamed myself for leaving them when there were so few to stand guard.

By this time I had got to the door and stood up. All was dark inside, so that I could make out nothing with my eyes. As for sounds, there was the steady snore of the sleeping men and a small, pecking noise that I could not account for.

With my arms before me, I walked carefully in. I should lie down in my own place (I thought, with a smile) and watch their faces when they found me in the morning.

My foot struck something that moved. It was a man's leg. He turned and made a sound, but did not wake.

And then, all of a sudden, a shrill voice filled the dark room with "Pieces of eight! Pieces of eight! Pieces of eight! Pieces of eight!" and on and on without a break, like the sound of a little mill.

Silver's green parrot, Captain Flint! It

was she that I had heard pecking at a piece of wood; it was she, keeping better watch than any man, who told of my appearance with her old watchword.

I had no time left me to get away. At the first sound of the parrot, the men awoke and were on their feet in a second. With a mighty curse, the voice of Silver cried:

"Who goes?"

I turned to run, fell against one man, turned again, and ran full into the arms of another, who, for his part, closed upon me and held me fast.

"Bring a light, Dick," said Silver, when they were sure I could not get away.

And one of the men left the house and was quick to return with a lighted stick.

Great heaps of coin and bars of gold

PART VI—CAPTAIN SILVER

Chapter XXVIII

In the Enemy's Camp

THE RED light from the burning torch showed me the worst thing I could have expected. The pirates were in possession of the house and the stores. There was the rum, there was the meat and bread, but not a sign of any of our men. I could only suppose that they had all been killed, and I wished that I could have died with them.

There were six of the pirates, all told; not another one of them was still living. Five of them were on their feet, looking stiff and sleepy, showing plainly that they were full of drink. The other one was pale and had a bloody bandage round his head, showing that he was hurt but a short time ago. I remembered the man who had been shot and ran back into the woods, and was sure this was he.

The parrot sat on Long John Silver's shoulder. He himself looked white and more stern than I was used to. He still wore his fine suit, but it was covered with mud and badly torn.

"So," said he, "here is little Jim, bless his heart! dropped in, like. Well, come, I take that friendly." And with that he sat down and began to fill his pipe.

"Give me a light with your fire, Dick," said he; and then when he had a good light, "That will do, son," he added; "put the fire in the wood heap; and you, gentlemen, bring yourselves to!—You need not stand up for Mr. Hawkins. He don't mind, you may lay to that. And so, Jim, here you are, and quite a pleasant surprise for poor old John! I seen you were smart when I first set eyes on you, but this here gets away from me clean, it do."

To all this, as you may suppose, I made no answer. They had set me with my back against the wall, and I stood there, looking

Silver in the face, square enough, I hope, to make them think I was not afraid, but with black fear in my heart.

Silver ran on again. "Now, you see, Jim, so be as you are here," said he, "I'll just give you a piece of my mind. I always liked you, I have, for a boy of spirit, just as I was at your age, and pretty fine, I call that. I always wanted you to join us and take your part, and be a gentleman of fortune till you die, and now, by the powers, you've got to.

"Captain Smollett is a fine seaman, I say, but is hard at giving orders. 'Duty is duty,' says he, and right he is. Just you keep clear of the captain. The doctor himself is gone dead against you—'ungrateful scamp' was what he said. The short and the long of the whole story is just about this: you can't go back to your own lot, for they won't have you; and without you start a third ship's company all by yourself, which might be lonely, you'll have to join with Captain Silver."

So far, so good. My friends, then, were still living, and though I believed only part of what Silver said, that my party was angry at me for leaving as I did, I was more glad than sorry at what I had heard.

"I don't say nothing as to your being in our hands," continued Silver, "though there you are, and you may lay to it. I'm all for being square. If you like the service, well, you will join. If you don't, Jim, why, you are free to answer no. Now, by the powers, can fairer be said?"

"Am I to answer, then?" I asked with a voice that trembled. Through all this talk I was made to feel the fear of death hanging over me, and my heart beat fast and loud.

"My boy," said Silver, "no one is hurrying you. Take your time. None of us would hurt you, Jim; time goes so pleasant in your company, you see."

"Well," said I, growing a bit bolder, "if I am to choose, I think I have a right to know what you mean, and why you are here, and where my friends are."

"What he means?" repeated one of the pirates, in a deep, rough voice. "Well, all of us would like to know that!"

"Better speak when you are called on, my friend," cried Silver to the one who spoke. And then in his first easy manner he replied to me, "Yesterday morning, Mr. Hawkins, in the dog-watch,[1] down came Doctor Livesey with a flag of truce. Says he, 'Captain Silver, you are sold out. The ship is gone.' Well, maybe we had been drinking and having a song to pass the time. I don't say no. But none of us had looked out. We looked out then, and, by the powers! it was gone.

"I never seen a lot of men look sicker, and you may lay to that. 'Well,' says the doctor, 'let's bargain.' I took for us all you see here: stores, rum, house, firewood you was so

[1]dog-watch, a watch of two hours kept either from four to six P.M. or six to eight P.M.

good as to cut, and, in a manner of speaking, the whole blessed business. As for them, they left. I don't know where they went."

He drew again quietly at his pipe.

"And if you should take it into your head to think you are still one of that party, here is the last word that was said: 'How many are you,' says I, 'to leave?' 'Four,' says he—'four, and one of us wounded. As for that boy, I don't know where he is, nor I don't much care. We're about sick of him.' Those were his words."

"Is that all?" I asked.

"Well, it is all you are to hear, my son."

"And now am I to choose?"

"And now you are to choose, and you may lay to that," said Silver.

"Well," said I, "I know pretty well what I have to look for. Let happen what may, it is little I care. I have seen too many die since I fell in with you. But there is a thing or two I have to tell you," and by this time I was quite excited; "and the first is this. Here you are in a bad way. Your ship is lost, your treasure lost, your men lost; your whole business has gone to nothing. And if you want to know who did it, it was I. I was in the apple barrel the night we sighted land, and I heard you, John, and you, Dick, and Hands, who is now at the bottom of the sea, and told every word you said before the hour was out.

"And as for the ship, it was I who cut her rope, and it was I who killed the men you had on her, and it was I who brought her where you'll never see her again, not one of you. The laugh is on my side; I have had the top of this business from the first. Kill me if you please, or let me live.

"If you do not hurt me, the past shall be forgotten, and when you fellows are in court for piracy, I'll save you all I can. It is for you to choose. Kill another and do yourselves no good, or spare me and keep a friend to save you from hanging."

I stopped, for I tell you I was out of breath, and to my wonder not a man of them moved, but all sat staring at me like as many sheep. And while they were so still, I began to talk once more.

"And now, Mr. Silver," I said, "I believe you are the best man here, and if you kill me, will you let the doctor know the way I took it?"

"I'll bear it in mind," said Silver, with a note in his voice that made me wonder whether he was laughing at what I asked or liked my courage.

"I can put one to that," cried the old hard-faced seaman, Morgan by name, whom I had seen in Long John's inn at Bristol. "It was him that knew Black Dog."

"Well, and see here," added the sea cook, "I can put another again to that, by the powers! for it was this same boy that took the map from Bill Bones. First and last Jim Hawkins has brought us trouble."

"Then here goes!" said Morgan with a curse. And he stepped toward me, drawing his knife as if he had been twenty.

"Stop there!" cried Silver. "Who are you, Tom Morgan? You thought you was captain here, perhaps. By the powers, but I can teach you better! Cross me, and you go where many a good man before has gone, some on deck, and some below, but all to feed the fishes. There never was a man looked me between the eyes and seen a good day again, Tom Morgan, you may lay to that."

Morgan stood where he was; but the others began to talk among themselves.

"Tom's right," said one.

"I stood enough from one," added another. "I don't mean to take nothing from you, John Silver."

"Did any of you gentlemen want to have it out with me?" shouted Silver. "Put a name on what you want; I guess you know, all right. Him that wants shall get it. Have I lived this many years to have a yellow dog come at me here at the end? You know the way; you are gentlemen of fortune by your own account. Well, here I am. Take a sword, him that dares, and I'll see the color of his inside before that pipe's empty."

Not a man moved; not a man answered.

"That is your kind, is it?" he added, returning his pipe to his mouth. "Not much good to fight though, are you? Perhaps you can understand the King's English. I was chosen the captain here. I'm captain here because I'm the best man by a long sea-mile. You won't fight, as a gentleman of fortune should; then, by the powers, you will take orders, and you may lay to that!

"I like that boy, now; I never seen a better boy than that. He is more a man than any pair of rats like you in this here house, and what I say is this: Let me see one of you lay a hand on him, and you may lay to it."

They waited a long time after this. I stood

up straight against the wall, my heart still going fast and hard, but now I had one ray of hope. Silver sat back against the wall, his arms crossed, his pipe in the corner of his mouth, as quiet as if he had been in church; yet he kept his eye on every man in the room. They, on their part, got together in the far end of the room, and the low sound of their voices kept going like a stream.

One after another they would look up, and the red light of the fire would fall on their faces; but it was not toward me, it was toward Silver that they turned their eyes.

"You seem to have a lot to say," remarked Silver without raising his voice. "Speak up and let me hear it."

"I asks your pardon, sir," returned one of the men. "You are pretty free with some of the rules; you might be kind enough to keep an eye on some of the rest. This crew has its rights like others, and by your own rules I take it we can talk together. I asks your pardon, sir, since you are captain at this present; but I asks my right and steps outside for a council."

And with a deep bow, this fellow, a long, ill-looking, yellow-eyed man, stepped toward the door and went out of the house. One after another the rest followed him, each bowing as he passed and adding some word. All marched out and left Silver and me alone.

Silver took his pipe out of his mouth.

"Now, look you here, Jim Hawkins," he said in a very low voice that I could no more than hear, "you are within half an inch of death, and what is a long sight worse, of torture. They're going to throw me off. But you mark, I stand by you through thick and thin. I never meant to; no, not till you spoke up. I was about ready to do anything, to lose that much money and be hanged, too. But I see you was the right sort. I says to myself, you stand by Hawkins, John, and he will stand by you. You're his last chance, John, and, by the powers, he's yours. You save your witness, and he'll save your neck!"

I began to understand a little bit.

"You mean all is lost?" I asked.

"That is just what I do!" he answered. "Ship gone, neck gone—that's the size of it. Once I looked into that bay, Jim Hawkins, and seen no ship, well, I'm hard, but I gave up. As for that lot, mark me, they're fools and cowards. I'll save your life, if so be I can, from them. But, see here, Jim, you save Long John from hanging."

I was all mixed up. I saw no hope for what he was asking—he, the old pirate, the ringleader through everything.

"What I can do, that I will," I said.

"Good!" cried Long John. "You speak up right as you can, and, by the powers, I have a chance."

He got up and stood for a moment. Then he said, "Understand me, Jim. I have a head on my shoulders. I know you have that ship safe somewhere. How you done it, I don't know, but safe it is. I guess Hands and O'Brien turned soft. I never thought much of either of them. Now you mark me. I ask no questions, nor I won't let others. I know when a game's up, I do; and I know a boy that is strong. Oh, you that's young—you and me might have done a power of good together!"

He got some rum in a cup.

"Have a drink?" he asked; and when I said no: "Well, I need a bit myself, for there is trouble on hand. And, talking of trouble, Jim, why did the doctor give me the map?"

My face showed my wonder, and he saw no need of more questions.

"Well, he did, though," said he, "and there is something under that, no doubt—something, Jim—bad or good."

And he took another drink, shaking his great fair head like a man who looks forward to the worst.

Chapter *XXIX*

The Black Spot Again

THE council of the pirates had lasted some
time when one of them came back into the
house, and with the same salute, which had
in my eyes a mean air, asked for the use of a
light for a moment. Silver gave it to him, he
left again, and the two of us were there together in the dark.

"There's a breeze coming, Jim," said Silver, who by this time was acting quite friendly
toward me.

I turned to the hole nearest me and looked
out. The fire had burned so low and now
gave so little light that I understood why the
men came into the house for the torch. About
half-way down to the fence they had gathered
together in a group. One held the light, another was on his knees, and I saw an open
knife shining in his hand.

The rest seemed to be watching closely

what this one was doing. I could just make out that he also had a book in his hand, and I was thinking it very strange that such men should have a book with them when the man rose once more to his feet, and the whole party began to move toward the house.

"Here they come," said I. And I left my place at the opening, for I did not want them to see that I had been watching.

"Well, let them come, my boy, let them come," cried Silver lightly. "I still have a shot in my gun."

The door opened, and the five men, standing close together, pushed one of their number in. At any other time it would have been funny to see him move so slowly, stopping as he put down each foot, but holding his closed right hand in front of him.

"Step up, son," cried Silver. "I won't eat you. Hand it over. I know the rules, I do, and I stand by them."

These words gave the fellow courage. He

moved more quickly, handed something to Silver, and stepped right back to the others.

Long John looked at what had been given him. "The black spot! I thought so," he said.

"Where might you have got the paper? Well, upon my word now, this is bad. You've gone and cut this out of a Bible! What fool has cut a Bible?"

"There!" said Morgan, "there! What did I say? No good can come of that, I said."

"Well, you've about fixed it now, among you," continued Silver. "You'll all hang now, I guess. What soft head had a Bible?"

"It was Dick," said one.

"Dick, was it? Then Dick had better say his prayers," said Silver. "This looks bad for him, and you may lay to that."

But here the long man with the yellow eyes broke in.

"Stop that talk, John Silver," he said. "We have given you the black spot in full council, as in duty bound; just you turn it over, as in duty bound, and see what we wrote there. Then you can talk."

"Thank you, George," replied Silver. "You always was quick for business, and has the rules by heart, as I'm pleased to see. Well, what is it, now? 'Deposed'[1]—is that it? Very pretty writing, to be sure. Did you write that, George? Why, you was getting to be quite a leading man in this here party. You'll be captain next, I shouldn't wonder. Bring me that light again, will you? This pipe don't draw."

"Come, now," said George, "you don't fool us no more. You think you're a funny man, but that don't help now. You just step this way and help vote."

"I thought you said you knowed the rules," returned Silver. "Well, you don't, but I do, and I wait here. I'm still your captain, mind, till you tell what you want and I reply. Until then, your black spot don't mean a thing. After that, we can see."

[1]**Deposed,** put out of office.

"Oh," replied George, "you don't need to have no fear; we are all square, we are. First, a nice mess you made of this here trip—you can never say no to that. Second, you let that doctor and his crowd out of here for nothing. Why did they want to get out? I don't know, but they wanted it, and that's plain. Third, you kept us from killing them as they went away. Oh, we see through you, John Silver; you want to play for time, that's what's wrong with you. And fourth, there is this here boy."

"Is that all?" asked Silver quietly.

"Enough, too," cried George. "We'll all hang and dry in the sun for your mistakes."

"Well, now, look here," said Silver; "I can answer these four points; one after the other I'll do it. I made a mess of this trip, did I? Well, you all know what I wanted; if you had done what I wanted, we should all be on board the ship right this night—every one of us living and well and full of fine food, and the money in the hold, by the powers!

"And who crossed me? Who forced my hand? Who stopped me as was the captain by rights? Who gave me the black spot the day we landed, and started this dance? And a fine dance it is—I'm with you there—looks like we should all be doing a dance soon at the end of a rope.

"But who done it? Why, it was Anderson and Hands and you, George Merry. You're the last one living of that crowd, and you have the face to stand for captain over me—you that is killing all of us! By the powers! but this tops the tallest story to nothing."

Silver stopped for a moment, and I could see by the faces of Merry and his party that these words had not been said in vain.

"That is just for number one," cried Long John, wiping his forehead, for he had been talking loud and fast. "Why, I give you my word, it makes me sick to speak to you. You have no sense, and you don't remember nothing. I never seen why your mothers ever let you come to sea. Sea! Gentlemen of fortune! I guess tailors is your trade."

"Go on, John," said Morgan, "speak up to the others."

"Yes, the others!" returned John. "A nice lot they are, to be sure! You say this trip is a mess. And you don't even know how bad it is. We're that near to hanging that my neck hurts with thinking of it. You've seen them hanging, birds about them, seamen pointing them out as they go out to sea. 'Who's that?' says one. 'That? Why, John Silver. I knowed him well,' says another. Now that's about where we are, every one of us, thanks to him and Hands and Anderson, and you other fools.

"And if you want to know about number four, and that boy, why, bless my bones! isn't he a hostage?[2] Are we going to waste

---

[2]**hostage,** a person given by his friends to an enemy to make sure that his friends mean to keep their promise. Here Silver knew that he was safe from the doctor's party as long as he kept Jim with him.

him? No, not us. He might be our last chance. Kill that boy? Not me!

"And number three. Well, there is a lot to say to number three. Don't you count it nothing to have a real college doctor come to see you every day—you, John, with your head broke, and you, George Merry, that had the shakes on you this very day, and has your eyes as yellow as eggs to this minute? And perhaps you don't know there is another ship coming to hunt for us, either? But there is, and not so long till then. And then you will be glad enough to have a hostage when it comes to that.

"And as for number two, and why I let that party go, well, you wanted me to. You even came on your knees and asked me to, you was that afraid of starving. Oh, that's nothing to you now, but you look there and see—that's why!"

And he threw down upon the floor a paper that I knew at once—none other than the map on yellow paper, with the three red crosses, that I had found in the captain's chest. Why the doctor gave it to him was more than I could understand.

If I was surprised when the map appeared, these men were a hundred times more so. They jumped at it like a cat at a mouse. It went from hand to hand, one tearing it from another. They cried out and laughed like children. You would have thought they not only had the gold, but had it safe at sea.

"Yes," said one, "this is Flint's map, sure enough; his marks, and no doubt of that."

"Very pretty," said Merry, "but how are we to get away with it, and us with no ship?"

Silver got up with a sudden spring, and held himself with his hand against the wall. "Now, I tell you this, George," he roared, "one more word out of you, and you have me to fight. How can we get it away? Why, how do I know? You tell me, you and the rest that lost me my ship, burn you! But not you, you don't know enough. But civil you can speak, and shall, George Merry, and you may lay to that!"

"Fair enough," said the old man Morgan.

"Fair! I think so," said Silver. "You lost the ship; I found the treasure. Who's the better man at that? And now I am through, by the powers! Take any man you please to be your captain now. I'm done with it!"

"Silver!" they cried. "Silver! Silver for captain!"

"So that's your song, is it?" cried the cook. "George, you'll have to wait another turn, my friend; and it's good for you that I am not a man that tries to get even. That was never my way. And now, mates, this black spot? It ain't much good now, is it? Dick has crossed his luck and cut up the Good Book, and that's about all. A Bible with a bit cut out is no good."

"Here, Jim, here is something for you," said Silver; and he tossed me the bit of paper.

It was round and small. One side had had nothing upon it, for it had been the last leaf of the Bible. Although the printed side had been made black with wood ashes, these had partly come off, and I could still read these words: "Without are dogs and murderers." On the other side had been written the one word "Deposed." I have that paper beside me at this minute.

That was the end of the night's business. Soon after, with a drink all round, we lay down to sleep. All Silver did to George Merry was to put him up for guard and promise to kill him if he should fail in his duty.

It was a long time before I could close an eye. Heaven knows I was troubled enough about the man I had killed that day and about my own danger. But more than that I was thinking of the game Silver was playing, keeping the pirates together with one hand, and reaching out with the other for every possible way to make his peace and save his own life.

He himself slept soundly; yet my heart went out to him, wicked as he was, to think of the many dangers which he must meet and the end which he feared.

Chapter XXX

On Parole[1]

WE WERE all awakened the next morning by a clear voice calling from the edge of the woods.

"Here's the doctor," it cried.

And the doctor it was.

Although I was glad to hear the sound, yet I knew I had done wrong in leaving my friends without asking the captain, and I was ashamed to face the doctor.

"You, doctor! Top of the morning to you, sir," cried Silver in a very friendly voice. "Bright and early, to be sure; and it's the early bird, as the saying goes, that gets the feed. George, get up, son, and help the doctor over the fence. All doing well, we are, well and happy."

So he ran on, standing at the top of the

[1]**Parole,** a promise by a prisoner that he will not try to escape.

hill, one hand on the side of the house—quite the old John in voice and manner.

"We've quite a surprise for you, too, sir," he continued. "We've a little stranger here, looking fine—slept like a tree right here by John—right side by side we was, all night."

The doctor was by this time over the fence and pretty near the cook, and I could hear the change in his voice as he said:

"Not Jim?"

"The same Jim as ever was," said Silver.

The doctor stopped still, although he did not speak, and it was some time before he was able to move.

"Well, well," he said at last, "duty before pleasure, as you might have said yourself, Silver. Let us have a look at the sick men."

A moment later he was in the house, and with just a nod to me, went on about his work. He seemed to have no fear at all, though he must have known that he was in great danger.

He talked to the men as if he were paying a visit to any quiet family in England. They took on the same manner and acted as if nothing had happened.

"You're doing well, my friend," he said to one, "and if ever any man had a narrow escape, it was you; your head must be as hard as iron. Well," to another, "how goes it? You are a pretty color; why, man, your liver is upside down. Did you take that medicine? Did he, men?"

"Aye, aye, sir, he took it sure enough," replied one.

"Because, you see, if I am to be pirates' doctor," said the doctor in his most pleasant way, "I can't lose a man for the king (God bless him!) and the gallows."

The pirates looked at each other, but said nothing.

"Dick don't feel well, sir," said one.

"Don't he?" returned the doctor. "Well, step up here, Dick, and let me see your tongue. No, I should be surprised if he did; a tongue like that would put fear into the French. Another fever."

"There," said another, "that come of tearing the Bible."

"That come—as you say—of being such fools," said the doctor, "and not being smart enough to know good air from poison and dry land from that vile swamp. I think all of you will have a fine time before you get free of this fever. Try to live on that low ground, would you? Silver, I am surprised at you. You know more than some, but you don't seem to know the first thing about the rules of health.

"Well," he added, after he had given all of them their doses, which they had taken in the most lamb-like way, "well, that's done for to-day. And now I wish to have a talk with that boy, please."

George Merry was at the door, choking over his medicine, but when the doctor said this, he turned quickly with his very red face and cried, "No!"

"Keep still!" Silver roared like a lion. "Doctor," he went on in his usual voice, "I was thinking of that, knowing as how you had a fancy for the boy. We all thanks you for all you done for us and believes in you, and takes your medicine down like so much rum. And I take it I have a way as will suit all. Jim, will you give me your word of honor as a young gentleman—for a young gentleman you are, although poor born—will you give me your word of honor not to try to get away?"

I gave him the promise he asked for.

"Then, doctor," said Silver, "you just get over that fence, and once you gets outside, I'll bring the boy down on this side, and I suppose you two can talk through the bars. A good day to you, sir, and all our duties to the captain and Mr. Trelawney."

The anger, which nothing but Silver's

black looks had kept down, broke out as soon as the doctor left the house. They told Silver he was playing double—trying to make a separate peace for himself—of not caring for their interests—in a word, of the exact thing that he was doing. This was so plain that I wondered how he could ever answer them.

But he was much more of a man than any one of them, and his victory of the night before made them see this. He called them the fools they were, said it was necessary that I should talk to the doctor, held up the map before their faces, and asked if they wanted to break their treaty on the very day they were to start hunting the treasure.

"No, by the powers!" he cried, "we breaks that treaty when the time comes, but till then I fools that doctor no matter how I has to do it."

Then he told them to light the fire and walked out on his crutch with his hand on my shoulder, leaving them angry but quieted more by his long speech than by any of the reasons he gave.

"Slow, boy, slow," he said. "They would kill us at the drop of a hat if we was seen to hurry."

Slowly, then, we walked across the sand to where the doctor waited on the outside of the fence, and as soon as we were at an easy speaking distance, Silver stopped.

"You make a note of this here, too, doctor," said he, "and the boy can tell you how I saved his life and got them all against me for it, and you may lay to that. Doctor, when a man is as near to his end as I be, would you think it too much, maybe, to give him one good word? And you remember it's not just my life now, but that boy's. You will speak fair for me, doctor, and give me a little hope."

Silver was a very different man once he was out there and had his back to his friends in the house. His face looked thin, his voice shook; never was a man more dead in earnest.

"Why, John, you're not afraid, are you?" asked the doctor.

"Doctor," said he, "John Silver is no coward. But I has to say I gets the shakes when I thinks of the gallows. You're a good man and true; I never seen a better one! And now I steps away and leaves you and Jim alone. And you put that down for me, too, for that's a lot, that is."

Saying this, he stepped back a little and sat down on a tree stump, turning now and again so he could see first the doctor and me, then the pirates as they went back and forth from the fire to the house, bringing out meat and bread for the breakfast.

"So, Jim," said the doctor sadly, "here you are. You always get back what you give, my boy. Heaven knows, I cannot find it in my heart to blame you, but this much I will say. When the captain was well, you dared not go away, but when he was ill and could not help it, it was cowardly!"

Here I began to cry. "Doctor," I said, "you might have some pity on me. I have blamed myself enough, and I should have been dead now if Silver hadn't stood for me. And, doctor, please believe this. I can die, and I dare say they will kill me—"

"Jim," the doctor cut in, and his voice was quite changed, "I can't have this. Jump over, and we can run for it."

"Doctor," said I, "I gave my word."

"I know, I know," he cried, "but we can't help that. I can take that all on my shoulders; but stay here, I cannot let you. One jump and you'll be out, and we'll run for it like deer."

"No," I replied. "You know right well you would never do such a thing; neither you, nor the squire, nor the captain, and no more will I. Silver trusted me; I gave my word, and back I go. But, doctor, you did not let me finish. I got the ship, and she lies in North Inlet on the south shore, just below high water. When it is half-tide, she must be high and dry."

"The ship!" cried the doctor.

Quickly I told him how I got her, and he listened without a word.

"There is a kind of fate in this," he said when I was done. "Every step it's you that saves our lives, and do you suppose by any chance that we are going to let you lose yours? That would be a poor return, my boy. You found out the plot; you found that man Gunn —the best thing you ever did, or will do if you live to be a hundred. And, by the powers! Talking of Gunn—Silver," he cried, "Silver, let me give you a piece of advice. Don't be in any great hurry after that treasure."

"Why, sir," said Silver, "I have to do my best. I can only save my life and the boy's by looking for that treasure."

"Well, Silver," replied the doctor, "if that is so, I'll say a little more; look out for a storm when you find it!"

"Sir," said Silver, "as between man and man, that's too much and too little. What you want, why you left this house, why you gave me that map, I don't know, now, do I? And yet I did what you said with my eyes shut and never a word of hope. But, now, this here's too much. If you don't want to tell me plain out what you mean, just say so, and I'll stop trying to be captain."

"No," said the doctor, after thinking a little, "I have no right to say any more; if I had, I give you my word, I would. But I'll go as far as I dare, and a step more, for the captain will blame me now, I dare say. And first, here is a bit of hope. Silver, if we both get away from here without being killed, I'll do my best to save you."

Silver was happy indeed at this. "You couldn't say more, I am sure, sir, not if you was my mother."

"Well," said the doctor, "now a piece of advice. Keep the boy with you, and if you need any help, call us. I'm off now to hunt that money for you, and that will show you I mean what I say."

And the doctor shook hands with me through the fence and set off into the wood.

Chapter XXXI

The Treasure Hunt — Flint's Pointer

J IM," said Silver when we were alone, "if I saved your life, you saved mine, and John Silver's not the one to forget it. With the tail of my eye I seen the doctor waving you to run for it—and I seen you say no as plain as hearing. Jim, that's one for you.

"This is the first bit of hope I had since we tried that attack, and it come through you. And now we go in for this treasure hunt, with sealed orders, too, and I don't like it. You and me must stick close, back to back like, and we'll save our necks no matter what happens."

Just then a man called from the fire that breakfast was ready, and we were soon sitting here and there on the sand eating. They had built a fire big enough to roast a whole cow, and it had now grown so hot that we could go near it only on the side from which the wind was blowing, and there only with care.

In the same wasting way they had cooked three times as much food as we could eat, and one of them, with a laugh, threw what was left upon the fire. I never in my life saw men so careless of their stores. They were daring enough to kill and be done with it, but from the way they wasted food and from the way their guards fell asleep while on duty, I knew they could not hold out long against us.

Even Silver, eating away, with the parrot on his shoulder, said not a word against their foolishness. And this surprised me the more because I thought he had never before seemed as cunning as he did just then.

"Mates, it's lucky you have me to think for you with this here head," he said. "I got what I wanted, I did. Sure enough, they have the ship. Where it is, I don't know yet, but once we finds the treasure, we gets out and finds out. And then us that has the boats, I guess, has the best chance."

Thus he kept running on with his mouth

full of hot bacon. So he built up their hopes, and, I think, his own at the same time.

"As for the boy," he continued, "that was his last talk, I guess, with them he loves so dear. I got my piece of news and thanks to him for that; but that's over and done. He goes with me when we hunt the money, and we'll keep him like so much gold, in case of accidents, you see. And once we get the ship and money both, and off to sea like a jolly family, we can talk Mr. Hawkins over and give him some, because he has been so kind."

It was no wonder the men were happy now. For my part, I was very much cast down. If this new plan of Silver's should work, he would follow it as quickly as any other. He was by no means to be trusted, and he had friends now in each party. Of course, he would rather be rich and free with the pirates than escape hanging by not more than an inch, which was the best he could ever hope for if he were on our side.

Even if things so happened that he had to keep his word with the doctor—even then what danger lay before us! What if the others found out that he was tricking them, and he and I had to fight for dear life—Silver with only one leg, and I, a boy—against five strong men!

Add to this double worry the strange things my friends had done—their leaving the stockade, their giving up the map, and then the doctor's words to Silver, "Look out for a storm when you find it." You will see then why I cared little for my breakfast and with what a troubled heart I set out behind the pirates on the hunt for the treasure.

Everyone in our party was armed heavily. Silver carried two guns, one before and one behind him—besides the sword at his belt and a pistol in each pocket. On top of all this, Captain Flint sat on his shoulder and gave us bit after bit of old sea talk. I had a line about my waist and followed Silver, who held the end now in his free hand, now in his great teeth. For all the world, I was led like a dancing bear.

The other men carried tools for digging and food for the day. All the stores, I saw, came from our supply, and I could see the truth of Silver's words of the night before. Had he not bargained with the doctor, all of them would have had to live on water and such birds and animals as they could kill. Water would not have been to their taste, and few sailors can shoot straight.

Well, so we set out—even the fellow with the broken head, who should have been resting in the shade. One after another we reached the shore, where we found the two boats in which they had come from the ship on that first afternoon. Both were to be taken along with us to make sure that my friends might not get one. And so, some in one boat, some in the other, we began the journey.

There was a good deal of talk about where

to begin the hunt. The cross was too large to be of much use as a guide, and the notes on the back of the map were not clear, as you may see:

"Tall tree, Spy-Glass shoulder bearing to a point N. of N.N.E."

"Skeleton Island E.S.E. and by E."

"Ten feet."

A tall tree was thus the principal mark. Now right before us the land was thickly covered with pines with one every here and there which rose high above its neighbors. It would take a close study of each to decide which was the right one. At length we landed at the mouth of the second river—the one which runs down the side of the Spy-Glass.

We climbed first through low, wet ground, then through a thick wood, then at last to a high flat country where we spread out in fan shape and went on for about half a mile. Suddenly one of the men stopped with a cry of terror.

"He can't have found the treasure," said Morgan. "That was clean on top."

Indeed, what he had found was something very different. At the foot of a big pine were the bones of a man with a few bits of cloth about them.

"He was a seaman," said George, who, more daring than the others, had gone up close to the bones. "Leastways, this is good sea cloth."

"Yes," said Silver, "like enough. Would you think to find a bishop here? But what kind of way is that for bones to lie?"

Indeed the body was not in a natural position. But for some little change (the work, perhaps, of birds that had fed upon him), the man lay perfectly straight—his feet pointing in one direction, his hands raised above his head, and pointing directly opposite.

"I've got a notion in my old fool head," said Silver, "that here is the compass. There's the tip-top point of Skeleton Island sticking out like a tooth. Just take a look along the line of the bones."

This was done. The body pointed straight toward the island.

"I thought so," cried the cook. "This here is a pointer. Right up there is our line for the north star and the jolly dollars. But, by the powers! if it don't make me cold inside to think of Flint. This is one of *his* jokes, and no mistake. Him and these six was alone here; he killed them every man; and this one he put here for a pointer, by the powers! They are long bones, and the hair was yellow. That would be Allardyce. You mind him, Morgan?"

"Yes, I do," returned he. "He took some of my money, he did, and he took my knife on shore with him."

"Speaking of knives," said another, "why don't we find one around here? Flint never was the man to pick a seaman's pocket, and the birds, I guess, would leave it be."

"By the powers, and that is true!" cried Silver.

"Not a thing left here," said George, still feeling around the bones; "not a thing. It don't look natural to me."

"No, it don't," agreed Silver, "not natural, and not nice, says you. And if Flint was living, this would be a hot spot for you and me. Six they were, and six we are; and bones is what they are now."

"I saw him dead with these two eyes of mine," said Morgan. "Bill took me in. There he laid with penny pieces on his eyes."

"Dead—sure enough he's dead and gone below," said the fellow with the broken head; "but if ever spirit walked, it would be Flint's. Dear heart, but he died bad!"

"That he did," put in another. "Now he would rage, and now he would call for drink, and now he would sing. 'Fifteen Men' were his only song, and I tell you I never rightly liked to hear it since. It were right hot, and the windows were open, and I hear that old song coming out clear as clear—and death on the man already."

"Come, come," said Silver, "stop this talk. He's dead, and he don't walk, that I know; leastways he don't walk by day, and you may lay to that. Care killed a cat. Go on now for the money."

We started, but the pirates no longer ran separate and shouting through the wood, but kept side by side and spoke in low voices. The fear of the dead Flint had fallen on their spirits.

Chapter XXXII

The Treasure Hunt — The Voice among the Trees

Because they were still afraid, and because Silver and the sick men needed to rest, the whole party sat down as soon as we had reached the top of the slope.

From this point we had a wide view on either hand. Before us, over the tops of the trees, we could see the Cape of the Woods; behind we saw not only the bay and Skeleton Island but also—clear across the low land to the east—the open sea. High above us rose the Spy-Glass with single trees here, great rocks there.

There was no sound but that of the sea and of the insects about us. There was not a man, not a sail on the sea. Indeed, we were alone.

Silver, as he sat, was taking his bearings.

"There is three 'tall trees,' " said he,

"about in the right line from Skeleton Island. 'Spy-Glass Shoulder,' I take it, means that lower point there. Child's play it will be to find the money now. I have half a mind to eat first."

"I don't feel good," said Morgan. "Thinking of Flint—I think it were—has done me."

"Well, my son," said Silver, "you may thank your stars he is dead."

"He were a mean one," said a third man, his voice shaking, "that blue in the face, too!"

"That was how the drink took him," added another.

"Blue! Well, I guess he was blue. Them is true words."

Ever since they had found the dead man and got this train of thought, their voices had gone lower and lower until they could hardly be heard.

All of a sudden, out of the middle of the trees in front of us, a thin, high, shaking voice began the old song:

"Fifteen men on the dead man's chest—
Yo-ho-ho and a bottle of rum!"

I never have seen men more terrified.
Every bit of color left their faces; some
jumped to their feet; some caught hold of
others; Morgan fell on the ground.

"Flint!" cried Merry.

The song had stopped as suddenly as it
began—broken off in the middle of a note, as
if someone had put a hand over the mouth
of the man singing.

Coming through the clear air among the
tree tops, I thought it sounded sweet and was
the more surprised at the effect it had on
the men.

"Come," said Silver, but he found it hard
to speak. "Stand by to go about. This is a
bad start, and I don't know the voice, but
this is someone trying to fool us—someone
that is flesh and blood, and you may lay to
that."

As he spoke, the color came back to his

face, and the others were beginning to take heart, when the voice sounded again—not singing but in a faint, far-away call.

"Darby McGraw," it cried again and again, and then a little higher and with a curse, "Bring me a drink, Darby!"

The men stood still, as if tied fast, long after the voice had died away.

"That fixes it!" gasped one. "Let's go."

"They was his last words," cried Morgan, "his last words before he died."

Dick had his Bible out and was praying. He had been well brought up before he came to sea and fell in with bad company.

I could hear Silver's teeth rattle in his head, but still he would not turn back.

"No one in this here island ever heard of Darby," he said; "not one but us that heard it just then." And then, rising to his full height, he cried, "Mates, I came here to get that money, and I'll not be beat by man or devil. I never was afraid of Flint in his life, and, by the powers, I'll face him dead. There is seven hundred thousand pound not a quarter of a mile from here. When did ever a gentleman of fortune turn his back to that much money for a drinking old seaman with a blue face—and him dead, too?"

"Wait there, John!" said Merry. "Don't cross a spirit."

The others were still too terrified to speak. Each one would have run away if he had dared, but fear kept them together and kept them close to John, as if his daring helped them.

"Spirit? Well, maybe," he replied, "but what do you say to this? There was an echo. Now, no man ever seen a spirit with a shadow. Well, how can a spirit have an echo, I want to know?"

His argument seemed very weak to me. but, to my surprise, it seemed to be enough for the others.

"Well, that's so," said Merry. "You have

a head on your shoulders, John, and no mistake. Come, mates! We was wrong, I do believe. And come to think on it, it was like Flint's voice, but not just so clear away like it, after all. It was like some other voice now— it was like—"

"By the powers, Ben Gunn!" roared Silver.

"And so it were!" cried Morgan. "Ben Gunn it were!"

"It don't make much difference, do it?" asked Dick. "Ben Gunn's not here in his body any more than Flint."

But the older men laughed at this.

"Why, nobody minds Ben Gunn," said one. "Dead or not, nobody minds him."

Their spirits rose quickly, and the color came back to their faces. Soon they were talking together, stopping at times to listen. Not long after, hearing no more sounds, they picked up their tools and set out again. One walked in front with the compass to keep them on the right line. It was true; dead or not, nobody minded poor Gunn.

It was fine open walking here with our way leading a little down the hill. There were not many trees, and the sun was very hot in the open spaces. Going north and west as we did, we drew near the shoulder of the Spy-Glass on the one hand. On the other hand, we saw the west bay where I had once been tossed about in Gunn's little boat.

We reached the first tall tree, but this proved to be the wrong one. So, with the second. The third was spread out much farther than the others and was much taller. It could be seen far out at sea and might well be taken as a landmark. But it was not its size that interested the pirates. The thought of the money that lay in the ground there had ended their fears. Their eyes burned in their heads; they walked faster; their only thoughts were of the life of wild spending which lay waiting for each one of them.

Silver found it very hard to keep up with them, and he was growing tired. He cursed roundly when the flies flew against his hot face. He pulled roughly at the line which held me to him, and from time to time he turned his eyes upon me with a look which I could not mistake.

In his great desire for the gold which was so near he cared for nothing else. His promise to the doctor and the doctor's warning were both things of the past. I am sure he was planning to take the treasure, find and board the ship under cover of the night, kill every good man on the island, and sail away loaded down with his crimes and his riches.

Troubled as I was, I found it hard to keep up even with Silver. Now and again I fell, and it was then that he pulled at the line so roughly and looked at me in such an angry way. Dick had fallen behind, for, with the heat, the long walk, and his fear, a fever was coming on just as the doctor had expected.

This troubled me the more, and, to top it all, I could not stop thinking that near this very spot Flint had, with his own hand, cut down his six companions—Flint with the blue face, who had died singing and calling for drink. This place that was now so quiet must have been filled with their cries. I even thought that I could still hear them.

We were now at the edge of a little wood.

"Now, men, all together!" shouted Merry, and broke into a run.

But suddenly, not ten yards from there, they stopped. A cry went up. Silver ran, and the next moment he and I, too, had come to a dead stop.

Before us was a great hole, which must have been dug some time before, for the sides had fallen in, and grass was growing at the bottom. Nothing else was to be seen except a broken pick and a few boards. On one of these we saw the word "Walrus"—the name of Flint's ship.

It was all clear. The money had been found and taken—the seven hundred thousand pounds were gone!

Chapter XXXIII

The Fall of a Chieftain

THERE was never such a change in this world. Each of the six men stopped as if he had been struck, but with Silver the blow passed in a moment. With all his soul he had been set upon getting that money. In a second every hope was gone, but he kept his head and made a complete change in his plans before the others had had time to think.

"Take that," he said softly to me, "and stand by for trouble." And he handed me a double-barreled pistol.

At the same time he quietly moved a little to one side, and in a few steps had put the hollow between us two and the other five. Then he looked at me as if to say, "This is a tight place," and indeed it was. He now had the air of an old friend, and I was so angry at these many changes that I could not help saying, "So you've changed sides again!"

There was no time for him to answer. The pirates, with a cry and a curse, jumped into the hole and began to dig with their hands, throwing the boards to the side as they did so.

Morgan found a small piece of gold which he handed from one to the other.

"That!" roared Merry. "Is that your seven hundred thousand pounds? And you are the man that never made a mistake, you wooden-headed fool!"

"Go on, boys," said Silver coolly. "You may find some nuts."

"Do you hear that?" screamed Merry. "I tell you that man there knew this all the time. Look in the face of him, and you can see it, mates."

"Ah, Merry," said Silver, "standing for captain again? You are a fine fellow, to be sure."

Almost out of their heads with anger, the men began to climb out of the hole, but this

I was glad to see—they all got out on the side which was away from Silver.

Well, there we stood, two on one side, five on the other, the hole between us, and not one wishing to give the first blow. Silver never moved. He watched them and looked as cool as I ever saw him. He was brave, and no mistake.

At last, Merry seemed to think a little talk would help.

"Mates," he said, "there is two of them alone there—one the old one-legged fool that brought us down to this, and the other that boy that I mean to get the heart of. Now, mates—"

He was raising his arm and his voice, and seemed ready to lead a charge. But just then —crack! crack! crack! three shots rang out. Merry fell into the hole; the man with the broken head fell full length on the ground; and the other three turned and ran for it as fast as they could go.

At the same moment the doctor, Gray, and Ben Gunn came out from among the trees with their guns smoking.

"Forward!" cried the doctor. "We must head them off from the boats!" And we set off as fast as possible.

Silver was most anxious to keep up with us and hopping on one leg went through an amount of work that no sound man ever could equal, as the doctor now says. As it was, he was quite a distance behind us and so tired that he was almost falling when we reached the top of a little hill.

"Doctor," he called, "see there! No hurry!"

Sure enough, there was no hurry, for in an open space we could see the three men still running in the same direction they had started, which was not toward the boats. We were already between them and the boats, and so we four sat down to rest, while Silver came up slowly.

"Thank you kindly, doctor," said he. "You came at just about the right time for us two. And so it's you, Ben Gunn!" he added. "Well, you're a nice one, to be sure."

"I'm Ben Gunn, I am," he replied. Then after a time, "And how do, Mr. Silver! Pretty well, I thank you, says you."

"Ben, Ben, to think as you've done me!" said Silver in a very low voice.

The doctor sent Gray back for one of the pickaxes which the pirates had left when they ran. Then as we walked down to the boats, he told in a few words what had happened since I left. It was a story which greatly interested Silver, and Gunn was the hero from beginning to end.

Gunn, as he had wandered about the island alone, had found the bones of the dead man. He had found the treasure; he had dug it up; he had carried it on his back, in many slow journeys, from the foot of the tall tree to a cave near the northeast end of the island.

There it had been, safe, for two months before we came.

The doctor had got the whole story from him on the afternoon of the fight. The next morning he had gone to Silver and had given him our store of food, for our new friend had enough goats' meat, which he himself had salted. The doctor had given everything for a chance to move safely from the stockade to the hill, where our men could be far from the fever swamp and could keep a guard upon the money.

"As for you, Jim," he said, "it went against my heart, but I did what I thought best for those who had stood by their duty, and if you were not one of these—well, none of us told you to run away."

The morning of his visit to the sick men in the stockade, he had seen that I was to be with the pirates when they went on their hunt. He had run all the way back to his own party, left Mr. Trelawney to care for the cap-

8ĳ

tain, and had taken Gray and Gunn with him to be on hand when we arrived.

Soon, however, he saw that our party had the start of him and had sent Gunn on to do his best alone. Gunn had thought of frightening the pirates and had done so well that Gray and the doctor were already there before we came.

"Well," said Silver, "it was good for me that I had this boy with me. You would have let old John be cut to bits and never given it a thought, doctor."

"Not a thought," returned the doctor lightly.

By this time we had reached the pirates' boats. With the pickax the doctor broke up one of them. Then we all got into the other and set out by sea for North Inlet.

This was a run of eight or nine miles. Silver, although he was very tired, was put at the oars with the rest of us, and we were soon rowing rapidly over a quiet sea. Soon, then, we rounded the southeast corner of the island, where four days ago we had pulled the ship in.

Later, as we passed Gunn's hill, we could see the black mouth of his cave and a man standing beside it. It was Mr. Trelawney. We waved to him and gave him three cheers, in which Silver joined with as much will as any.

Three miles more, and what should we meet but the *Hispaniola* sailing by herself. The last high water had lifted her, and if there had been much wind, we should never have seen her more. We anchored her again, then pulled to a little bay, which was the nearest point for Gunn's cave, and Gray returned alone to the ship, where he was to spend the night on guard.

As we landed, Mr. Trelawney met us. To me he was pleasant and kind, saying nothing either good or bad about my running away.

At Silver's pleasant salute he said, "John Silver, you are a scoundrel—an unspeakable scoundrel—but I am told I am not to bring you to court. Well, then, I will not. But the dead men, sir, hang about your neck like millstones."

"Thank you kindly, sir," replied Long John.

"How dare you to thank me!" cried Mr. Trelawney. "Stand back!"

Then we all entered the cave. It was a large place with a little spring of clear water. The floor was sand. Before a big fire lay the captain, and in a far corner were great heaps of coins and bars of gold. This was the gold for which we had come and which had already cost the lives of seventeen men from our ship. How many lives it had cost in the gathering, how much blood, how many good ships, how many lies, how many shot of cannon, no man living could tell. Yet here were Silver and Gunn—both had helped with these crimes and both expected to get some of the money.

"Come in, Jim," said the captain. "You

are a good boy in your line, Jim, but I don't think you and me will go to sea again. You are too free in your ways for a ship's boy. And is that you, John Silver? What brings you here, man?"

"Come back to do my duty, sir," returned Long John.

"Ah!" said the captain, and that was all he said.

What a supper I had of it that night with all of my friends around me! Never, I am sure, were people more happy. And there was Silver, sitting back almost out of the light, but eating with a will and quick to spring forward when we wanted anything. He even joined in quietly when we laughed—the same gentle, well-mannered seaman of the journey out.

Chapter XXXIV

And Last

THE NEXT morning we fell to work early, for carrying so large an amount of money nearly a mile to the shore and then three miles by boat to the ship was a great deal of work for so small a number of men. The three pirates still free on the island did not greatly trouble us. One guard on the hill was enough to save us from any surprise from them. Besides, we thought they had had enough of fighting.

We worked rapidly. Gray and Gunn came and went with the boat, while the rest of us carried the treasure to the shore. Two of the bars, carried by a rope, made a good load for a grown man—one that he was glad to walk slowly with. For my part, as I could not carry much, I was kept busy sorting the coins and putting them into bags.

I think I never had more pleasure than in doing this, for I found pieces of all shapes and sizes and values and from all countries. And as for number, I am sure they were like the leaves on the trees, so that my fingers hurt from the sorting of them.

Day after day this went on; by evening a fortune had been stored in the ship, but there was another fortune waiting for the morning. And all this time we heard nothing of the other three pirates.

At last—I think it was on the third night— the doctor and I were walking over the hill, when, from out of the dark below, the wind brought us a sound between screaming and singing. Then again it was quiet.

"Heaven help them," said the doctor; "it is the pirates!"

"All drunk, sir," said Silver from behind us.

Silver, I should say, was allowed to go and come as he pleased. He must have seen how much we looked down upon him; still he seemed to think himself as much a member of our party as if he had always remained our friend. I think none treated him better than a dog except Ben Gunn, who was still afraid of him, and myself, who did have something to thank him for.

So the doctor answered him very shortly. "Drunk or raving?" he said.

"Right you are, sir," said Silver, "and little difference it makes to you and me."

"My feelings may surprise a man like you, Mr. Silver," returned the doctor. "But if I were sure they were raving—and I am very sure one of them is sick—I would go to them and give them what help I could, no matter what might happen to me."

"You would be very wrong, sir," said Silver. "You would lose your life, and you may lay to that. I'm all on your side now, and I don't wish for to see the party lose a man, let alone you, seeing as I knows what you has done for me. But those men down there could not keep their word—not if they wanted to. And what is more, they could not believe as how you could."

"No," said the doctor, "you are the man to keep your word, we are sure of that."

And that was about the last we heard of the three. After talking it over, we decided we should have to leave them on the island. At this Ben Gunn was delighted, and Gray felt more at ease. We left them all we could of our powder and shot, salt meat, medicines, and clothing. Then at the wish of the doctor we added a large present of tobacco.

That was almost the last thing we did on the island. Before that we had stored the treasure and had put on board water and some of the salt meat. Then, at last, one fine morning we sailed out of North Inlet, flying the same colors that the captain had used at the stockade.

The three fellows must have been watching us more closely than we thought, as we soon found. As we sailed away, they came down to the shore, and there we saw them on their knees with their arms held out to us. They begged us not to leave them to die in such a place, but for God's sake to have mercy on them. Then, seeing that the ship did not stop, one of them seized his gun and sent a shot whistling over Silver's head.

After that we kept under cover, and when next I looked, they were gone, and the shore line was no longer clear in the distance. Then, before noon, to my great joy, even the highest rock on the island was gone from our view.

We were so short of men that every person on board had to work. Only the captain lay in his chair in the stern and gave his orders, for though he was much better, he was still too weak to go back to all of his old duties. We sailed for the nearest port in Spanish America, for it would not have been safe to try the journey home until we had more hands. As it was, we were all worn out before we reached the port.

It was just as the sun was setting that we sailed into a beautiful bay and were met by many small boats full of negroes and Indians selling fruits and offering to dive for bits of money. The sight of so many good-natured faces, the taste of fresh fruits, and the lights in the town were a most happy change after our dark and bloody stay on the island.

The doctor, Mr. Trelawney, and I went on shore to spend the early part of the night. Here we met the captain of an English ship, fell in talk with him, and went on board his ship. There we had such a pleasant time that day was breaking when we returned to the *Hispaniola*.

Ben Gunn was on deck alone, and as soon as we came on board, he told us that Silver was gone. Gunn had allowed him to escape in a shore boat some hours ago. This he had done, he said, to save our lives—which he said we would surely have lost if "that man with one leg had stayed on board." But this was not all, as we found. Silver had taken with him one of our bags of gold worth perhaps three or four hundred pounds.

Well, to make a long story short, we got a few more hands on board, had a safe journey home, and reached Bristol just as our friends there were beginning to think of starting a search for us. Only five of those who had started returned home. "Drink and the devil had done for the rest," to be sure, but we were not in quite so bad a case as the ship they sing about:

"With one man of the crew alive,
    What put to sea with seventy-five."

Each of us got a good part of the treasure and used it wisely or not, as was his nature. The captain is old now and no longer sails a ship. Gray saved his money, but more than that, he became a very careful sailor and is now mate and part owner of a fine ship. He is married and is the father of a family. Ben Gunn got a thousand pounds, which he spent or lost in less than three weeks, for in that time he was back again begging. Just as he had feared on the island, he was given a gate to tend. The country boys laugh at him, but they like him, and he can be heard singing loudly in the church every Sunday.

Of Silver we have never heard any more. That daring seaman with one leg has at last gone clean out of my life, but I dare say he met his negro wife and perhaps lives in comfort with her and his parrot. It is to be hoped so, I suppose, for his chances for comfort in another world are small.

The bars of silver and the arms still lie, for all I know, where Flint left them; and there they shall lie for all of me. Nothing could ever bring me back again to that cursed island, and the worst dreams I ever have are when I hear the waves breaking along its coast or hear the sharp voice of the old parrot ringing in my ears: "Pieces of eight! Pieces of eight!"

The Legend of Sleepy Hollow

Do you be-
lieve in ghosts? Ichabod
Crane did. This story tells
how he met a famous ghost
and how he lost his lady-
love.

In the very act of throwing his head

The Legend of Sleepy Hollow

Written in 1819 by Washington Irving . . . One of America's favorite ghost stories . . . And one of the funniest ever written.

Sleepy Hollow

THERE is one broad part of the Hudson River named by the old Dutch sailors the Tappan Zee, where they always wisely brought their boats through with great care and prayed to Saint Nicholas to keep them when they crossed. Near the Tappan Zee lies a small market town or country village, which is generally known by the name of Tarrytown.[1] This name was given, we are

[1] Tarry, stay.

told, in former days by the good housewives of the country around because their husbands always stayed so long at the inn there on days when they went to sell their vegetables. I do not say that this is a fact, but tell it only because it is of interest.

Not far from this village, perhaps about two miles, there is a little valley, among high hills, which is one of the quietest places in the whole world. A small brook runs through it with a low singing sound that makes one want to stop and rest, and the calls of the birds are almost the only noises that are ever heard. If ever I should wish for a place where I might go from all the world and dream away the rest of a troubled life, I know of none more promising than this little valley.

Because the place is so still and because the people who live here are so quiet, this valley has long been known as Sleepy Hollow. Its young men are always called the Sleepy Hollow boys all through the country.

A feeling of being in a dream seems to hang over the land and to fill the air. Some say the place was bewitched[2] by a doctor in the early days of the country; others say that an old Indian chief gathered his men together there in mysterious meetings long before the country was discovered by Master Hendrick Hudson.[3] Certain it is, the place still continues under some power that holds the minds of the good people, causing them to walk as if they were dreaming all the time.

They believe all kinds of strange things, too, and often see strange sights and hear strange music and voices in the air. The valley has haunted spots; and stars shoot more often across the hills here than in any other part of the whole country.

The Headless Horseman

The spirit, however, that visits this valley most and seems to be the captain of all the

---

[2]**bewitched,** put under a magic spell. [3]**Hendrick Hudson,** the man who discovered the Hudson River.

powers of the air[4] is a figure without a head, riding on a horse. It is said by some to be the spirit of a soldier whose head was carried away by a shot in a battle during the Revolutionary War, and who is often seen by the country people hurrying along in the dark of night as if on the wings of the wind.

He rides out of the valley at times to roads that are near, mostly to a church at no great distance. Indeed, certain of the men, who have written histories of these parts, who are known to tell the truth, and who have been careful in gathering the facts, say that the body of the soldier lies under the earth of the churchyard. They say also that every night the ghost rides forth to the place of the battle, hunting for his head, and that he rushes back like the wind because he is late and in a hurry to get back to the churchyard before day.

Such in general is the story that is told in the valley, and the ghost is known in all the

[4]powers of the air, spirits or ghosts.

country homes by the name of the Headless Horseman of Sleepy Hollow. Not only the people who have lived all their lives in the valley see such sights, but so do those who come to live there for a time. However wide awake they may have been before they entered this quiet place, they are sure in a little while to see and hear many things that they do not understand.

In such little Dutch valleys, found here and there in the great state of New York, the manners of the people remain always the same, while changes in other parts of this growing country pass without touching them. Though many years have passed since I walked through Sleepy Hollow, yet I believe I should still find the same trees and the same families living there just as they did long ago.

Ichabod Crane

In this valley there was, in a far-away time of American history—that is to say, some thirty years ago—a man of the name of Ichabod Crane, who came to Sleepy Hollow for the purpose of teaching the children of the place.

The name of Crane[5] suited him. He was tall, but very thin, with narrow shoulders, long arms and legs, hands that hung a mile out of his sleeves, big feet, and his whole body was most loosely put together. His head was small and flat at the top, with big ears, large green eyes like glass, and a long pointed nose, so that it looked like a weathercock[6] set upon his thin neck to tell which way the wind was blowing. To see him walking along a hill in the wind with his clothes flying about him, one might have thought he was some scarecrow[7] running away from a corn-field.

His school-house was a low building of one large room, made of logs. The windows were

---

[5]**Crane,** a bird with a long neck and long legs. [6]**weathercock,** a little wood figure that is set on top of a house and that turns in the wind. [7]**scarecrow,** a figure, perhaps of wood, dressed like a man, set up in a field or garden to scare the birds from the plants.

of glass, but some that were broken were covered with pieces of old writing paper. When school was over, the building was kept closed by a little stick through the handle of the door, and large sticks set against the wooden blinds,[8] so that, though it might be easy to get in, it would be hard to get out if one were caught.

The school-house stood there alone, but in a rather pleasant place just at the foot of a hill. A brook ran close by, and growing at one corner was a tree, from which the school-master got his sticks. From here the low sound of children's voices saying over their lessons might be heard on a quiet summer's day, with now and then the voice of the teacher commanding, or perhaps the sound of the stick as he helped some lazy child along the path of learning.

To tell the truth, he wanted to do just what was right and believed the old saying.

---

[8]**blinds,** window-shades.

"Spare the rod and spoil the child."[9] Ichabod's school children were not spoiled.

I would not have you think, however, that he was one of those cruel teachers who like to hurt their children. Quite different from that, he punished as fairly as a man could. He was easy on some weak little fellow who was afraid of the least touch of the stick, but he gave plenty to some hard, wrong-headed boy who grew mean. All this he called "doing his duty by their fathers and mothers." He never used his stick without telling the boy that "he would remember it and thank him for it the longest day he lived."

When school hours were over, he was even the friend of the larger boys and played with them; and on afternoons when there was no school, he would take some of the smaller ones home, who had pretty sisters, or mothers who were known for their good cooking.

[9]**rod**, stick. **Spare the rod and spoil the child.** A child who is not whipped at times may grow into a spoiled child.

Indeed, it was well for him to be a good friend to the children. The pay for teaching his school was small and might not have been enough for his food alone, for he ate much, even though he was thin. But in that part of the country, the teacher lived in the homes of the farmers whose children were in his school. He went to their houses in turn, a week at a time, going the rounds among the neighbors with all that belonged to him tied up in a handkerchief.

Ichabod had many ways of making himself both pleasant and of service, so that his stay would not be too hard upon the farmers. For some of them thought that school cost a great deal and that school-teachers had life very easy. He helped often in the lighter work of the farms, helped to make hay, fixed fences, took the horses to water, drove the cows to the fields, and cut wood for the winter fire. Here he did not seem like a teacher at all, but was always gentle and kind. The mothers thought well of him because he was so good to the young children. He would sit with a little child on his knee for whole hours at a time.

With his other work he was the singing-master of the country and made a little money by teaching the young people to sing. He was proud on Sundays to take his place at the front of the church to sing with the others. He thought the people noticed him more than they did the minister. Certain it is, his voice sounded above all the others. There are strange notes still to be heard in that church and which may even be heard half a mile off, quite across the water by the mill on a still Sunday morning, which are said to have come from the nose of Ichabod Crane.

So in many little ways the good teacher got on well enough and was thought by all who did not know the work of learning to have an easy time of it.

The schoolmaster is generally an important man among the women in the country, being thought far above the country fellows and, indeed, almost as important as the minister himself. When he appeared, the lady of the house would hurry to get a dish of cakes and to bring out the good cups and the good silver.

Our schoolmaster, therefore, was happy in the smiles of all the country girls. How proudly he walked among them in the church-yard between services on Sundays, talking and laughing. He would read for them all the writing[10] on the gravestones, or he would walk along with a whole crowd of them to the water by the mill, while the country boys stood back.

Since he was always moving from one farm-house to another, he became a kind of traveling newspaper, carrying all the news from house to house, so that people were glad to have him come. The women, too, thought

[10]**read . . . writing.** Very few people could read in those days.

well of him because of his great learning, for he had read several books quite through and knew perfectly a whole book about witches.

Ichabod's Belief in Ghosts and Witches

He firmly believed in witches. He believed all the stories of ghosts that were supposed to be seen in the valley. No story was too big for him. It was often his delight, when school was out for the afternoon, to lie on the thick bed of grass beside the little brook that ran by his school-house and there read over the stories in his book about witches until it grew so dark he could not see the pages.

Then, as he went his way by field and stream and awful forest to the farm-house where he happened to be staying, every sound of Nature was something to fear, even the noise of the birds moving among the leaves. The fireflies, too, which were brightest in the darkest places, now and then frightened him as one would cross his path. At such times

he would sing to drive the spirits away, and
the good people of Sleepy Hollow, as they sat
by their doors of an evening, were often filled
with wonder at hearing his song coming from
the far hill or along the dark road.

Another of Ichabod's pleasures that were
part fear was to pass long winter evenings with
the old Dutch wives as they sat by the fire, with
a row of apples cooking in the heat, and listen
to their wonderful stories. They would talk
for hours of ghosts and haunted fields, and
haunted brooks, and haunted bridges, and
haunted houses, and particularly of the Headless Horseman of the Hollow.

He would delight them, in turn, by stories of witches and of terrible sights and sounds.
He would frighten them, too, by talking of
shooting stars and with the awful fact that the
world did truly turn round and that they were
half the time standing on their heads.[11]

[11]**standing on their heads.** People used to believe the
earth was flat and did not know that it moved.

There was pleasure in all this while sitting warm among the company in a room that was lighted from the dancing fire and where, of course, no ghost dared to show its face. However, that pleasure was always followed by the fears of his walk home. What dreadful shapes and shades[12] waited along his path when the snow lay on the ground!

How he would look at every light streaming across the fields from some window in the distance! How often he jumped in fear at some bush covered with snow, which stood like a ghost all dressed in white beside his path! How often did he stop at the sound of his own steps and stand afraid to look over his shoulder because there might be something walking close behind him! And how often did he shake with fear at the wind rushing among the trees, thinking that it was the Headless Horseman on one of his night rides!

All these, however, were just fears of the

[12]shades, ghosts.

night, sights that he only thought he saw. Though he had seen many strange things in his time, day always put an end to them. He would have passed a pleasant life of it if his path had not been crossed by a being that causes more trouble to man than all the ghosts and all the witches put together, and that was —a woman.

Ichabod's Love

Among the young people who gathered one evening in each week to study singing was Katrina Van Tassel, the daughter and only child of a rich farmer.

She was a pretty girl of eighteen and was known far and wide not only for her beauty but also for the money she would have some day. Katrina knew that she was pretty, and she liked to catch the boys' eyes, as might be seen from her dress, which was most suited to make her look well. Her short skirt showed the prettiest foot in the country round.

Ichabod Crane had a soft and foolish heart toward girls, and it is not to be wondered at that such a pretty one soon pleased him, more especially after he had visited her in her father's house.

Old Baltus Van Tassel was a perfect picture of a rich, happy, kind-hearted farmer. He did not often send his eyes or his thoughts away from his own farm, but here everything was happy and well cared for. He liked being rich, but he was not proud. He was glad to have plenty, but he made no great show of it.

His home was on the banks of the Hudson in one of those green, quiet places, almost like nests, in which the Dutch farmers like to live. A large tree spread its broad branches over it, at the foot of which a spring of the softest and sweetest water rose in a little well and ran away shining through the grass to a near-by brook.

Close to the house was a large barn that might have served for a church. Every window showed the good things of the farm. The men were busy in it from morning till night. Birds were flying about its roof. Fat pigs stood in their pens, from which ran forth, now and then, little pigs with their noses up as if to smell the air. Snow-white geese were riding on a stream of water, leading a whole company of ducks. Turkeys walked about the farmyard.

Before the barn door marched the brave cock, proudly beating his wings and crowing in the joy of his heart—and sometimes tearing up the earth with his feet and then gladly calling his family of wives and children to come and get the rich bit which he had discovered.

The school-teacher's mouth watered as he looked upon all this fine food that was ready for winter. As he rolled his great green eyes over the fat farm lands, the rich fields of wheat and Indian corn, the trees heavy with fruit, and the warm home of Van Tassel, his heart longed for the girl who would some day own all these. He even thought how they might be turned into money which could be used to buy large pieces of wild land in the new country in the West. Indeed, his busy fancy already called up the picture of the pretty Katrina with a whole family of children, in a wagon loaded with furniture, and he, himself, riding a horse, setting out for the new lands of the West.

When he entered the house, he wanted more than ever to become one of the Van Tassel family. In the large room in the middle of the house the family spent most of their time. Here rows of shining dishes met his eyes. In one corner stood bags of wool ready to be made into cloth, and in another corner was cloth ready to be made into clothes. Ears of Indian corn and apples on a shelf waited until they were needed.

From the moment Ichabod saw these delights, the peace of his mind was at an end, and his only study was how to win the fair daughter of Van Tassel. In this, however, he had more real trouble than a knight of long ago. The knight usually had only giants and bad fairies and dragons to fight and had to make his way only through gates of iron and walls of stone to come to the lady of his heart. All this was as easy as cutting his way through a Christmas pie, and then the lady married him as a matter of course.

Ichabod, however, had to win his way to the heart of a rich country girl, who knew very well what she liked and what she wanted. He had to win against many young men who were also trying to get Katrina, and, while keeping an eye upon each other, were ready to fly out together against any new fellow.

Brom Bones

Among these, the one to fear most was a big, loud fellow of the name of Abraham—or Brom, as he was called—Van Brunt. Brom was known through all the country round, which was full of stories of things his strong arms had done. His shoulders were broad, his black hair was short and curly, and his face bold but pleasant.

He was proud, but full of fun, too. From his big body and the great power of his arms and legs, he was known generally as Brom Bones. He was famous as a brave horseback rider who would dare to do anything. He was first at all races and cock fights. He was always ready for a fight, himself, but he liked fun even more than a fight.

He had three or four friends who looked upon him as their captain, and at the head of them he would ride through the country to everything that went on for miles around. In cold weather he would wear a fur cap with a fox's tail on it, and when people at a country party saw that well-known cap at a distance among a party of men riding hard, they always expected something to happen.

Sometimes his crowd would be heard rushing past the farm-houses in the middle of the night, talking loudly. Then the old people in their beds would listen a minute till the noise passed and say, "There goes Brom Bones and his fellows!" The neighbors looked upon him with wonder and yet with good-will, and when any wild trick was played, they knew Brom Bones was at the bottom of it.

Brom had for some time wished to win the fair Katrina, and although he must have been about as gentle as a bear at making love, yet it was said that she did not destroy his hopes. Certain it is that when he talked with her, that was a sign for all others to keep away.

When his horse was seen standing at Van Tassel's fence on a Sunday night, a sure sign that his master was courting, all other young fellows passed by to some other girl's house.

Such was the fellow who wanted the same girl that Ichabod Crane wanted. A stronger and wiser man than Ichabod would have given up.

Ichabod and Brom

To go openly against Brom Bones would not have been possible, for Brom was not a man to be stopped in his love-making. Ichabod, therefore, went on in a quiet and gentle manner. As singing-master, he often visited the farm-house. He had nothing to fear from the mother and father, as many young men do.

Balt Van Tassel was an easy, good-natured soul. He loved his daughter even better than his pipe and let her have her way in everything. His little wife, too, had enough to do to keep house and look after her farmyard; for, as she said, a duck and a goose are foolish things and must be looked after, but a girl can take care of herself. So while she was busy in her house, honest Balt would sit smoking his evening pipe, watching a little wood soldier, who, with a sword in each hand, was fighting the wind at the very top of the barn. So Ichabod would talk with the daughter, sitting by the side of the spring under the big tree or walking with her in the evening, which is the time for love-making.

From the moment Ichabod Crane showed his interest in Katrina, the interest of Brom Bones seemed to grow less. His horse was no longer seen standing at the fence on Sunday nights. A dreadful anger rose between him and the teacher of Sleepy Hollow.

Brom would have fought with Ichabod and have settled their quarrel that way, but Ichabod knew too much of those strong arms of his enemy to fight with him. He had heard Bones say that he would "double the school-master up and lay him on the shelf in his own school-house," and he was too wise to give him the chance.

Brom did not like this way of letting things go on. It gave him nothing to do but play tricks on his enemy. Brom and his crowd smoked out the singing-school by stopping up the chimney. They got into the school-house at night and turned everything over, so that the poor schoolmaster began to think that all the witches in the country held their meetings there. And every time he could, Brom would make poor Ichabod look like a fool before the girl of his dreams. He even taught his dog to cry so that people laughed, and then said that this was Katrina's new singing teacher.

The Invitation

Matters went this way for some time. Then, on a fine afternoon, Ichabod was sitting sadly on the tall chair where he usually watched over his school. In his hand he held a ruler. The stick lay upon three nails on the wall behind him, a constant fear to those who did what they should not. On his desk might be seen several articles that he had taken from the boys—apples, pop-guns, fly traps, and whole armies of little paper game-cocks. It

seemed that some child had just been punished, for all the boys and girls were now busy
with their books or whispering behind them,
with one eye on the schoolmaster, and a kind
of buzzing quiet was over the room.

Suddenly a boy came riding up on the
back of a wild little horse. He ran loudly up
to the school door and asked Ichabod to attend
a party to be held that evening at Herr Van
Tassel's. Then the boy on his horse went over
the brook and up the Hollow, very important
and very much in a hurry.

In a moment all was alive in the school-
room that had been so quiet. The children
raced through their lessons. Those who were
quick left out half, and those who were slow
had a little touch of the stick from behind to
help them over a hard word. Books were
thrown here and there without being put
away, and the whole school was let go an hour
before the proper time.

Ichabod now took at least a half-hour to

make ready for the party, brushing up his best, and indeed only, suit of black and combing his hair before a piece of looking-glass on the school-house wall.

That he might appear in a fine manner before his lady, he asked the farmer with whom he was staying to let him have his horse. The farmer, a cross old Dutchman of the name of Hans Van Ripper, let him take the animal, and Ichabod started proudly forth.

Ichabod and Gunpowder

I should tell you about him and his horse. The animal was a broken-down horse that had worked for many years on the farm and that had little life in him except in his mean temper. His bones showed, his coat of hair needed to be brushed, and his neck was crooked. He could not see out of one eye, but his good eye had the light of a very devil in it. In his day, he must have had some fire or spirit, if we may judge from his name, which was Gunpowder. The cross Van Ripper, who used to ride hard, had always liked this horse and perhaps had put some of his own spirit into the animal; for old and slow as he now looked, there was more of the devil in him than in any young horse in the country.

The figure of Ichabod suited the horse. His knees came almost as high as the horse's shoulders. He carried his whip straight up. As his horse walked on, Ichabod's arms stuck out so that they looked like a pair of wings moving up and down. A small hat rested on the top of his nose, for he had only a narrow little forehead, and the tails of his black coat flew out almost to the horse's tail.

That is the way he looked as he went out the gate of Hans Van Ripper, and it was such a sight as is not often met with in the daylight.

It was, as I have said, a fine day. The sky was clear. Nature was dressed in rich and golden colors. The forests had put on their dark brown and yellow, and frost had turned the leaves of some of the young trees red.

The Party

It was toward evening when Ichabod arrived at the home of Herr Van Tassel, which he found filled with people from all over the country—old farmers in home-made suits, blue stockings, big shoes with shining buckles; their wives in close caps and long dresses; and the girls dressed like their mothers.

Brom Bones was the most important person there, having come to the gathering on the horse he liked best, Daredevil—an animal, like himself, full of spirit and mischief, and which no man but him could ride. Brom liked horses that were wild and given to all kinds of tricks. He would not have a gentle horse.

A great plenty of food waited for the Van Tassels' company. There were cakes and pies and meats—milk—but I have not time to talk of the food. I must get on with my story. Ichabod was not in so great a hurry as I, but took time to eat all that he could hold.

He was a kind person, whose heart warmed with thanks as he became filled with food and whose spirits rose with eating as some men's do with drink. He could not help, too, rolling his large eyes round him and smiling at the thought that he might one day be lord of all he saw. Then, he thought, how soon he would turn his back upon the old school-house.

Old Baltus Van Tassel moved about among the company, with a face spread with joy, round as the full moon. He would shake their hands and tell them to "fall to, and help themselves."

And now music sounded, calling all to the dance. Ichabod was almost as proud of his dancing as of his singing. His whole body was busy when he danced. Not any part of him was still. How could the schoolmaster help being happy? The lady of his heart danced with him, smiling in reply to all his smiles, while Brom Bones, jealous, sat by himself in one corner.

Stories of the Headless Horseman

When the dance was at an end, Ichabod joined some of the older people, who, with old Van Tassel, sat smoking and telling long stories about the war. Then there were stories of ghosts and of strange things people had seen and heard. Many were told about cries that were heard at the tree where Major André[13] was taken and which stood near. They told of a woman dressed in white who appeared in the dark and cried on winter nights before a storm.

Most of the stories were of the Headless Horseman of Sleepy Hollow, who had been seen several times lately riding over the country and whose horse, it was said, stood each

[13]**André,** an English spy who was hanged during the war.

night among the lonely graves in the dark churchyard.

This dark church seems always to have been a place for troubled spirits. It stands on a hill, and its white walls show through the trees. At the foot of the hill is silver water, and in the distance are the hills of the Hudson. It looks like a quiet place where the dead might rest in peace.

On one side of the church extends a little wood, along which runs a large brook among broken rocks and fallen trees. Over a deep, black part of the stream, not far from the church, was once built a wooden bridge. The road that led to it and the bridge itself were thickly shaded by trees, which made it dark even during the day and made it terribly black at night. Such was one of the places where the Headless Horseman most often appeared.

The story was told by old Brouwer, who did not believe in ghosts, of how he met the Horseman returning from his ride into Sleepy

369

Hollow, and was forced to get up behind him; how they rode up hill and down hill until they reached the bridge, when the Horseman suddenly threw old Brouwer into the brook and sprang away over the tree-tops with the sound of thunder.

Brom Bones then said that as he was returning one night from the near-by village of Sing-Sing, he met the Horseman riding. Brom offered to race with him, and Brom would have been first, too, for Daredevil beat the ghost horse. But just as they came to the bridge, the Horseman rushed on and disappeared in fire.

These stories were told in the low voice in which men talk in the dark, with their faces lighted only when they light their pipes. Ichabod listened to all that was said. Then he, too, told parts from his book about witches and added stories of the strange sights which he had seen in his walks at night in Sleepy Hollow.

The Homeward Journey

At last the party began to break up. The old farmers gathered their families together in their wagons and were heard for some time driving along the roads and over the hills in the distance. Some of the girls were seated on horses behind their young men, and they were heard laughing along the wood until the sounds died away. At last all was still at the home of Balt Van Tassel.

Ichabod stayed behind a moment, as a young man in love does, to speak to Katrina, sure that he was now on the way to win her. What they talked of, I will not say, for in fact I do not know. Something, however, I fear me, must have gone wrong, for he certainly walked off after a while with an air quite sad.

Oh, Woman! Woman! Could that girl have been playing off any of her tricks? Had she been leading the poor teacher on just to help her win another? Heaven only knows, not I! But Ichabod left with the manner of a man who had been stealing chickens rather than seeking to win a fair lady's heart.

Now, without looking to right or to left to notice the rich lands of Van Tassel, he went straight to his horse and woke him from dreams of mountains of corn and whole valleys of sweet grass.

It was the very time of night for witches when Ichabod, heavy-hearted, traveled home along the sides of the hills which rise above Tarrytown, and which he had traveled so happily in the afternoon. The Tappan Zee spread its waters before him, with here and there a boat riding quietly close to shore. In the dead of night he could even hear the barking of a watch-dog from the other side of the river, but that friend of man seemed very far away from Ichabod. Now and then, too, the long crow of a cock would sound far, far off, from some farm-house among the hills, but it was like a dream in his ears. There was no sign of life near him, except from some little animal in the wood as it turned in its bed.

All the stories of strange things that Ichabod had heard in the evening now came crowding back into his mind. The night grew darker and darker. Sometimes the clouds even covered the stars. He had never felt so alone.

Also he was coming to the place of which many of the stories were told. In the middle of the road a large tree stood high above the other trees. Its branches took a different shape from the others, turning down almost to the earth and then rising again in the air. It was called Major André's tree because the poor André had been taken prisoner close by. The people all knew of the awful sights and sounds around the tree.

As Ichabod came near, he began to whistle. He thought his whistle was answered, but it was the wind through the dry leaves. A little nearer he thought he saw something white hanging in the middle of the tree. He stood still and stopped whistling. But on looking more closely, he saw that it was only a place where white wood showed. Suddenly he heard a groan. Ichabod began to shake from head to foot. It was only one large branch rubbing upon another. He passed the tree safely. But other fears lay in his path.

About two hundred yards from the tree a small brook crossed the road and entered the wood. A few logs laid side by side made a bridge over the stream. On that side of the road where the brook ran among the trees, the deep shade made everything dark.

To pass this bridge was the hardest part of Ichabod's journey. It was at this very spot that poor André was taken, and behind these very trees had been hiding the men who surprised him. This has ever since been a place of fear. Every school-boy who has to pass it alone after dark is afraid.

As Ichabod came to the stream, his heart began to jump. He tried to be brave, however. He gave his horse a few kicks and tried to rush across the bridge. But instead of going forward the old animal stepped to the side and ran right against the fence. Ichabod, whose fears were now increasing, pulled the lines on the other side and kicked hard with his other foot. But it was of no use. His horse took a step forward, it is true, but it was only to jump to the other side of the road into the bushes.

The schoolmaster now used both whip and foot on old Gunpowder, who rushed forward a moment but came to a stand just by the bridge so suddenly that he nearly sent Ichabod flying over his head.

Ichabod Meets the Headless Horseman

Just at this moment Ichabod's ear heard a step by the side of the bridge. In the dark of the wood, beside the brook, he saw a strange shape, big and black. It did not move, but seemed all gathered up as if ready to spring upon him.

The hair of the poor schoolmaster rose upon his head in fear. What was to be done? To turn and fly was now too late. And, anyway, what chance was there of escaping a ghost, if such it was, which could ride upon the wings of the wind?

Trying to be brave, his words trembling, he called, "Who are you?"

He received no reply.

He asked again in a shaking voice.

Still there was no answer.

Once more he beat the sides of Gunpowder and, shutting his eyes, started to sing a church song.

Just then the black object moved and all at once stood in the middle of the road. Though the night was dark, Ichabod could make out the form of the strange being. He appeared to be a horseman—large—riding a black horse of big body. He made no offer of hurting Ichabod or of talking to him, but kept off to one side of the road, riding along on the blind side of Gunpowder, who now seemed not quite so much afraid.

Ichabod did not want the company of this fellow. He remembered Brom Bones's meeting the Headless Horseman and so made his horse go faster in the hope of leaving the stranger behind. The other, however, came on just as fast. Ichabod pulled up and fell into a walk. The other did the same. Ichabod's heart stood still. He tried to sing again, but his dry tongue was sticking to the roof of his mouth, and he could not make a sound.

Something in the still manner of this object was terrible. On mounting a bit of rising ground from which the horseman could be seen more clearly against the sky, Ichabod saw that he was headless! His horror was increased to see that the head which should have rested on the horseman's shoulders was carried before him on the saddle.

Ichabod was so afraid he could not think

what was best to do. He beat Gunpowder, hoping by a sudden start to get away, but the horse behind started full jump with him. Away they went, through thick and thin, stones flying at every step. Ichabod's clothes, too, were flying in the air as he leaned away over the horse's head.

They had now reached the road which turns off to Sleepy Hollow. But Gunpowder, who seemed to have lost his sense, instead of taking the right way, made the wrong turn and rushed down the hill to the left. This road leads through a place shaded by trees, to where it crosses a bridge close beside the white church.

As yet Gunpowder had been so much afraid that he had kept Ichabod a little in front of the other horseman, but just as he got almost to the bridge, the saddle gave way and began to slip off. Ichabod caught at it and tried to hold it, but he could not. He had only time to save himself by throwing his arms around Gunpowder's neck, when the saddle fell to the ground and he heard the horse behind step upon it.

For a moment, the thought of cross old Hans Van Ripper came to his mind, for it was the old Dutchman's best saddle. But this was no time for little fears. The ghost was close upon him, and since Ichabod could not ride at all well, he had all he could do to keep his seat.

An opening in the trees gave him hope that the church bridge was near. A star shining on the water of the brook told him that he was right. He saw the walls of the church under the trees. He remembered the place where Brom Bones had said the ghost disappeared. "If I can but reach the bridge," thought Ichabod, "I am safe."

Just then he heard the black horse blowing close upon him. He even thought he could feel the wind hot upon his neck. Again he beat Gunpowder, who ran upon the bridge;

he rushed over the boards; he reached the other side; and now Ichabod looked behind him to see whether the horseman would disappear in fire. He saw the fellow rising in his stirrups and in the very act of throwing his head at him. The poor schoolmaster tried to dodge, but the awful thing hit his head with a great noise. Down fell Ichabod into the dust, and Gunpowder, the other horse, and the ghost passed by like the wind.

The Disappearance of the Schoolmaster

The next morning the old horse was found without his saddle, eating grass at his master's gate. Ichabod did not appear at breakfast. Dinner hour came, but no Ichabod. The boys came to school and walked about the banks of the brook—but no schoolmaster. Hans Van Ripper began to wonder what had happened to his saddle.

The neighbors started to hunt for Ichabod, and after a while they came upon the

marks his horse's shoes had made. In one part
of the road leading to the church the saddle
was found, lying in the dust. Marks of the
horse's feet led to the bridge, and on the bank
of the broad part of the brook, where the
water ran deep and black, was found the hat
of poor Ichabod and close beside it a pumpkin broken in pieces.

The neighbors hunted in the brook, but
the body of the schoolmaster was not to be
discovered. Hans Van Ripper looked after
the things that belonged to Ichabod. There
were a few clothes and a book of church songs.
They also found his book about witches and
a book of dreams in which was a paper with
several lines in honor of Katrina Van Tassel.

These books were burned by Hans Van
Ripper, who from that time forward decided
to send his children no more to school, saying
that he never knew any good to come of this
same reading and writing. Any money that
the schoolmaster had—and he had received his

pay but a day or two before—he must have had with him.

The event was talked of at church on the following Sunday. People gathered in the churchyard, at the bridge, and at the spot where the hat and the pumpkin had been found. The stories of Brouwer, Brom, and of others were called to mind. When they talked over all of them and then this present case, they began to shake their heads and decided that Ichabod had been carried off by the Headless Horseman. No one troubled his head any more about him. The school was moved to a different place, and another schoolmaster came to teach.

It is true that an old farmer, who had been down to New York on a visit several years after, said that Ichabod Crane was still alive; that he had left the country because he was afraid of the ghost and of Hans Van Ripper, and because he felt bad at having been sent away by Katrina. He added that Ichabod had gone to live in another part of the state; had kept school and made a study of law at the same time; had opened his own law office; had written for the newspapers; and at last had held a high place in the court.

Brom Bones, who, soon after Ichabod left, took the fair Katrina as his wife, always looked as if he knew a great deal when the story of Ichabod was told. He laughed loudly when people spoke of the pumpkin—which led some to think that he knew more of the matter than he would tell.

The old country wives, however, who are the best judges of these matters, say to this day that Ichabod was taken away by some strange means, and the story is often told by the neighbors round the winter evening fire. The bridge was more than ever an object of fear and wonder, and that may be the reason the road has been changed of late years to pass the church from the other side.

The school-house soon fell down. It was

said the ghost of the poor schoolmaster often came there. Certain it is that boys, going slowly home of a still summer evening, have often thought they heard Ichabod's voice at a distance singing a sad song in the quiet of Sleepy Hollow.

Rip Van Winkle

This story tells of the good Dutch people who lived along the Hudson River in early times, of strange things that happened in the Catskill Mountains, of the power of a woman's tongue, and of what happened to a hen-pecked husband.

Slowly Rip's fear left him.

Rip Van Winkle

Another short story by Washington Irving . . . And one of his best-liked . . . Taken from The Sketch Book . . . *1819.*

Rip Van Winkle and His Wife

ANYONE who has made a journey up the Hudson River must remember the Catskill Mountains. They are a branch of the great Appalachian Mountains[1] and are seen away to the west of the river, rising high and standing like lords above the country around.

At the foot of these mountains, light smoke might be noticed rising from a village, whose roofs are seen among the trees just where the blue of the hills meets the fresh green of the

[1]**Appalachian Mountains,** mountains that extend north and south in New York and other states in the East.

nearer fields. This little village was settled by the Dutch long ago in the early times of the country, just about the beginning of the government of the good Peter Stuyvesant[2] (may he rest in peace!). Some of the first houses of the town were still standing a few years ago, built of yellow bricks brought from Holland.[3]

In that same village and in one of these very houses (which, to tell the truth, was a very poor house) there lived many years ago, while the country still belonged to England, a kind, simple fellow of the name of Rip Van Winkle. He was one of the family of Van Winkles who were once brave soldiers in the days of Peter Stuyvesant, and were with the good Stuyvesant in battle.

Rip, however, was not much like a soldier. I have said that he was a kind, simple man; he was also a good neighbor, and he let his wife

[2]**Peter Stuyvesant,** head of the government of this part of the country when it belonged to Holland. [3]**Holland,** a country in Europe, the home of the Dutch.

order him about until he was quite henpecked.[4]

Indeed, it may have been that because he
did what his wife told him, he would always do
as others wished. For those men who are
ordered about by cross wives are almost always
patient and easy to get along with. Their manners are made gentle by angry words at home.
A man who is always scolded by his wife is
usually not quick to become cross, himself. A
scolding woman may therefore in some ways
be good for a man, and, if so, Rip Van Winkle
was blessed with his wife.

Certain it is that all the good wives of the
village liked him. They took his part in all
family quarrels and said that Dame[5] Van Winkle had caused the trouble. The children of
the village, too, would shout with joy when he
appeared. He helped in their games, made

---

[4]**henpecked,** ordered about by his wife until he had no
will of his own. [5]**Dame,** Mrs.

toys for them, showed them how to fly kites and shoot marbles, and told them long stories of ghosts, witches, and Indians. When he went about the village, he was followed by a crowd of them hanging on his coat tails, climbing on his back, and laughing and playing with him. And not a dog would bark at him in the whole town.

The great trouble with Rip was that he did not like to work. It was not because he could not stick to one thing long at a time; for he would sit on a rock, with a heavy rod, and fish all day, even though he did not catch a single fish. He would carry a gun on his shoulder through the wood for hours, up hill and down hill, to shoot a few squirrels. He would help a neighbor at any time in the hardest work and was busy enough at all the country parties for husking Indian corn or building stone fences.

The wives of the village, too, used to ask him to go here and there for them and do bits of work that their husbands would not do. In a word, Rip was ready to do anything but attend to his own business. He never did his own work, and he did not keep his own farm in order at all.

In fact, he said it was of no use to work on his farm. No piece of ground in the whole country was so bad as his. Everything about it went wrong, and would go wrong, no matter if he did work. His fences were always falling to pieces. His cow would run away or get into the garden. Weeds were sure to grow more quickly in his fields than in other men's. The rain always began just when he had some work to do outside.

Rip had lost so much of the farm that his father had left to him that there was now little more than a garden of Indian corn and potatoes. Yet not one of his neighbors' farms was so badly kept as his small piece of land.

His children, too, were in rags and as wild as if they belonged to no one. His son Rip was just like him. It seemed that young Rip not only got his father's old clothes but had his father's ways, too. He generally was seen running along behind his mother, wearing a pair of his father's old trousers and having a great deal of trouble in trying to hold them up with one hand, as a fine lady does a long dress in the rain.

Rip Van Winkle, however, was one of those happy men who take the world easy, eat white bread or brown—the one that can be got with less thought and trouble—and would rather not have enough to eat than work to make some money. If left to himself, he would have whistled away all his life and been happy. But his wife was always scolding because he would not work and because he did not take better care of his family. Morning, noon, and night her tongue was going, and everything he said or did was sure to bring a storm of words from her.

Rip had one way of replying to her. He

would draw up his shoulders, shake his head, roll up his eyes, and say nothing. This, however, always brought a fresh scolding from his wife, and Rip would go to the outside of the house—the only side which, in truth, belongs to a henpecked husband.

Rip's dog Wolf was his best friend. Wolf had no more peace at home than had his master, for Dame Van Winkle said that he was partly the cause of Rip's leaving his work so often.

True it is, Wolf was as brave an animal as ever hunted in the woods, but even a brave dog would run away from such a tongue as this woman had.

The minute Wolf entered the house, he would lower his head, and his tail would hang low to the floor or curl between his legs. He went about as if he had been doing something wrong. He did not dare to look at Dame Van Winkle, and if she touched a stick of firewood or the broom, he would fly to the door crying.

The Company at the Inn

Times grew bad indeed for Rip Van Winkle as the years rolled on. A cross woman never grows sweeter with age, and the more she uses her tongue, the sharper it becomes. For a long time, when Rip was driven from home, he would go to the inn, for there on a seat before the door a crowd of men was always gathered under the picture of the King of England. This picture was the sign by which the inn was known.

Here they used to sit in the shade through a long lazy summer day, talking over things that had happened in the village or telling sleepy stories about nothing. Sometimes when an old newspaper happened to be left behind by a man who was passing through the village, Derrick Van Bummel, the school-teacher, read it to them. Derrick was a neat, learned little man, who was not afraid of the biggest word in the paper. At these times they talked

very wisely about things that had taken place
months before.

Nicholas Vedder was the leader of the men
who gathered here. Nicholas owned the inn,
and he was one of the oldest and wisest men
in the village. He took his seat at the door of
the inn from morning till night, just moving
enough to get out of the sun and keep in the
shade of a large tree. The neighbors could
tell the time of day by his moving just as if
he had been a sun-dial.[6]

It is true, Nicholas did not often speak,
but just sat smoking his pipe. The other men,
however, could tell what he was thinking.
When he did not like what was read or told,
he would smoke his pipe in short, quick, angry
puffs. When pleased, he would draw in the
smoke slowly and blow it out again in light,
quiet clouds, and sometimes, taking the pipe

[6]**sun-dial.** A sun-dial tells the time of day by the way the
shadow from the sun falls upon it. Men told time by sun-
dials before clocks were made.

from his mouth and letting the smoke curl about his nose, would nod his head to show that he thought the same.

From even this pleasant place poor Rip was driven by his wife. She would suddenly break in upon the quiet crowd and scold all the men. Not even Nicholas Vedder, himself, escaped the sharp tongue of this woman. She said he helped to keep her husband from work.

Rip's Escape to the Woods

At last Rip did not know what to do. The only way he could get away from the work of the farm and from his scolding wife was to take his gun and go off into the woods. Here he would sit sometimes at the foot of a tree and divide his little bag of bread and butter with Wolf. Rip felt sad for Wolf because Dame Van Winkle was never kind to the dog.

"Poor Wolf," he would say, "Dame Van Winkle is not good to you; but never mind, my boy, while I live, you shall have a friend to stand by you." Wolf would wag his tail, look up into his master's face, and if dogs can feel sad, I believe he was sad for Rip, too, with all his heart.

On one of his long walks in the woods on a fine day, Rip, without watching how far he was going, had climbed to one of the highest parts of the Catskill Mountains. He was shooting squirrels, and the quiet hills had sounded again and again with his gun. Very tired, he lay down, late in the afternoon, on a little round green hill covered with mountain plants.

The mountain was steep below. From an opening between the trees he could see all the lower country for many a mile of rich forest. He saw at a distance the Hudson River, far, far below him, moving on its way. A purple cloud or the sail of a lazy boat showed here and there on its still water, which at last lost itself in the blue mountains.

On the other side he looked deep down between two hillsides to a wild glen[7] filled with rocks, the bottom dark and covered with large stones. For some time Rip lay just looking about him. Evening was coming on. The long blue shadows of the mountains began to fall over the valleys. He saw that it would be dark long before he could reach the village, and he shook his head sadly when he thought of meeting Dame Van Winkle.

Strange Happenings in the Mountains

As he was about to go down, he heard a voice from a distance calling, "Rip Van Winkle! Rip Van Winkle!" He looked around but could see nothing but a bird flying alone across the mountain. There seemed to be no one who could have called, and he turned again to go. Again he heard the same cry ringing through the still evening air, "Rip Van Winkle! Rip Van Winkle!"

[7]glen, a little valley.

At the same time Wolf's hair stood up, and giving a low growl, he came close to his master's side, looking down into the dark as if he was afraid. Rip now felt afraid, too. He looked down into the narrow glen and saw a strange figure slowly climbing up the rocks, carrying something heavy on his back. Rip was surprised to see a man on this wild mountain, but thinking it was some neighbor, he hurried down to help him carry his load.

The man looked very strange. He was a short, square old fellow, with thick hair and a gray beard. His clothes were like those of many years before: a cloth coat with a belt around the middle, several pairs of short trousers, the top ones very large, with rows of buttons down the sides, and bunches at the knees.

He carried on his shoulders a heavy keg,[8] which seemed to be full of liquor, and made signs to Rip to come and help him with it. Though still a little afraid, Rip came quickly,

[8]keg, a small barrel.

and taking turns at carrying the keg, they climbed up a narrow valley which looked as if a mountain stream had once run through it.

As they went up, Rip every now and then heard long, low sounds like thunder in the distance. The noise seemed to come out of a deep opening between tall rocks toward which their path led. He stopped for a moment, but supposing it to be one of those thunder-storms which often take place in the mountains, he went on.

Soon they came to a hollow, around which stood high rocks, with branches of trees over their edges like a roof, so that you could see very little of the blue sky and the bright evening clouds. During the whole time Rip and the old man did not speak, though Rip wondered greatly what could be the reason for carrying a keg of liquor up this wild mountain. Yet there was something so strange about the whole business that he did not dare ask questions.

When they entered the hollow, new objects of wonder appeared. In the center was a small company of odd-looking men playing ninepins.[9] They were dressed most strangely. Some had on short coats. Others had long knives in their belts. Most of them had big full trousers like his guide's. Their faces, too, were odd. One had a large beard, a broad face, and small eyes like a pig's. The face of another seemed to be all nose, and he had on a white hat with a red cock's tail on it. All of the men had beards, of different shapes and colors.

There was one who seemed to be the captain. He was a fat old gentleman with a wrinkled, brown face. He had a long coat with a broad belt and short sword, a high hat with a feather, red stockings, and high-heeled shoes. They all looked like the men in a picture which Rip had seen hanging in the house of

[9]ninepins, a game like bowling played with nine large wooden pins and a wooden ball.

Dominie Van Shaick in the village, and which had been brought over from Holland at the time the town was settled.

What seemed most strange to Rip was that, though these men were playing a game and seemed to be having a good time, their faces were very sad. They did not even talk. Rip could hear nothing except the noise of the balls which, when they rolled, sounded along the mountains like thunder.

As Rip and his guide came up, the men stopped their play and looked at him. Rip was frightened, and his knees began to shake. The old man set down the keg and made signs to Rip to serve drinks to the company. Rip did so, but he was still afraid. They drank without speaking and then returned to their game.

Slowly Rip's fear left him. He even dared, when no one was looking, to taste the liquor, which he found very good. In a minute he took a long drink, then another, and another.

He took so many that soon he could not think rightly, his eyes began to swim, his head fell forward, and he went sound asleep.

The Next Morning

On waking, he found himself on the green hill where he had first seen the old man. He rubbed his eyes. It was morning. The sun was shining brightly. The birds were singing. "Surely," thought Rip, "I did not sleep here all night." He remembered what had happened the evening before. The strange old man with the keg of liquor—the mountain path—the wild glen—the sad game of ninepins —the drink he had had. "Oh! that drink! that bad drink!" thought Rip. "What shall I tell Dame Van Winkle?"

He looked around for his gun, but instead of a clean, shining gun, he found a rusted one there beside him. It was old and ready to fall to pieces. He now thought those fellows of the mountain had played a trick on him by giving him something to drink and then taking his gun. Wolf, too, was gone, but he might have run just out of sight. Rip whistled after him and called his name, but no dog was to be seen.

He decided to go back where he had been last night, and if he met any of the men, to ask them to give him back his dog and his gun. As he rose to walk, his legs were stiff and hard to move. "These mountain beds are not good for me," thought Rip, "and if this visit here should give me a cold and lay me up for a while, I shall have a bad time with Dame Van Winkle."

With some trouble he started down into the glen up which he and the old man had come the evening before. But to his great surprise a mountain stream was now running down it, rushing from rock to rock and filling the air with its noise. He, however, made his way up its sides, although many times he almost fell.

RIP VAN WINKLE

At last he came to where the opening through the rocks had been, but there were no signs now of such an opening. The rocks made a high wall over which the stream flowed and fell into a small, deep lake, black from the shadows of the forest. Here, then, poor Rip stopped. He again called and whistled for his dog, but Wolf did not come.

What was he to do? The morning was passing away, and Rip wanted his breakfast. He did not like to go away without his dog and without his own gun. He did not want to meet his wife, but he could not stay here in the mountains with nothing to eat. He shook his head, put the old gun on his shoulder, and with a heart full of trouble, turned his steps toward home.

Rip's Return to the Village

As he came near the village, he met a number of people, but he did not know any of them. Rip was surprised, for he thought he knew all the people in the country round. Their clothes, too, were different from any he had ever seen. They all looked at him in surprise, also, and then they would put their hands to their faces. When this had happened many times, Rip put his hand to his face and found his beard had grown a foot long!

He now entered the village. A crowd of strange children ran after him, laughing at him and pointing to his gray beard. The dogs, too, barked at him, and Rip saw that he did not know one of them. The very town was changed. It was larger and had more people. There were rows of houses where there had been none before, and those that he had often visited were gone. Strange names were over the doors—strange faces at the windows—everything was strange.

His mind seemed to be fooling him. He began to think that both he and the world about him were completely bewitched. Surely this was his village, which he had left only the day before. There stood the Catskill Mountains—there ran the Hudson at a distance—there were every hill and valley just as they had been always.

Rip did not know what to think. "That drink last night," said he, "has mixed up my poor head."

He had trouble finding the way to his own house. He was afraid as he went up to it, expecting every minute to hear the voice of Dame Van Winkle. He found the house falling to pieces. The roof had fallen in, the windows were broken, the doors hung open and would not close. A dog, whose very bones showed and which looked like Wolf, was walking about. Rip called his name, but the dog showed his teeth and went on. Rip felt very sad, indeed. "Even my dog does not know me," he said.

He entered the house, which, to tell the truth, Dame Van Winkle had always kept clean and in order. There was nothing in the house. No one seemed to live in it. Rip forgot his fear of Dame Van Winkle. He called loudly for her and for his children. The rooms sounded for a moment with his voice, and then all was still again.

He now ran out of the house and hurried to the inn, but it, too, was gone. A large wooden building stood in its place, with large windows, some of them broken, with old hats and skirts sticking in them. Over the door was painted, "The Union Hotel, by Jonathan Doolittle." Instead of the big tree that used to shade the quiet little Dutch inn, there was now a tall pole from which was flying a flag made up of stars and stripes.

All this was so strange that Rip could not understand. He saw on the sign, however, the picture of the King of England, under which he had smoked many a pipe. But even this was changed. The red coat was changed for one of blue and tan, a sword was held in the hand, on the head was a three-cornered hat, and under the figure was painted, in large letters, "GENERAL WASHINGTON."

There was, as usual, a crowd of people about the door, but none that Rip remembered. All of the people seemed changed. They were all busy and rushing about. He had never before seen men in a hurry at the inn. He looked for Nicholas Vedder with his broad face and long pipe, or for Van Bummel, the school-teacher. In place of these, a man was talking loudly to the people about the rights of citizens—elections—members of Congress—and other words which did not mean anything to Rip.

Soon the men about the door saw Rip Van Winkle with his long gray beard, his old gun, his strange clothes, and a crowd of women and children after him. The men gathered round him, too, and looked him over from head to foot. The man who had been talking ran up to him and, drawing him away a little, asked on which side he voted. Rip could not make any answer, for he did not know what the man was talking about. Another short but busy little fellow pulled him by the arm and asked in his ear whether he was a Federalist or a Democrat,[10] but Rip could not understand.

Then an old gentleman in a three-cornered hat, who seemed to think himself very important, made his way through the crowd. Standing right before Rip, he demanded in a stern voice what brought him to the election with a gun on his shoulder and a crowd running after him, and whether he was going to make trouble in the village?

"Gentlemen," cried Rip, "I am a poor, quiet man. I live in this village and am a true subject of the king, God bless him."

Then the people all shouted, "A spy! A spy! Away with him!"

The man who seemed to think he was very

---

[10]**Federalist or Democrat.** At that time there were Federalists and Democrats just as we now have Republicans and Democrats.

important asked Rip what he had come there
for and whom he was hunting. Rip told him
that he had come to look for some of his neighbors who used to be about there; that he did
not mean to cause any trouble.

"Well, who are your neighbors? Name
them."

Rip thought a minute and asked, "Where
is Nicholas Vedder?"

No one answered for a little while. Then
an old man replied in a thin voice, "Nicholas
Vedder? Why, he is dead and gone these
eighteen years! At his grave there was a piece
of wood set up that used to tell all about him,
but that is gone, too, now."

"Where is Brom Dutcher?"

"Oh, he went off to the army in the beginning of the war. Some say he was killed in
battle. Others say he was drowned in a storm.
I don't know—he never came back again."

"Where is Van Bummel, the school-
teacher?"

"He went off to the wars, too. He was a great general and is now in Congress."

Rip's heart failed at hearing of these sad changes in his home and friends and finding himself alone in the world. He could not understand why the men spoke of such a long time and of such strange things as war—Congress—citizens. He could not ask after any more of his friends, but cried out, "Does no one here know Rip Van Winkle?"

"Oh, Rip Van Winkle," said two or three. "Oh, to be sure. That's Rip Van Winkle over there by the tree."

Rip looked and saw a young man who was just like himself as he was when he went up the mountain. He seemed as lazy and was surely as ragged. Poor Rip could not think. He doubted whether he was himself or another man. And there was the man with the three-cornered hat asking who he was and what was his name.

"God knows," cried Rip. "I'm not myself

—I'm another person—that's me over there—
no—that is another man got into my shoes. I
was myself last night, but I fell asleep on the
mountain, and they have changed my gun,
and everything is changed, and I don't know
my name or who I am."

The people began now to look at each
other, and smile, and point to their heads.
Some talked, too, of taking the gun from him
so that the old fellow could not make any
trouble.

Rip Finds His Daughter

At that moment a pretty young woman
came through the crowd to look at him. The
fat child she carried in her arms was afraid of
Rip and began to cry. "Be still, Rip," said
the mother; "The old man will not hurt you."

Rip noticed the name of the child. He
thought he remembered the manner of the
mother and her voice. "What is your name,
my good woman?" asked he.

"Judith Gardenier."

"And your father's name?"

"Oh, poor man, Rip Van Winkle was his name, but it is twenty years since he went away from home with his gun, and never has been heard of since. His dog came home without him. But whether he killed himself or was carried away by the Indians, no one can tell. I was just a little girl then."

Rip had but one more question to ask. He asked it with shaking voice. "Where's your mother?"

"Oh, she, too, died a short time ago in a fit of anger."

Rip felt a little better to know that he need not fear Dame Van Winkle.

He took his daughter and her child in his arms. "I am your father," cried he. "I was young Rip Van Winkle once. I am old Rip Van Winkle now. Does nobody know poor Rip Van Winkle?"

All were surprised until an old woman

among the crowd put her hand above her eyes, and, looking under it in his face for a moment, said, "Sure enough! It is Rip Van Winkle. It is himself. Welcome home again, old neighbor. Where have you been all these twenty long years?"

Rip's story was soon told, for the whole twenty years had been to him but as one night. The neighbors opened their eyes wide when they heard it. Some were seen to smile at one another and put their tongues in their cheeks. The very important man in the three-cornered hat turned down the corners of his mouth and shook his head.

It was decided, however, to ask old Peter Vanderdonk what he thought, for he was slowly coming up the road. One of Peter's family once wrote a history of this part of the country, and Peter was one of the oldest men in the village and knew all of its history.

He remembered Rip Van Winkle at once and said that his story was true. He told the crowd that it was a fact that strange beings had always lived in the Catskill Mountains. That it had been said that Hendrick Hudson, who discovered the river and the country, kept a kind of watch there every twenty years with the men of his ship, the Half Moon; that in this way he was allowed to visit the places he had liked while he was living. That his father had once seen them in their old Dutch clothes playing ninepins in the mountains; and that he himself had heard, one summer afternoon, the sound of their balls like thunder in the distance.

To make a long story short, the crowd left Rip and returned to the more important matter of the election. His daughter took him home to live with her. She had a good house and a strong, happy farmer for a husband, whom Rip remembered as one of the little boys who used to run along with him in the street. As for Rip's son, who had been standing by the tree, he worked on the farm, but,

like his father, he would rather do anything
else than his own duties.

Rip now went back to his old walks and
ways. He soon found many of his old friends,
though all of them had become old men. Rip
liked better to make friends among the young
people. They liked him, too.

Having nothing to do at home, he took his
place once more on the seat at the inn door
and was honored as one of the wise men of the
village and one who could tell good stories of
the old times "before the war." It was some
time before he could understand the things
that had happened during his long sleep—how
there had been a Revolutionary War—that the
country no longer belonged to England—and
that instead of being a subject of the King of
England, he was now a free citizen of the
United States.

Rip, in fact, knew little of such things.
The changes of government made little difference to him. There was one kind of gov-

ernment under which he had suffered, and that was a woman's government. Now that was at an end. He had got free of his wife and could go in and out as he pleased without being afraid of Dame Van Winkle.

He used to tell his story to all the men that came to Mr. Doolittle's inn. At first he would change some points every time he told it, which was, perhaps, because he had not been awake very long. But it at last settled down to the story that I have told.

Some people would not believe it. They said that Rip had been out of his head. The old Dutch people, however, all believed it. Even to this day they never hear a thunderstorm of a summer afternoon about the Catskills without saying Hendrick Hudson and his men are at their game of ninepins. It is the wish of all the henpecked husbands in the village, when life becomes tiresome to them, that they might have a drink like the one Rip Van Winkle had that night in the mountains.

As You Like It

*D*id you ever think you would like to go away from home and have strange adventures? This is the story of a beautiful princess who was driven from home and went into a wild forest, dressed as a boy.

They found the name Rosalind.

As You Like It

*From a play by Shakespeare
. . . First presented about
1600 . . . Written as a story
by Charles Lamb in 1807
. . . Has had a long run on
the stage—about three hundred years . . . Still very well
liked.*

The King in the Forest

LONG ago, far across the ocean in the country of France, there lived a good king, who ruled over a small kingdom. All his people loved him. But the good king was driven away from his throne and from his palace by his younger brother, Frederick. Then the younger brother made himself the king, took the palace, and ruled the kingdom.

The true king was even forced to leave the kingdom. So he took a few friends who were true to him and went into the Forest of Arden. Here he lived with these friends who had left their homes to follow him. For the false king, Frederick, had taken the men's homes, their lands, and all that they had.

At first the men were sad in the strange forest, but soon they were happy together in this new way of living. Life was easy for them in the wood, and in time they began to like it better than the busy life that they had known before. Every day more fine young men came to join them there, and they all made a merry company.

In the summer they would lie on the soft grass in the cool shade of the large trees, watching the wild deer play. They liked the beautiful brown deer so much that they were sorry when they must kill the gentle animals to give themselves meat to eat.

But when the cold winds of winter came, the king felt the change from his warm palace. However, he was brave. He would say, "These cold winds that blow upon my body cut me, but they at least are true. They do not make up pleasant things to say to me just to win my favor, as some men have done. They bite me sharply, but they do not hurt me so badly as some men did when they took all that I gave them and never thanked me. I find that even when life is hard, men may still get some good things from it, just as medicine to quiet pain is taken from the head of an ugly toad."[1]

The good king was wise, too. Far from the busy city he listened to the trees which said to him, "Be strong," and to the brooks which said to him, "Be patient."

The Two Princesses

The king had a daughter who was named Rosalind. When the king was driven away from his home by his brother, Frederick kept Rosalind at his court as company for his own daughter, Celia. The two girls loved each

[1]**toad.** In those days men had strange ideas about health and often made strange medicines from parts of animals.

other dearly, and even though their fathers had quarreled, Rosalind and Celia were yet good friends.

Celia tried always to be very kind to Rosalind. She wanted Rosalind to be happy. When thoughts of her poor father made Rosalind sad, Celia did everything to please her, to help her forget her trouble.

Orlando

One day Celia and Rosalind sat together on the grass at the side of the palace. Celia said in her usual kind way, "I beg you, Rosalind, my sweet cousin, smile and be merry." While she spoke, a boy came running to them and said, "Two men are going to wrestle to show their strength before the king. If you ladies wish to see, come now to the court in front of the palace." Thinking that the sport might make Rosalind forget her sadness, Celia decided to go.

In those times, princes often had games

and even rough sports take place in their courts before the eyes of fair ladies. So Rosalind and Celia went to see the men wrestle.

However, when they had found seats among the crowd, they feared they might not like the sight. One of the men was large and strong and had been wrestling many years. He had even killed weaker men who had tried their strength against him. The other one was very young, and it did not seem that he could have such strength as the older man, nor could he know so well how to wrestle. All the people who watched thought that the younger man would be hurt or killed.

When the king saw Rosalind and Celia, he came to them and said, "My dear girls, have you come to see these men wrestle? I think you will find little pleasure here because one man is so much bigger and stronger than the other. The younger one should not try to meet the older one's great strength. I have asked him not to try it, but he has decided to

425

do it. I will call him to us, and you two girls may ask him not to do this dangerous thing. Perhaps he will listen to your wishes."

The girls were pleased to speak with the young man, for they did not wish him to be hurt. First Celia asked him not to wrestle with the stronger man. Then Rosalind spoke to him. Her words were kind, and she seemed to care so truly that the young man wanted more than ever to show this beautiful girl how strong and brave he was. He only decided more firmly to do his best.

However, though he would not do as the girls asked, his manner was most pleasing. He said, "I do not like to say no to the wishes of such fair and fine ladies. But let your beautiful eyes and gentle wishes go with me as I try my strength against a stronger man. Then I shall surely win. However, if I fail, I have been shamed before. If I am killed, I do not care. I have no friends who would feel sad over me. I have nothing in the world. I only fill a place that another might fill better when I have left it." As he turned to go, the girls were more troubled for him than before.

Then the men began to wrestle. Celia wished that the fine young man might not be hurt, but Rosalind felt most for him. He had said that he had no friends who would feel sad if he should die. Rosalind thought that his life, indeed, must be a sad one like her own. She watched him very closely, and as she watched him, she fell in love with him.

With the two kind girls looking on, the strange young man felt himself grow braver and stronger. He wrestled wonderfully. The girls could not believe their eyes. In the end, he won. The older man was hurt so badly that for a while he could not speak or move.

Frederick, the king, was much pleased with the brave young man. He called the lad to him and asked his name and who his father was. It was his wish to keep the young man there and to help him.

The stranger replied that his name was Orlando and that he was the youngest son of Sir Rowland de Boys.

Sir Rowland de Boys, the father of Orlando, had been dead for some years. When he was living, he had been the true subject and friend of the real king, Rosalind's father, who had been driven into the Forest of Arden.

When Frederick learned that Orlando was the son of his brother's friend, he did not care to have anything more to do with the young man. He turned and walked away, feeling very cross. Frederick did not want to help the son of any friend of the real king. Yet he thought Orlando was a brave man, and as he went, he said, "I wish that you had been the son of any other man."

Rosalind's Love

However, Rosalind was delighted to hear that the young man whom she liked so well was the son of Sir Rowland. She remembered

Sir Rowland, and she said to Celia, "My father loved Orlando's father. If I had known he was Sir Rowland's son, I could not have kept back my tears when he decided to wrestle."

When the girls saw that Orlando was hurt because Frederick had turned away from him so suddenly and so cruelly, they went to him. They spoke kindly to him, and when they were going away, Rosalind turned back to smile. Taking a golden chain from around her neck, she gave it to Orlando. "Friend," she said, "wear this chain for me. I have nothing else to give, or I would give you a finer present."

Orlando took the chain. In those days, in a battle or a game a young man often wore a lady's favor to help him win. The favor might be a chain, or a ring, or a ribbon.

When the girls were alone in their rooms, Rosalind still talked of Orlando. Then Celia saw that Rosalind was in love with the handsome young man and asked, "Is it possible that you should fall in love so quickly?"

Rosalind replied, "The king, my father, loved Orlando's father dearly."

"But," answered Celia, "that is no reason for your loving Orlando dearly. If that were so, then I should hate him, for my father hated his father. But I do not hate Orlando."

Driven from the Palace

The false king, Frederick, was troubled because Orlando made him remember that the real king still had many good and noble friends. Now for some time Frederick had not been pleased with Rosalind. The people liked her because she was beautiful and kind and good, and they were sorry for her because of her father's trouble. Frederick feared that the people might think more and more of Rosalind and less of himself. So he turned against her.

While the girls sat talking of Orlando, Frederick entered the room. In an angry voice he said to Rosalind, "Leave my palace at once.

You must go from my kingdom and follow your father into the Forest of Arden."

"Father, let Rosalind stay for my sake!" cried Celia.

"For your sake," answered Frederick, "I have already let her stay too long a time."

Then Celia fell to the floor at her father's feet, saying, "Let her stay here with me. We have been together all the years since we were children. We have learned our lessons together. We have played together. I love her as I would a sister. I cannot live without her."

To these words Frederick replied cruelly, "The people love her more than they love you, Celia. You are a fool to want Rosalind to stay, for you would seem more bright and beautiful if she were gone. You need not ask that I let her stay, for I mean what I have said. I will not change my word. Rosalind must go." Then Frederick turned and left the room.

Since Celia knew that her father would not

let Rosalind stay, she decided at once that she would go with her cousin into the forest. The girls began to get ready to leave their home. As they made their plans, Celia said, "It is not safe for two girls to travel through the country alone in such rich clothes as we are wearing. I am afraid someone will hurt us, thinking that we have money. Let us dress as simple country girls."

Rosalind replied, "It would be safer if one of us was dressed like a man. Then no one would be quick to stop us."

So they quickly decided that Rosalind should put on man's clothes because she was the taller. Rosalind dressed like a young country fellow, and Celia wore the dress of a country girl.

When they were ready, Rosalind said, "Let us say that we are brother and sister. I shall say that my name is Ganymede."

Celia answered, "And I shall say that I am Aliena."

The Journey to the Forest

So, dressed in the clothes of country people, the girls took all the money they had and started on their long journey, for the Forest of Arden was far from Frederick's kingdom.

The Lady Rosalind (or Ganymede, as she must now be called) seemed taller and looked very brave in her new clothes. Since she had to go, she was happy that her kind friend Celia would go with her. They walked many hard miles, but Rosalind was merry because Celia was with her. It seemed as if she were truly a strong Ganymede and as if Celia were a simple country girl.

All day long they walked and walked. At night they stopped to sleep at inns along the road. However, when they entered the Forest of Arden, there were no places where they could find the food and rest they needed.

Ganymede had kept his sister gay with his happy talk. But at last he sat down by the road and said, "I am very, very tired." Even though he had on the clothes that a man should wear, he wished to cry like a woman. As for Aliena, she said that she could not go on one step more.

Then Ganymede tried to remember that it is a man's duty to be strong and to make the way easy for a woman. Wishing to appear brave before his new sister, he said, "Come, my sister Aliena, let us be happy again. We are now near the end of our journey. We are in the Forest of Arden."

However, playing that he was a brave young man did not long help them to be gay. It is true that they were in the Forest of Arden, but in that big wood they did not know where to find Rosalind's father, the good king. Their journey might have come to a sad end there, for they might have got lost and have died for want of food. As they sat by the road, not able to go on, they lost all hope.

Then, to their surprise, a man happened

to pass that way. Ganymede stood up and tried to speak like a man. "Good man," he said, "if we can get help in this place for love or money, please take us where we can rest. This young girl, my sister, is very tired, and she has had nothing to eat for a long time."

The man replied, "I work for a farmer who lives near here, but my master is going to sell his house. He is not prepared to receive company. You may, however, come with me. He will let you rest as well as you can."

The promise of help gave new strength to Ganymede and Aliena, and they followed the man to the farmer's home. It was a pretty place. Since the farmer wanted to sell it, the girls bought the house themselves, for they needed a place to live. They also asked the man who had brought them there to stay and serve them.

The house was small but clean. There was food in it, too. So Ganymede and Aliena decided to live there until they could learn in what part of the forest Rosalind's father was living.

There they rested a long time from their journey. Soon they began to like their new home and the forest, and they almost believed that they were a farmer boy and girl.

Yet sometimes Ganymede remembered that once he had been the Lady Rosalind and that he had loved the fine young man, Orlando. Ganymede thought that Orlando was many, many miles away—as far away as all the miles he and Aliena had traveled. Yet at that very moment Orlando was also in the Forest of Arden. This is how it happened.

Oliver and Orlando

When Orlando was just a boy, his father had died. The father left the child in the care of his older brother, Oliver. The father told Oliver to send Orlando to school so that he might learn the things that a gentleman should learn. He also told Oliver to give his younger brother all the things that one of their noble family should have.

However, Oliver did not do as his father had ordered him. He did not send Orlando to school but kept him at home and gave him no attention.

But Orlando was always quick to learn, and even though he had not been to school, he knew a great deal. By nature he was so fine and noble that he was like a young man who had been brought up with the greatest care.

Oliver grew to hate Orlando because the boy was so good and because his manners were so pleasing. At last he even wished to destroy Orlando. For this reason he had sent Orlando to try his strength that day at Frederick's court against the stronger man. Oliver had hoped that his brother would be killed.

Orlando knew that Oliver hated him, and that is why he told Rosalind and Celia that he had nothing in the world. He felt that no one cared for him.

When Oliver heard that his mean hopes had failed and that Orlando, instead of being killed, had gained great honor, he was very angry. He swore that he would set fire to Orlando's room when Orlando was sleeping there.

However, a faithful old man named Adam, who had served the father of these two brothers, heard Oliver say what he planned to do. Adam loved Orlando because Orlando was like his father, Sir Rowland. So Adam went to meet Orlando as the young man was coming from the king's court.

When he saw Orlando, he ran to him and cried, "Oh, my gentle young master, why have you shown yourself so strong and brave? The good report of you has come to your home too swiftly before you."

Orlando could not understand. "What do you mean, good Adam?" he asked. "What is the matter?"

Then old Adam said, "Your brother Oliver

has heard how well you wrestled, and he hates you for it. He hates you because all the people like you. Now, since he knows how you have made more honor for yourself, he plans to kill you by setting fire to your room while you sleep."

Orlando could not believe such a thing.

Adam continued, "Do not come home, my dear young master. Go away so that you may escape death tonight."

Adam knew that Orlando had no money. Oliver had all the money and gave none to Orlando. So Adam had brought with him his own little bit of money in a bag.

"I have some gold pieces here," he said, holding out the small bag. "I saved this money when I worked for your father. I laid it by so that I might have something when I should be too old to work. Take this money now. God will take care of me when I can work no longer. Here is the gold. I give it all to you. Let me go with you and serve you. I am old, but I will do all that a young man could do."

"Oh, my good Adam!" cried Orlando. "How faithful you have been through all the years. You shall come with me if you wish. We shall go away together. I take your money now because I must, but some day I shall pay you back more than you have given me."

Then the kind old Adam and his young master started out, not knowing where to go. They walked miles and miles until they came to the Forest of Arden. There they found themselves in the same want that Ganymede and Aliena had felt. They had no food, and they could see no house where they could go to rest. Still they had to keep on.

At last Adam cried, "Oh, master, I shall die if I do not have food. I can walk no more."

Orlando was sad to see poor Adam so weak. Taking the old man up in his arms, he carried him to the cool shade under the trees. Softly he said, "Do not give up, Adam. Rest your

440

tired body here a while. I will find food for you." Then Orlando went away a distance to find food and drink for Adam.

Orlando's Meeting with the King

It happened that he soon came to the part of the forest where the good king was living. There Orlando saw the king and his friends just sitting down to eat their dinner under the large trees.

Orlando was so hungry that he could not think what was right to do. He ran up to the men, drew his sword, and prepared to fight to take their dinner from them. "Stop," he cried. "Do not eat one bite. I must have this food."

In surprise the good king asked, "What is the matter, young man? Why do you act so wildly? Are you a rough fellow who has no manners?"

Orlando replied, "I am about to die for want of food."

Then the kind king said, "Sit down and

eat with us. Eat all that you wish. There is plenty."

Hearing the king speak such gentle words, Orlando put up his sword. He was ashamed that he had acted so. "Pardon me for being rude," he said. "You men who sit here seem to have seen better days. You seem to have once lived where you could hear church bells ring. You seem to have sat at great dinners. If your eyes have ever filled with tears, listen to my trouble and help me."

"It is true we have seen better days," the king answered. "Though we now live in this wild forest, we once lived as other men do. We have heard church bells ring. We have had tears in our eyes when we have been sad for a friend. Therefore, young man, sit down with us, eat all that you wish, and tell us how we can help you."

Orlando replied, "Not far from here lies a poor old man who has come with me many hard miles. Tired and hungry, he could walk no more and fell down upon the grass. Until he has food, I can eat nothing myself."

"Go, bring the old man here," said the good king. "We shall not eat till you return with him."

Then Orlando ran away through the forest as fast as a deer. Soon he came back carrying the tired old Adam in his arms.

When the king saw them, he said, "Put the man down here. Both of you shall eat until you are filled." The men gave old Adam food. When he had eaten for a while, the old man felt well and strong again.

After dinner the king asked Orlando, "Who are you, my young man?"

Orlando answered, "I am the son of your old friend, Sir Rowland de Boys."

The king cried, "Sir Rowland's son! My old friend's son! How glad I am to see you! You may stay with me and my men here where all is safe."

So Orlando and Adam decided to make

their home there with these kind men. In this way it happened that Orlando came into the Forest of Arden not many days after Ganymede and Aliena had bought the farmer's house for their home.

The Meeting of Orlando and Ganymede

One day as Ganymede and Aliena walked in the wood, they found here and there the name Rosalind cut into the trees. Sometimes words of love to Rosalind were cut there, too. Ganymede and Aliena were greatly surprised, for who in this strange place could know the Lady Rosalind?

While they stood wondering, they saw Orlando walking a little distance away. As he came nearer, they saw that the chain Rosalind had given him was about his neck.

Seeing these two, Orlando thought they were a country boy and girl. He could not see that Ganymede was truly the fair Lady Rosalind, who had been so kind to him at the palace. He did not know that this boy was Rosalind to whom he had lost his heart.

However, when he saw the nice-looking fellow with the pleasing manner, he began to talk with him. He thought that in some strange way this farmer boy was like his pretty Rosalind. Ganymede, of course, did not seem like a fine lady. He acted like a country boy, as he had to act. He talked as a man talks with a man.

Laughing, he said to Orlando, "Some fellow who is in love goes through this forest cutting the name Rosalind into the trees. He writes love lines there, too. They all speak of this same Rosalind. If I could find this one who is in love, I would tell him a cure for his trouble."

Orlando answered, "I must be honest, my good boy. I am he who is in love. Tell me the cure for this sweet, sad feeling that I have."

Ganymede replied, "Come to my home here in the forest every day. My sister and I live here with our serving-man. I shall talk to you of Rosalind. When we have talked about her, you may learn that you do not truly love this Rosalind. Or perhaps you may grow tired hearing about her. In this way, you will grow out of your love for her."

Orlando said, "I do not believe that that can happen. I do not think that I can stop loving the beautiful Rosalind. But I shall come to your home every day, and we shall see whether your plan will make me grow tired of my love. Indeed, I am not happy loving Rosalind and not seeing her."

So Orlando came to the house where Ganymede and Aliena lived. He and Ganymede talked much of Rosalind. Yet day after day Orlando loved Rosalind more, and not less, and he never dreamed that this country boy, Ganymede, was his own Rosalind.

However, he said to Ganymede all that he felt in his heart for Rosalind. It pleased him to say it almost as much as it pleased Ganymede to listen. Ganymede kept his secret and was delighted that all these fine love speeches were said to the right lady.

Many happy days passed for these young people there in the Forest of Arden. The sweet Aliena saw that her dear Ganymede was happy again, and she let him do as he pleased. She smiled at his meeting Orlando every day, and did not even say that they had not yet gone to see the good king. Orlando had told them where the king was living in the forest.

One day by chance Ganymede met the king in the wood and talked with him a little while.

The king asked, "Who are your father and mother, my young farmer?"

Ganymede answered, "My father and mother were as good as yours."

The king smiled, because he did not guess that the boy belonged to a king's family. When Ganymede saw that the king was well and happy, he decided to wait a few days before telling him the farmer boy was his own Rosalind.

Orlando Rescues Oliver

One morning, as Orlando was going to visit Ganymede, he saw a man sleeping on the ground. A large green snake was close by. Orlando stopped. When the snake saw him, it slipped away among the bushes. As he walked nearer, he saw a lion closely watching the sleeping man, and ready to spring on him.

Then Orlando thought that some power had guided him here to save this man. However, when he looked closely into the man's face, he saw that it was his own brother, Oliver, who had planned to kill him. For just a moment, Orlando wanted to run away and leave Oliver to the lion. But Orlando was gentle and kind and could not leave his brother to die. So he took his sword, killed the lion, and saved Oliver's life. In the fight the lion tore one of Orlando's arms with his sharp teeth.

Oliver saw that his brother, to whom he had been so cruel, had saved his life by killing the lion. Now Oliver was sorry for all that he had done, and very, very much ashamed. His eyes filled with tears. "Forgive me, Orlando," he said, "I shall never do such things again."

Orlando was glad to have his brother for his friend. He gladly forgot all that he had suffered because of Oliver, and the brothers put their arms about each other. Oliver had followed Orlando to the forest to kill him. But from that hour when Orlando saved his life, Oliver loved Orlando as a brother should.

But now Orlando's arm, which the lion had torn, hurt badly. Orlando was so sick and weak that he could not walk through the forest to visit Ganymede.

Then he asked Oliver, "Will you do something for me, my kind brother? Follow this path through the wood until you come to the farmer's home by a spring of water. There a young boy named Ganymede lives. I often talk to him of my Rosalind, whom I love. Tell him that I have been hurt and cannot come to see him today."

So Oliver went to Ganymede's home, as Orlando had asked him to do, and told Ganymede and Aliena that Orlando had saved his life. He finished by saying, "Orlando was very, very brave. If he had not come, I should surely have been killed. I am his brother, but I have not been good to him. I have hated him. Now I shall always love him."

Oliver was sorry for all that he had done to his brother, and now he spoke so well of Orlando that Aliena began to look upon Oliver with interest. As she watched his handsome face, she liked him. Oliver felt that she was kind. She seemed to him very sweet, and at that moment he fell in love with her. At the same time Aliena knew that she loved Oliver.

During this time, however, while love was coming into the hearts of Aliena and Oliver,

Oliver had been telling Ganymede how badly Orlando was hurt. As Ganymede listened, he fell in a faint. When he was well again, he held his shoulders straight and said, "I was only playing when I fell. Tell your brother that this faint was not real."

However, Oliver saw how white Ganymede's face was, and he knew that Ganymede had not been playing. He wondered that a farmer boy like Ganymede should be so weak. So he said, "If you were playing, my good friend, you play the part well; but if I were you, I should rather try to be a strong man."

Ganymede replied, "I do try, but I should have been born a woman."

Oliver had a long visit with Ganymede and Aliena. When he returned to his brother Orlando, he had much to tell.

Among other things he said, "Ganymede grew sick when he heard that you had been hurt. I saw the fair Aliena at the house, and I fell in love with her in the short time that I talked with her. I am sure she loves me, for her eyes were very kind." Orlando listened with interest to his brother's story of Aliena.

Oliver continued, "I shall take Aliena for my wife. I love her, and I cannot live without her. I shall become a farmer and live here in the forest with my country wife. You may have my house and all the land back home."

Orlando answered, "Do as you please. Make Aliena your wife tomorrow if you wish. I shall ask the good king and his friends to come to see you wed. Go now and talk with Aliena. Ask her to become your wife tomorrow. She is alone now, for look, here comes her brother!"

At once Oliver started away to see Aliena.

Ganymede's Promise

Then Ganymede, whom Orlando had seen walking through the forest, came up to Orlando. "How are you feeling, my good Orlando?" he asked. "Are you hurt badly?"

Orlando answered, "I am much better. My hurt is almost well."

Ganymede replied, "I am glad, for I suffered when I knew that you suffered."

"Ganymede," Orlando said, "my brother loves your sister, the pretty Aliena. And he says that she loves him. I have told Oliver to go to Aliena and ask her to become his wife tomorrow. He has gone to talk with her. How I wish, Ganymede, that the fair Lady Rosalind were to become my wife on that same day."

"You do wish it?" Ganymede asked. "You truly wish to make Rosalind your wife tomorrow?"

"With all my heart I wish it," Orlando answered.

"Then, if you love her, tomorrow you shall see her," Ganymede said. "I promise you that Rosalind will come tomorrow."

Orlando jumped to his feet, forgetting that he had been hurt. "Could you bring her, Ganymede?" he cried. "Are you not playing with me when you say that she will come here to the Forest of Arden?"

"This is not in fun, Orlando," Ganymede replied. "Rosalind will be in my house tomorrow. And if you ask her to be your wife, she will."

Ganymede could keep his promise, to be sure, because he was the Lady Rosalind, dressed in boy's clothes.

Orlando shook his head and said, "I cannot believe that you can bring my Rosalind. Do you mean what you have promised me?"

"I do," Ganymede answered. "Tomorrow put on your best clothes. Ask the good king and all your friends here in the forest to come to my house to see you wed. If you desire the Lady Rosalind, she will be there, and you may make her yours."

The Wedding

The next morning the king and his men found seats before the house of Ganymede and

Aliena. They were waiting to see Aliena become the wife of Oliver and Rosalind the wife of Orlando.

Oliver and Aliena walked before this company. With them came Orlando, but Rosalind had not appeared. The company began to wonder and to look about for Rosalind. Many of them thought that Ganymede had spoken only in fun when he promised Orlando that Rosalind would come. The good king, who had heard that his daughter would be brought here to the forest in some strange way, asked Orlando, "Do you believe what this farmer boy has promised?"

Orlando answered, "I am not sure."

At that moment Ganymede came out to the king. "My good king," Ganymede said, "if I bring your daughter here, will you give her to Orlando for his wife?"

"I will," replied the king, "and I would, even if I had rich lands to give with her."

Ganymede then said to Orlando, "Will

you take Rosalind for your wife if I bring her here?"

"I will," answered Orlando, "though I were a king with many rich lands."

Then Ganymede and Aliena left the company and went into the house. There Ganymede quickly took off his boy's clothes and dressed in her own court clothes. So he was quickly the Lady Rosalind herself. Aliena changed from the clothes of a country girl to her own rich dress, and once again she was the fine Lady Celia.

While the two girls were in the house, the king said to Orlando, "There is something about that boy Ganymede which makes me think of my own daughter Rosalind."

Orlando replied, "I, too, have seen that he is very like her."

At that moment, Rosalind and Celia came out of the house, dressed in their fine court clothes. At once the company rose to their feet before such beauty.

Rosalind ran to her father and fell to her knees at his feet.

It was hard for the king to believe his own eyes when Rosalind appeared. However, Rosalind told her father how the false king, Frederick, had driven her away and how she had come into the forest to live as a farmer boy.

The king said that she might be Orlando's wife. Then Orlando and Rosalind and Oliver and Celia were wed at the same time.

In this wild forest no great dinner could be served to the merry party. Yet there never was a happier wedding day. As they all sat down to their simple dinner in the cool shade, they did not need anything else to fill their hearts with joy.

The Return of the King to His Palace

Suddenly a man appeared among them to tell the true king good news. The kingdom was again his own! The false king, Frederick, had heard that Rosalind and Celia had gone into the Forest of Arden. He knew that every day many men went there to join the good king. So Frederick had marched with an army to the forest, planning to kill the true king and all his friends.

As he entered the wild forest, a strange old man met Frederick and had a long talk with him. The old man was so gentle and good that Frederick became ashamed of his wicked ways and gave up his plan to kill the good king. He felt so sorry for all that he had done that he decided never to go back to the palace or even return to the kingdom.

Soon word came from Frederick to the true king that all the kingdom was his again and that all his friends might return to their homes and families. This good news made the day perfect, and no happier wedding dinner has ever been eaten since that glad day in the Forest of Arden.

Gareth and Lynette

This is a story of the days when knights were bold. It tells how a young prince dressed himself as a poor boy and how, at last, because he was very brave and patient, he was made a knight of King Arthur's Round Table.

They came together, spear on helmet.

460

Gareth and Lynette

One of the oldest stories in the English language . . . Written about 1400 by Thomas Malory . . . Made into a poem by Alfred Tennyson in 1872—nearly five hundred years later.

Gareth's Promise to His Mother

GARETH was the last of three tall sons at home. He was, in truth, taller than his brothers, Gawain and Modred. One day in spring he looked upon the river which was high and rapid from late heavy rains. A young tree lost its hold upon the earth and so was washed away.

"How it went down!" cried Gareth; "as a false knight or a bad king would fall before my sword—if a sword were mine to use. O river, you are full only of water. I am full of living blood. You do the will of Him who made you, and you do not know it. And I, who know and have fine strength, stay on at home here like a child. The queen, my mother, treats me as if I were still a child.

"I long[1] to go to Arthur's[2] court to fight with all my power against the wrong. I must not stay at home when I might serve King Arthur. Why, Gawain, when he came home here with Modred in the summertime, asked me to try my strength against him in a joust[3] with the spear. Modred was the judge. Gawain is a proved knight, and he said, 'You have half won against me.'

"But Modred, biting his thin lips, said nothing. I did not care, for Modred is never too pleased with me.

"I shall go to my mother and weary her

---

[1]long, wish. [2]Arthur, a good king who, the stories say, ruled over England many hundred years ago. [3]joust, a fight between two knights on horseback, usually with spears.

ears,[4] begging her to let me go to King Arthur's court."

So Gareth went, and waiting near her chair, asked, "Mother, though you think me still a child, do you love your child?"

She laughed. "You are foolish to ask."

"Then let me go to King Arthur's court."

The queen said, "Have you no pity that I am alone? Your father is an old, old man. Both of your brothers are in Arthur's hall. I have loved you best of my three sons. Stay with me. The wars are hard, and you have never known the pain of a broken arm or leg. Stay here at home and hunt the deer in our forests by our fast-falling streams. You will grow stronger day by day, for hunting is fine pleasure. And some day I will find for you a fair, sweet wife. Stay, my best son!"

"Follow the deer?" asked Gareth. "I would follow Christ, the King. I would live pure,

---

[4]**weary her ears,** ask her again and again.

speak true, right all wrong, follow the king. For what other reason was I born? I would walk through fire to serve the king."

The queen, his mother, saw that he would never turn from his one purpose to go to Arthur's court. She answered, "Will you walk through fire? So, go then if you must. But I demand one promise of you before you ask the king to make you a knight."

Gareth cried, "If it is one hard promise or a hundred, yet will I go. Say quickly what it is that you demand of me."

His mother, looking at him, spoke slowly. "Prince, you shall not tell your name when you go to Arthur's hall. No one shall know that you are the son of a true king and queen. You shall ask for work in Arthur's kitchen and there serve up his meat and drink, among the kitchen-knaves,[5] for twelve months and a day."

The queen believed that her own fine

[5]knaves, servant boys.

Gareth, when he saw that his only way to Arthur's Round Table[6] was through kitchen service, would be too proud to go. She thought that he would then stay with her in her castle, far from wars and fighting.

Gareth waited for a moment, and then answered, "Even then I should be free in soul, and I should see the jousts. Since you are my mother, I must do the thing you ask. I will go and ask for work among the kitchen-knaves and tell my name to no one, not even to King Arthur."

Yet Gareth stayed at home a little while. His mother's eye was always on him, full of fear that he would go. Then one morning early, before day brought full light, he rose and called two men that had served him all his young life. Before his mother heard him, he was gone.

[6]**Round Table.** King Arthur had a large round table about which his knights sat to talk with him about matters of their kingdom. Sometimes King Arthur's men themselves are called the Round Table. That is the meaning here.

The Journey to Camelot

The three were dressed like common men. As they turned their faces to the south, the birds sang in the trees, and the hills were green and bright with flowers.

After many days they set their feet on a wide plain. Before them they saw Camelot, the castle of the king, standing upon a hill that rose between the field and forest. At times the top of the high city flashed through clouds. At times only the great gate that opened on the field was shining. And then again the whole fair city was not seen at all.

Those who went with Gareth were afraid at this strange thing. One cried, "Let us not go on, my lord. This is a magic city, built by fairy kings."

The second said, "Lord, we have heard from our wise man at home that this king is not the real king, but was made king by magic and has driven his enemies out by magic. Let us have nothing to do with such a king as this one."

Then the first one added, "Lord, there is no city here. This is a dream."

Gareth laughed at them, and they came on to Camelot's gate. There was no gate like this under heaven. Upon it the Lady of the Lake[7] was cut in stone, her dress flowing from her sides like water. From one hand a sword hung down, and from the other, a small lamp. To her right and to her left were pictures which told brave stories of Arthur's wars.

The two with Gareth looked so long upon the figures in the battles that the pictures seemed to move.

The men called to Gareth, "Lord, the gate has come alive!"

Then Gareth fixed his eyes so long upon the gate that even to him the figures seemed to move. Soon, out of the city, music sounded.

---

[7]**Lady of the Lake,** a magic figure who gave Arthur his sword.

Back from the gate the young men started, and out to them there came an old, old man with a long beard.

"Who are you, my sons?" the old man asked them.

Gareth answered, "We are farmers, sir. We have come to see the wonders of the king. But your city moved so strangely in the clouds that my men here doubt whether the king is king at all. They think he has come from fairyland and doubt whether the city is not built by magic, or whether there is any city. This music now has frightened them. Tell them the truth."

Then the wise old man answered, "My son, I have seen the good ship sail with bottom up and with sail down in the heaven. I have seen castles standing on their tops in air. Now this is truth. As you say, the city was built by magic. Fairy kings and queens came from the mountain, with harps in their hands, and built it to the music of their harps. It is a magic city where nothing is what it seems, except the king. And some men say that Arthur is not real, that only the city stands there truly.

"If you go within that gate, you will fall under Arthur's power. He will ask you for the highest promises. They will be hard to keep. Yet every man should promise them and live by them. If you are afraid, do not go in, but stay outside among the cows here in the field. If you heard music just now, per-haps they are still building, for the city is built to music. Therefore it is never built at all, and therefore built forever."

Gareth was angry. "Old man," he said, "why do you make fun of me? I spoke fairly to you."

"I am not making fun of you but you of me. For you are not the man you seem to be. But I know who you are. And you go to Arthur, seeming to be what you are not—to King Arthur who hates even the shadow of a lie."

So saying, the old man turned and went away across the field.

Then Gareth said, "My men, I do not like a lie. Our coming thus makes me ashamed. I did it out of love for my mother. And to good King Arthur I will make things right as early as I may."

Though Gareth did not know, the old man was Merlin himself, master of magic in King Arthur's court—Merlin who knew all things.

King Arthur's Court

Gareth and his men entered the gate of Camelot. All about the castle, pictures, cut in stone, told of the deeds of Camelot's kings. Now and then a knight passed into the hall, or out. His sword sounded against his armor. The sound was good in Gareth's ear. Out of the windows looked beautiful women, and everywhere the people walked as if before a great, good king.

When Gareth came into the hall, he heard a voice—the voice of Arthur. There sat the king far above the heads of others on his rich throne, judging the cases which his people brought before him. Gareth felt his young heart beat hard and turned his head away, thinking, "The king will see that I am not what I appear to be, and he will hate me for this one half-lie."

However, on he went. Though he feared that he would meet his brothers, Sir Gawain and Sir Modred, he did not see them. In all the brave eyes of those tall knights that stood about the throne, he saw clear honor shining like the morning star, with trust in their great king, with love of Right, the light of glory they had won, and glory they would win.

Then a woman came crying to the king. "Grant me this favor, O Sir King!" she said. "I am your enemy. With your own hand you killed my lord in battle. I was against you, too. I have no right to ask a favor of you, but

471

this I must ask. My husband's brother shut my son in the castle and gave him no food so that he died. Now this man has taken all my lands. Grant me some brave knight to do the battle for me and give justice to the man who has killed my son and taken all I have."

A good knight stepped toward Arthur, crying to him, "A favor, O Sir King! I am of this woman's family. Let me right her wrong."

Then Sir Kay, master of the food and drink, cried out, "A favor, O Sir King! Grant this woman nothing, for she has lied. Send her away with nothing."

However, Arthur said, "We are the king to help those who have suffered wrong through all our land. Woman, you may go. You who offered to fight for her, go and lay low the man, yet do not kill him. Then bring him here that I may judge the right, and if he has done these wrongs, so shall he die."

Next there came into the hall a man sent

by King Mark. Mark was a king not honored in the land. The man put down a cloth of gold upon the floor before the throne and fell to his knees upon it. He said that Mark was on his way to Camelot to ask King Arthur to make him a knight. The cloth of gold Mark sent to Arthur as a gift.

Cried Arthur, "Take the cloth! Tear it to pieces! Throw it upon the fire, where the oak-tree is burning there. Mark! Does he try to buy me with a gift? Shall the shield of false King Mark stand with these of my good knights?"

Gareth looked down the side of the long hall and saw three rows of shields cut in stone and under every shield the name of a knight. Some shields were colored, some were only cut, some had nothing on them. In Arthur's hall when a brave man had done one noble deed, his arms were cut in the stone. When he had done two, his arms were colored, also. If he had done none, there was no sign upon the shield—only his name under it. Gareth saw that Gawain's shield was colored, rich and bright, but Modred's had nothing on it.

Arthur spoke again. "Mark is not fit to be a king, or fit to be my knight. Rise, man. Go back to Mark and tell him not to come to me. Sir Kay will give you food and find you what you need."

Then many others came, asking their favors.

Last Gareth came, leaning heavily upon his men. He asked, "A favor, O Sir King!" His voice was all ashamed. "I ask three gifts. Grant me to serve you just for my meat and drink, among your kitchen-knaves, for twelve months and a day. You see how weak I seem, and hungry. And do not ask my name. Later will I ask two other gifts."

A Kitchen-Knave

The king said to him, "You look to be a good young man and to be worth a greater favor. Yet if this is what you ask, then Kay, master of the meats and drinks, shall be your master."

Gareth rose and stepped away.

Then Kay said, "Look at the fellow! He must not have had enough to eat. If he works, I shall fill him up until he is as fat as any pig."

Sir Lancelot was standing near. "Sir Kay," he said, "you may know dogs. You may know horses. But you do not know a fine man when you see one. This boy is noble. He has not told all he knows. Be kind to him, for fear he will shame you for having judged him wrongly."

Kay answered, "If the boy were noble, he would have asked for horse and arms. You leave my man to me."

So Gareth took his place in Sir Kay's kitchen. He had his food with the young boys by the door and lay down at night with dirty kitchen-knaves.

Lancelot always spoke to him pleasantly.

Kay, who did not like him, would hurry him and make him work much harder than the other boys at drawing water or cutting wood or heavier duties. However, Gareth did all that he was told the best he could. Even his least service seemed fine and good because he did it well.

Gareth loved to hear the boys talk of Arthur and of Lancelot. They told how Arthur had saved Lancelot's life two times, and Lancelot saved Arthur's once.

If their talk ever was not clean, Gareth would not listen to them, but would walk away. At first they laughed at him, but later they honored him.

When the boys played at games, no one could throw a stone as far as Gareth. If there was a joust and Sir Kay let him go, Gareth would hurry to see it. And when he saw the knights' arms shining in the light, he was beside himself with joy.[8]

[8]beside himself with joy, very happy.

A Kitchen-Knave Made Knight

For one month he worked among the kitchen-knaves. Then his mother sent him his arms and freed him from his promise. Gareth went at once to Arthur. He found the king alone and told him all.

King Arthur said, "My son, your good mother let me know that you were here. Now I have promised you two other gifts. Tell me what you wish."

"First make me your knight," said Gareth, "nor tell anyone my name even yet. And the second gift I ask is that I may right the wrong for the first person that asks a favor of you."

"You ask to be my knight. My men promise to be strong and to be gentle, to be true in love, and to do as I command."

Gareth, lightly springing from his knees, said, "I promise all." Then King Arthur answered, "So be it. We shall tell your name only to one, our noblest, truest Lancelot."

"As you wish, my king," said Gareth. "Let Lancelot know."

The great king smiled upon the boy. Then he called Lancelot where Gareth could not hear and told him, "I have promised Gareth to let him right the first wrong that we hear of. So listen in the hall, and when he starts away upon his horse, take your horse and follow him, far behind. Cover the lions on your shield so that he may not know you. See that he is not killed."

That same day a beautiful young girl came to the hall. She was as pretty as a flower.

Arthur asked, "What is your name? What is your need?"

"I am Lynette," she said. "I need a knight to battle for my sister Lyonors. She is shut up in her own castle by four knights—all brothers. One guards her there. The other three watch at three places by the winding river where one must cross to bring help to her. Therefore I have come for Lancelot."

Arthur remembered Gareth. He asked, "Who are these four who keep your sister prisoner?"

"Their names," she said, "are Morning Star, Noon-day Sun, Evening Star, and Night. But this last one is oftener called Death. They are all mighty men, and therefore I have come for Lancelot."

Sir Gareth rose. His eyes were shining. "A favor, O my King!" he called. "Let me go. I have been your kitchen-knave, and I am strong through meat and drink. I can fight a hundred such as these. Let me go."

King Arthur said, "Go."

At this Lynette's fair face turned red in anger. "Sir King!" she cried. "I asked for your chief knight, and you have given me a kitchen-knave!"

Then before a man could stop her, she ran from the hall, took her horse, and went through the gate, saying to herself, "Kitchen-knave!"

As Gareth left the hall to follow her, he saw there by the door King Arthur's gift, worth half a town, a war horse of the best. And there were, too, a shield, a helmet,[9] a spear, and a bright cloak. Gareth took the arms, got upon his horse, put the cloak about him, and passed out through the gate.

Lynette was riding now more slowly through the field. "Why did the king do this?" she asked herself. "If Lancelot could not come, could he not at least give me one of his proved knights rather than this, his kitchen-knave?"

Gareth came up to her. Few looked so strong and brave as this young knight in his new, shining arms. He said, "Lead, and I follow."

Lynette held her nose high. "Stay back," she said. "You smell of the kitchen. And look, knave! Your master comes behind to take you back with him."

[9]helmet, steel covering for the head.

Gareth Proves His Might

There came Sir Kay. "We need you at your work, young kitchen-knave," called Kay. "Go back. I am your master."

"You are not my master now," replied Gareth.

"We shall fight to see," Kay answered.

They fought with swords, and Kay fell, cut deep in his shoulder.

Gareth cried to Lynette, "Lead, and I follow." Then she rode fast away before him. When the stones stopped flying from her horse's feet and her tired animal had slowed down, then Gareth came up to her.

Lynette spoke to him. "Why do you ride here beside me? Do you think I like you better since you have shown your strength against Sir Kay? You should be washing dishes. To me you smell of the kitchen as before."

"Lady," Sir Gareth answered gently, "say what you will. I will go on until I finish."

Gareth smiled, but she did not. Away she rode through the thick forest. Gareth followed, and again she called him, "Kitchen-knave!" So they went along till evening.

As the sun set, they heard a man's voice calling. A serving man ran out of the dark wood, crying, "They have taken my master and tied his hands and feet to throw him into the lake."

"I should help this man," said Gareth, "but, fair lady, my first duty is to you."

"Lead, and I follow," said Lynette.

Gareth answered, "Follow! I lead!"

He rode into the forest. There six tall men were pulling another into the lake. A stone was tied about his neck. Gareth laid low three men with heavy blows, but three men ran away. He took the stone from off the man and made free his hands and feet.

"You have saved my life," said the strange man. "What can I give you for this?"

Gareth said, "Nothing! I serve the king."

The man replied, "I well believe you are his knight." But Lynette laughed.

As night was coming on, the stranger took them to his castle and gave them food. He set Gareth down beside Lynette at table, but at once she rose. "No kitchen-knave shall sit with me," she cried.

The lord looked first at her and then at Gareth. Then taking Gareth to another place, he sat down beside him and began to eat. "Friend," he said, "whether you are a kitchen-knave or whether it is just her fancy, I ask not. However, you are strong and fine, and you have saved my life. Now you go on to fight alone with mighty men. Should you not turn back and ask that Lancelot come?"

Gareth answered, "I will go on, even to fight these mighty ones."

So in the morning the lord whose life he had saved sent the two on their way.

To Lynette, Gareth called, "Lead, and I follow."

She replied proudly still, "I shall not ride in front. I shall allow you to ride by me a little while. But will you not go back? For we are near one who will surely kill you."

"I will go on," said he.

Gareth Meets Three of the Brothers

They came to the stream where the first enemy waited for them near the bridge. He was Sir Morning Star. His clothes were red and gold.

Gareth watched him make ready for the fight.

Then Lynette said to Sir Gareth, "There is yet time to run away down the valley before he charges. You need not care. You are not a knight but a knave."

Said Gareth, "You still speak badly of me, but I shall win in this."

The two men ran together on the bridge. Both their spears bent but did not break, and both men fell. Quickly they rose and drew their swords, and Gareth pushed his enemy back and down the bridge.

Then Lynette called out, "Well done! Well done, my kitchen-knave."

Gareth's shield was cut in two, but Gareth laid him that cut it on the ground.

The enemy cried, "Take not my life."

Gareth answered, "If this lady ask it of me, I will not take your life."

Lynette's fair face grew red. "I ask of you! Never shall I ask one small thing of you!"

"Then, Sir Morning Star, shall you die!" cried Gareth.

But Lynette called, "Do not kill one higher than yourself, knave."

Gareth said, "Rise, fellow. Go to King Arthur's hall. Say that his kitchen-knave has sent you. Your shield is mine. Lady, lead, and I follow."

Fast away she went. When he came up with her, she said to him, "I thought, knave, when I watched you fighting on the bridge, that the kitchen smell was not so strong. Now the wind has changed, and it is twenty times as strong."

Then she sang a song which said, "My love has smiled on me."

After a while she spoke. "The second brother, whom we next meet, is stronger than the first. Turn back. You need not care. You are not a knight but a knave."

Gareth laughed and answered, "I will tell you a story of a knave. In my kitchen one boy had a cross dog to which he would throw his coat and say, 'Take care of that.' And no one dared to touch it. You are such a coat, which the king gave me to guard, and I am such a dog. If I am a knave but fight like a true knight, does that not serve as well to free your sister?"

"It makes me like you less," she said.

At the next river crossing they met the second brother, Noon-day Sun. His arms were shining in the light. He pushed his horse to meet Sir Gareth in the middle of the stream. They fought with swords. So mighty were the blows against him Gareth feared that he would lose. But the other's horse drew back and fell, and Noon-day Sun was carried away by the water. Gareth went into the stream after him, and helped him from the water; then he took his sword from him in fair fight and sent him to the king.

"Lead, and I follow," he said to fair Lynette.

Quietly she led.

"Has not the good wind changed again?" he asked. "Do I not seem a little better to you now?"

"No," she answered. "Not one bit. You did not win. His horse fell, for I saw it."

Then she sang another song which said, "Two times my love has smiled on me."

At length, evening came. Where they must cross the river again, they came to the third enemy, the one who called himself the Star of Evening.

Lynette cried to him, "Both of your brothers have fallen before this strong young man, and so will you, Sir Star, for you are old."

"I am old," said Sir Evening Star. "Old and hard, and strong as twenty boys."

Gareth said, "He who threw Sir Morning Star can throw Sir Evening Star."

They ran together in an awful battle on the bridge. Gareth threw the Star of Evening from his horse. They drew their swords. Sir Evening Star fell to his knees, and rose, and fell again, and rose. It seemed that Gareth could not win.

All the time Lynette was calling, "Well done, knave-knight! Well done, O good knight-knave! As fine as any knight! You are truly one of Arthur's best. The wind will never change again."

Gareth, hearing, had greater strength, and

yet it seemed he could not win. Then at length he broke the other's sword in two. Sir Star then jumped upon him, his arms round Gareth's neck to choke him, but Gareth called up all his power and threw Sir Star of Evening from the bridge into the stream.

Again Gareth said, "Lead, and I follow."

Lynette replied, "I lead no longer. Ride by my side. You are the finest of all kitchen-knaves. I am ashamed that I have talked so to you."

"You could not know me," Sir Gareth said. "Now since your words to me are fair, there is no knight—not even Lancelot—who has the strength to throw me."

Then Lynette sang a song which said, "Three times my love has smiled on me."

Lancelot Appears

Lynette knew that food for their supper, sent by her sister Lyonors, waited for them at a place near by. As they turned off the road to find the food, Lynette looked back, and cried, "Look! For someone rides behind!"

It was Lancelot who came, but the blue lions on his shield were covered as King Arthur had ordered. So Gareth did not know him. Lancelot, seeing the star on the shield which Gareth had taken from the fallen knight, thought him Sir Morning Star. "Stay!" he called. "I fight for my friend!"

They closed in fight, and before Lancelot's spear, which was the wonder of the world, Gareth fell. When he found the grass within his hands, he laughed.

Lynette said to him, "Why do you laugh? You have lost your fight. You were too proud."

Then Lancelot knew that it was Gareth, and he cried, "Prince! O Gareth, I saw the star upon your shield and thought you were our enemy. I came to help you, not to hurt you. I am Lancelot, and glad to find you safe."

Gareth answered, "You! Lancelot! I knew

yours was the spear that threw me! Therefore
I laughed. Had I fallen before some other's
strength, then I should be ashamed. But I
am not sad to fall before your spear."

Still Lynette was not pleased with Gareth.

Then Lancelot said to her, "My lady, are
you wise to call him shamed who only has
been thrown? I have been thrown, not once,
but many a time. By being thrown one learns
to throw another."

Then to his young friend he spoke. "Sir
Gareth, both you and your good horse are
tired. Yet I felt you strong and brave. You
have done well. You have freed the river of
our enemies. You have answered the girl
gently when she spoke badly of you. Prince
and knight you are, and truly one of the
Round Table of our king."

The three then found the food that had
been left for them. And after supper Gareth
fell into sleep.

Lynette said softly as she looked on him,

"Sleep soundly. You have cause to sleep. Rise strong. I seem as gentle to him as a mother, but such a mother as has been not too gentle all day and now blesses her child as he sleeps. It seems as if the world should all be peace and love."

She gently clapped her hands and said to Lancelot, "I am so glad to find that my good knave is both knight and noble. But I promised this last wicked brother, Sir Night, when he let me pass to come to Arthur's court, that I would bring you, Lancelot, back to fight with him. If you go with us, he will fight you first, and so Sir Gareth will not win completely."

Lancelot replied, "This fellow, Night, may know my shield. Let Gareth then change his shield for mine, if he will, and take my horse; for my brave animal is fresher and loves a battle as well as he that rides him."

"Lord Lancelot," she said, "how kind you are in this, as you are always kind."

Then Gareth woke. He took the shield with the blue lions. "O noble Lancelot," he cried, "I feel fire flow through me from this shield. I shall not shame you, Lancelot, wearing it. On! Let us go!"

On they went through the quiet field to Sir Night—or Death, as he was often called.

Suddenly Lynette, who was at Gareth's side, cried, "Let Lancelot do this battle. You have done wonders, but this time you will not win. Give Lancelot back his shield. I fear to see you hurt. You have thrown three, but you can never throw the fourth."

"Why not?" asked Gareth. "Tell me what you know of him. But still I will go."

"I have not seen him, Prince," she said. "He never rides by day. I have heard him pass in the night, but I have never heard his voice. He is said to have the strength of ten, and he kills even children. O Prince, I asked for Lancelot first. Let Lancelot meet Sir Night."

But Gareth laughed and said, "Sir Night is mine!"

Lancelot gave him wise and cheering words to help him in the fight, while Lynette said, "Heaven keep you."

Gareth Meets Sir Night

For a while they traveled on. Then Lynette lifted one arm and softly said, "There." Now they stood before the castle of the Lady Lyonors. They watched, and all at once Lyonors came to a high window and waved her hand to them.

Then out ran Night, upon a night-black horse, in night-black armor, with white bones painted on it. Ten steps he came in the half-light and then waited. He did not say a word.

Gareth called, "Fool, why do you appear so terrible? Must you frighten men first so that you may win over them? Men say you have the strength of ten. Can you not trust the body which God gave you?"

Night did not answer.

Lady Lyonors cried out in fear, for she knew that if Gareth lost, Sir Night and Death would keep her always. Even Sir Lancelot feared for Gareth.

All at once Sir Lancelot's horse lifted a foot quickly, and Death's dark war-horse jumped forward, too. Together came Gareth and Night, spear on helmet—in a great cloud of dust. One was thrown to the ground. It was Sir Night. Quickly Gareth took his sword and cut Death's helmet wide open. Half fell to the right and half to the left, and there within appeared the face of a bright boy! He was fresh as a new-born flower!

"Sir," he cried, "save me. My brothers did this wicked work. They made me stay to keep the Lady Lyonors. They never dreamed that you would have strength to pass them all and come to me."

Gareth answered kindly to one only a little younger than himself. "My fair child!

Why were you wild enough to call for Lancelot, the chief knight of Arthur's hall, to come to fight you?"

"Fair sir, the others made me do it. They are against the king and Lancelot, the king's friend. They hoped that Lancelot would come to save the Lady Lyonors and that they might kill him thus."

Then happy daylight came across the hills. Lady Lyonors and all her house made merry over Death, with song and dance, for they had been afraid of only a fair boy. So all was well, and Gareth won the day.

He that told the story long ago said that Gareth took the Lady Lyonors to be his wife, but he that told it later said that Gareth took Lynette.

The Golden Touch

Did you ever wish you could have everything you asked for? "The Golden Touch" tells how King Midas received everything he asked for and still was not happy.

But Marygold made no answer.

The Golden Touch

*A story of the days when the
world was young . . . But
people were much the same
as now . . . Written in 1851
by Nathaniel Hawthorne,
an American author.*

King Midas and His Love for Gold

ONCE upon a time,
there lived a very rich man who was also a
king and whose name was Midas. He had a
little daughter, whose name I either never
knew or have quite forgotten. So, because
I like odd names for little girls, I choose to
call her Marygold.

This King Midas liked gold better than
anything else in the world. He valued his
crown chiefly because it was made of gold.
If he loved anything better, or half so well,
it was the one merry little girl who played

around her father's chair. But the more Midas loved his daughter, the more did he desire and seek to become richer. He thought, foolish man, that the best thing he could do for this dear child was to gather for her the biggest pile of yellow, shining money that had ever been gathered together since the world was made. Thus he gave all his thoughts and all his time to this one purpose.

If ever he happened to look for one second at the gold clouds that lighted up when the sun set, he wished that they were real gold, and that they could be put safely in his strong box. When little Marygold ran to meet him with yellow flowers in her hands, he used to say, "Pooh, pooh, child! If these flowers were as golden as they look, they would be worth picking."

And yet in the early days, before he became interested only in being rich, King Midas had liked flowers. He had planted a garden in which grew the largest and most beautiful and sweetest roses that any man ever saw or smelled. These roses were still growing in the garden, as large, as pretty, and as sweet as when Midas used to pass whole hours looking at them and drinking in their sweet smell. But now, if he looked at them at all, it was only to think how much the garden would be worth if each rose were pure gold. And though he once had liked music, the only music for poor Midas now was the ring of one piece of money against another.

At length (as people always grow more and more foolish if they do not take care to grow wiser and wiser) Midas seemed not to think rightly at all. He would hardly touch or even look at any object that was not gold. He would pass a large part of every day in a dark room under his palace. It was here that he kept his gold. To this dark place Midas went when he wanted to be very happy.

Here, after locking the door, he would

take a bag of gold money, or a gold cup as big as a washbowl, or a heavy golden bar, or a big measure of gold dust, and bring them from the corners of the room into the one bright sunbeam that fell from a small window. He valued this sun for no other reason than that his gold would not shine without its help. Then he would count over the pieces of money in the bag; throw the bar into the air and catch it as it came down; let the gold dust run through his fingers; look at his face in the bright cup; and whisper to himself, "Oh, Midas, rich King Midas, what a happy man you are!"

Midas called himself a happy man but felt that he was not quite so happy as he might be. He would never reach his greatest pleasure until the whole world was his—a world to be filled with yellow gold which would be all his own.

Now I need not tell such wise people as you are that in the old, old times when Midas lived, a great many things happened which we should think wonderful if they were to happen in our own day and country. And, on the other hand, a great many things take place now which not only seem wonderful to us, but would have been hard for the people of old times to believe. On the whole, I think our own times are the stranger of the two; but, however that may be, I must go on with my story.

The Gift of the Stranger

Midas was having a pleasant time in his treasure room one day as usual when he noticed that a shadow was falling over his gold. When he looked up suddenly, what should he see but the figure of a stranger standing in the bright and narrow sunbeam! He was a young man, with a bright, happy face. Whether it was the thoughts of Midas that made a yellow color over everything, or whatever the cause might be, he could not help feeling that the smile which the stranger gave him had a kind of golden light in it. Certainly, although this figure shut out the sun, there was now a brighter light on all the gold than before. Even the far corners were lighted up as with yellow fire when the young man smiled.

As Midas knew that he had carefully turned the key and that no man could possibly break into his room, he, of course, decided that the stranger must be something more than just a man. It is no matter about telling you who he was. In those days when the earth was new, beings with strange powers visited it and interested themselves in the joys and sorrows of the people. Midas had met such beings before now, and he did not mind meeting one of them again. Indeed, this young man looked so friendly and so kind that no one could have expected him to hurt Midas. Rather, he appeared as if he came to do Midas a favor. And what could that favor be, except to increase the gold Midas already had?

The stranger looked about the room, and when his bright smile had lighted up all the golden objects that were there, he turned again to Midas.

"You are a rich man, friend Midas!" he said. "I doubt whether any other four walls on earth contain so much gold as you have gathered here in this room."

"I have done pretty well—pretty well," answered Midas, but he did not seem quite happy. "However, after all, it is only a little, when you think that it has taken me all my life to get it together. If one could live a thousand years, he might have time to grow rich!"

"What!" cried the stranger. "Then you are not satisfied?" Midas shook his head.

"What else do you want? I should like to know."

Midas thought a little while. He had a

feeling that this stranger had come here with both the power and the purpose to give him what he wished. Now, therefore, was the happy moment when he had but to speak, and he would get anything that might come into his head to ask. So he thought, and thought, and thought of how to get more gold, but he could not think of any plan that would give him enough.

At last a bright thought came to King Midas. It seemed as bright as the shining gold which he loved so much.

Raising his head, he looked the stranger in the face.

"Well, Midas," the stranger said, "I see you have decided upon something that will give you all you want. Tell me your wish."

"It is only this," replied Midas. "I am tired of gathering my gold with so much trouble and seeing the pile so small after I have done my best. I wish everything that I touch to be changed to gold!"

The stranger's smile became so very broad that it seemed to fill the room like a great sun, shining into the shade of a valley where the yellow leaves—for so looked the gold—lie in the light.

"The Golden Touch!" cried he. "That is a fine wish. But are you sure that this will be all you wish for?"

"What else could I want?" said Midas to the stranger.

"And will you never be sorry that you have it?"

"What could make me sorry?" asked Midas. "I ask nothing else to make me perfectly happy."

"Be it as you wish, then," replied the stranger, waving his hand in leaving. "To-morrow, when the sun rises, you will find that you have the Golden Touch!"

The figure of the stranger then became very bright, and Midas had to close his eyes. On opening them again, he saw only the sunbeam shining in the room, and all around him the gold which had taken his whole life to gather.

Whether Midas's sleep was as usual that night, the story does not say. However, his mind was perhaps like that of a child to whom a beautiful new toy has been promised in the morning. Day was just coming over the hills when Midas sat up in his bed, and, reaching his arms out, began to touch the objects that were near. He wanted to prove that the Golden Touch had truly come as the stranger had promised.

So he laid his finger on a chair at the side of the bed and on other things, but they remained just the same as before. Indeed, he felt very much afraid that he had only dreamed about the promise, or else that the stranger had been playing with him. How dreadful it would be if, after all his hopes, he would have to go on increasing his gold as he had, instead of making it by a touch.

THE GOLDEN TOUCH

The King's Happiness

All this while, it was still early morning, with one bright line of light along the edge of the sky, where Midas could see it. He lay down again, thinking that he had been fooled, and was growing sadder and sadder, until the sun came in through the window and made the wall above his head yellow.

The light fell in a strange way on the cover of the bed. When he looked more closely, what was his surprise and delight when he found that this cover had been changed into cloth of the purest and brightest gold! The Golden Touch had come to him with the coming of the sun!

Midas started up. He ran about the room, touching everything that happened to be in his way. He touched one of the bed posts, and it turned into gold. He pulled back a window curtain in order to see more clearly what he was about, and it became heavy in

509

his hand—gold. He took up a book from the table. At his first touch it became like one of the beautiful, gold-edged books that one often sees; but when his fingers ran through it, the leaves became thin golden plates on which nothing could be read.

He quickly put on his clothes and was delighted to see himself in a fine suit of gold cloth, which was as soft as his clothes had been although it was heavy upon his body. He took out his handkerchief, which little Marygold had made for him. That also became gold, with the thread which the child had used running along the edge in pure gold.

For some reason, this last change did not quite please Midas. He would rather that his little daughter's present should have stayed just the same as when she climbed upon his knee and put it in his hand.

However, it was not worth while to trouble himself about such a little thing. Midas now took his glasses from his pocket and put them on his nose in order to see more clearly what he had done. In those days the common people did not have glasses, but kings had them. Else how could Midas have had any?

To his great surprise, however, fine as the glasses were, he discovered that he could not see through them. This was the most natural thing in the world; for, when he took them off, they were plates of yellow gold, and, of course, were worth nothing to see with, though worth a great deal as gold. It seemed to Midas rather hard that, with all his money, he could never again be rich enough to own a pair of glasses with which he could see.

"But it does not matter," said he to himself. "We can expect to have no great good without giving up something to get it. The Golden Touch is worth a pair of glasses at least, if not one's very eyesight. My own eyes will serve for most purposes, and little Marygold will soon be old enough to read to me."

Wise King Midas was so happy over his

good fortune that the palace seemed too small to hold him. He therefore ran down the stairs and smiled when he saw that the stair rail became a bar of bright gold as his hand passed over it. He turned the door-key (it was gold when his fingers left it) and went into the garden. Here, as it happened, he found a great number of beautiful roses in bloom and others in bud. They smelled very sweet in the morning air. Their color was one of the fairest sights in the world; so gentle, so quiet, so happy did these roses seem.

But Midas knew a way to make them more precious, as he thought, than roses had ever been before. So he took great pains in going from bush to bush and using his magic touch again and again until every flower was changed to gold. By the time this good work was completed, King Midas was called to breakfast, and as the morning air had made him very hungry, he hurried back to the palace.

A Strange Breakfast

What a king's breakfast was in the days of Midas, I do not know, and have not time now to find out. I believe, however, that on this morning the breakfast was hot cakes, some nice little fish, potatoes, fresh eggs, and coffee for King Midas himself, and a bowl of bread and milk for his daughter Marygold. This is a breakfast fit to set before a king, and whether he had it or not, King Midas could not have had a better one.

Little Marygold had not yet appeared. Her father ordered her to be called and, seating himself at table, waited to begin his own breakfast until the child should come. To be fair to Midas, he did truly love his daughter and loved her more this morning because of the good fortune that had come to him. It was not long before he heard her coming along the hall, crying as if her heart was broken. This surprised him, because

Marygold was one of the happiest little people whom you would meet in a summer's day and did not have a dozen tears in her eyes in a year.

When Midas heard her, he decided to make her happy again by a pleasant surprise. So, reaching across the table, he touched his daughter's bowl (which was a glass one with pretty figures all around it) and changed it to shining gold.

"Well! Well! my little lady!" cried Midas. "What is the matter with you this bright morning?"

Marygold, with great tears in her eyes, held out her hand in which was one of the roses that Midas had changed by his touch.

"Beautiful!" said her father. "And what is there in this fine golden rose to make you cry?"

"Oh, dear father!" answered the child as well as she could while crying. "It is not pretty, but the ugliest flower that ever grew.

As soon as I was dressed, I ran into the garden to gather some roses for you, because I know you like them and like them better when they are gathered by your little daughter. But, oh, dear, dear me! What do you think has happened? Such a sad, sad thing! All the beautiful roses, which were so sweet and had so many colors, are ruined. They are grown quite yellow, as you see this one! What is the matter with them?"

"Why, my dear little girl, do not cry about that!" said Midas, who was ashamed to say that he himself had caused the change which made her so sad. "Sit down and eat your bread and milk. Would you not rather have a golden rose like that, which will last hundreds of years, than one that lasts only a day?"

"I do not care for such roses as this!" cried Marygold, throwing it away. "It has no smell, and it is so hard it hurts my nose."

The child now sat down to the table, but she felt so sad over her poor roses that she did not even notice the change in her glass bowl. Perhaps this was better, for Marygold always took pleasure in looking at the strange figures of trees and houses that were painted on her bowl, and these figures were entirely lost in the yellow of the gold.

Midas had poured out a cup of coffee, and, as a matter of course, the coffee-pot was gold when he set it down. He thought that it was a very fine pot for a man of his simple tastes, and began to wonder how he would keep his treasures safe. Articles of gold could not be safely kept in the kitchen.

As he was thinking these things, he lifted a spoonful of coffee to his lips and was surprised to see that the moment his lips touched the coffee, it became yellow, and the next minute it was hard gold!

"Oh!" cried Midas, not so pleased.

"What is the matter, father?" asked little Marygold, looking at him with tears still standing in her eyes.

"Nothing, child, nothing!" said Midas. "Eat your bread and milk before it is quite cold."

He took one of the nice little fish on his plate, and, to see what would happen, he touched its tail with his finger. It was at once changed into a gold fish, though not one of those goldfishes which people often keep in glass bowls. No; but it was really a gold fish. It was a very pretty piece of work, as you may suppose, but King Midas, just at that moment, would much rather have had a fish that he could eat.

"I do not quite see," thought he to himself, "how I am to get any breakfast."

He took one of the hot cakes and had only cut it when, though a moment before it had been of the whitest meal,[1] it now was the yellow color of Indian meal. To say the truth, if it had been a hot Indian cake, Midas would have liked it a good deal more than he did

[1]meal, flour.

now when he saw that it, too, was changed into hard gold.

He took an egg, and the same thing happened to it as to the fish and the cake.

"Well, what shall I do?" thought he, leaning back in his chair and looking at little Marygold, who was now eating her bread and milk very happily. "This breakfast would cost a great deal, and I can eat none of it!"

Hoping that by hurrying he could escape what he now did not like so much, he quickly took up a hot potato and got it into his mouth to swallow it quickly. But the Golden Touch was too fast for him. He found his mouth full, not of soft potato, but of hard gold, which so burned his tongue that he cried out and, jumping up from the table, began to dance about the room in both pain and fear.

"Father, dear father!" cried little Marygold, who was a loving child, "what is the matter? Have you burned your mouth?"

"Dear child," answered Midas sadly, "I do not know what is to become of your poor father."

The Terrible Power of the Golden Touch

And truly did you ever hear of such an unhappy case in all your lives? Here was the richest breakfast that could be set before a king, and, because it was so rich, it was good for nothing. The poorest working man sitting down to his piece of bread and cup of water was far better off than King Midas, whose fine food was in truth worth its weight in gold.

And what was to be done? Already, at breakfast, Midas was very hungry. Would he be less so by dinner time? And how would he feel by evening when his supper would be of the same kind of food as that now before him! How many days, think you, would he live on this rich food?

These thoughts so troubled wise King Midas that he began to doubt whether, after all, to be rich was what one should want most in the world. However, this was only a passing thought. So pleased was Midas with the shine of the yellow gold that he still would not have given up the Golden Touch for so little a thing as breakfast. What a price that would be for one breakfast! It would have been the same as paying millions and millions of dollars (and as many more millions as would take forever to count up) for some fish, an egg, a potato, hot cakes, and a cup of coffee!

"It would be quite too much," thought Midas.

Yet he wanted his breakfast so badly, and he was so troubled that he sighed out loud. Our pretty Marygold could stand it no longer. She sat a moment, looking at her father and trying with all her might to find out what was the matter with him. Then she started from her chair and, running to Midas, put her arms about his knees. He bent down and kissed her. He felt that his little daughter's love was worth a thousand times more than the gold he had made by the Golden Touch.

"My sweet, sweet Marygold!" cried he.

But Marygold made no answer.

What, oh, what had he done? How terrible was the gift which the stranger had given him! The moment the lips of Midas touched Marygold's face, a change had taken place.

Her sweet, pretty face, so full of love as it had been, now took on a bright yellow color, with yellow teardrops on her cheeks. Her beautiful brown curls took on the same color. Her soft little body grew hard and stiff within her father's arms. Midas's wish for gold had caused his little Marygold to be changed from a happy child into a golden figure.

Yes, there she was with that look of love and of care for her father hard in the gold of her face. It was the prettiest and most awful sight that any man ever saw. She was just as she had been. However, that made her father suffer the more when he looked at the golden figure, which was all that was left him of a daughter. Midas had often said lovingly to the child that she was worth her weight in gold. And now those words had become true. Now at last, when it was too late, he felt of how much greater value was a warm and gentle heart that loved him than all the gold that could be piled between the earth and the sky!

It would be too sad a story if I were to tell you how Midas, with his greatest wish come true, now rubbed his hands together and cried; and how he could not bear to look at Marygold, or yet to look away from her. Except when his eyes were fixed on the figure, he could not believe that she was changed to gold. But, looking again, he would see that there was the golden child with a yellow teardrop on its yellow cheek, and a look so sad and gentle that it seemed it must make even the gold soft, and make her a real child again. This, however, could not be. So Midas could only put his hands over his face and wish that he were the poorest man in the wide world if the loss of all his gold might bring back the rose color to his dear child's face.

The Stranger's Return

While he was so troubled, he suddenly saw a stranger standing near the door. Midas lowered his head without speaking, for he knew it was the same figure which had appeared to him the day before and had given him the terrible power of the Golden Touch. The stranger still smiled and seemed to make a yellow light all about the room, and upon the golden child, and all the other objects that had been changed by the touch of Midas.

"Well, friend Midas," said the stranger, "tell me, how do you get along with the Golden Touch?"

Midas shook his head. "I am very sad," said he.

"Very sad, indeed!" replied the stranger.

"How does that happen? Have I not kept my promise truly? Have you not everything that your heart wished?"

"Gold is not everything," answered Midas. "I have lost all that my heart cared for."

"Oh! So you have discovered that since yesterday?" asked the stranger. "Let us see, then. Which of these two things do you think is worth more—the gift of the Golden Touch, or one cup of clear, cold water?"

"Oh, blessed water!" cried Midas. "It will never cool my dry lips again!"

"The Golden Touch," continued the stranger, "or a piece of bread?"

"A piece of bread," answered Midas, "is worth all the gold on earth!"

"The Golden Touch," asked the stranger, "or your own little Marygold, warm, soft, and loving, as she was an hour ago?"

"Oh, my child, my dear child!" cried poor Midas, rubbing his hands. "I would not have given that sweet smile upon her face for the power of changing this whole big earth into gold!"

"You are wiser than you were, King Midas," said the stranger, looking seriously at him. "Your own heart, I see, has not been changed entirely to gold. If it were, there would, indeed, be no hope for you. However, you appear to be still able to understand that the common things, such as all people have, are worth more than the money that men long for and work so hard for. Tell me, now, do you truly wish to lose the Golden Touch?"

"I hate it!" replied Midas.

A fly settled on his nose, but it at once fell to the floor, for it, too, had turned to gold.

"Go, then," said the stranger, "and walk out into the river that flows past the bottom of your garden. Take a large cup of water from this river and sprinkle it over any object that you wish to change back as it was. This may help you."

King Midas bowed low, and when he lifted his head, the shining stranger was gone.

You will believe that Midas lost no time taking the largest cup he could find (it became gold when he touched it) and hurrying to the riverside. As he ran along by the bushes, he noticed in surprise how their leaves turned yellow behind him, as if summer were over and fall had come there, and no place else. On reaching the river bank, he jumped straight into the water without waiting so much as to pull off his shoes.

"Poof! poof! poof!" sounded through his nose as his head came up out of the water. "Well, this is a pleasant bath, and I think it must have washed away the Golden Touch. And now for filling my cup!"

King Midas's Change of Heart

As he put the cup into the water, his heart was glad when it changed from gold back as it had been before he touched it. He felt, also, a change within himself. A cold, hard, and heavy weight seemed to have gone from him. No doubt his very heart had been changing itself into gold, but was now soft again, as a heart should be. Noticing a pretty little blue flower on the bank, Midas touched it with his finger and was delighted to find that it remained blue instead of becoming yellow. The terrible power of the Golden Touch had, therefore, been taken from him.

King Midas hurried back to the palace. I suppose the servants knew not what to think when they saw their master so carefully bringing home a big cup of water. However, that water, which was to make things right again, had greater worth to Midas than an ocean full of gold. The first thing he did, as you need not be told, was to sprinkle it over the golden figure of little Marygold.

As soon as it fell on her, you would have laughed to see how the red color came back to the dear child's face! How surprised she was to find herself so wet and her father still throwing more water over her!

"Please do not do that, dear father!" cried she. "See how you have wet my nice dress, which I put on only this morning!"

For Marygold did not know that she had been a little golden figure, nor could she remember anything that had happened since the moment that she ran to poor Midas at the breakfast table.

Her father did not think that he need tell his dear child how foolish he had been, but he would show her how much wiser he had become. For this purpose, he led little Marygold into the garden, where he sprinkled all the roses with the water from the river, and more than five thousand roses took again their natural bloom.

There were two things, however, which so long as he lived used to make King Midas remember the Golden Touch. One was that the sands of the river that flowed past his garden were always bright like gold; the other, that little Marygold's hair had now more of a golden color than he had noticed in it before she had been changed by his kiss. The change of color seemed to him to make her hair more beautiful and richer than when she was a baby.

When Midas had grown to be quite an old man and used to hold Marygold's children on his knee, he would tell them this wonderful story, pretty much as I have now told it to you. Then he would smooth their shining hair and tell them that their hair, too, had a rich color of gold, which they had got from their mother.

"And, to tell you the truth, my dear young people," said King Midas, "ever since that morning I have not liked the sight of any other gold, except this!"

TEACHER'S NOTES

This collection of stories provides a type of reading material which is urgently needed—that is, easy reading material of adolescent reading interest but of intermediate-grade difficulty.

Many cases of reading disability are found among children who, although handicapped by neither physical nor mental defects, have for various reasons failed to develop adequate reading habits and skills. Often these children are as keenly interested in reading as are their more fortunate classmates, yet they are denied the pleasure of reading because of the difficulty of available materials. Among pupils of junior or senior high school age this problem becomes acute, and it is essential first to arouse an interest in reading, then through this interest to correct faulty habits and develop necessary skills.

The best means for arousing a desire for reading is an interesting book which can be read easily, because rapid progress, real enjoyment, and the consciousness of success are distinctly motivating and inspiring.

No grade level is prescribed for this volume. The main purpose of the book is to fit the pupil wherever he may be. The material of SIX GREAT STORIES has been adapted in such a way as to preserve the interest, plot, and style of the originals,* but at the same time to remove every obvious reading difficulty. In this manner the stories are made attractive and understandable to a host of pupils who would otherwise be unable to enjoy them.

*"Gareth and Lynette" is here adapted not from Malory's revision but from Tennyson's, and "As You Like It" is adapted from Lamb's version.

530

Concepts and vocabulary are definitely controlled in the interest of comprehension. Ninety-five per cent of the reading text is unlocked by a basic or core vocabulary of one thousand words. These words have been selected for their familiarity to modern children and their utility to the text. With a total vocabulary of approximately nineteen hundred words, SIX GREAT STORIES has a smaller vocabulary load than the average fourth-grade reader.

The treatment of the text, however, goes much further than the simplification of vocabulary. Every factor of reading difficulty has had careful consideration in the process of adaptation. Controlled experiments conducted by the editors proved that these stories in their revised form can be read independently and are enjoyed by seventh- and eighth-grade pupils of fourth-grade reading ability. Moreover, the stories in this form are often preferred to the original by junior-high pupils of average reading ability because the plots can be followed at a more normal reading tempo than when the process is retarded by a large percentage of words, idioms, and sentence patterns too difficult for any save adult readers.

We feel confident, therefore, that much can be accomplished in remedial work with slow readers if they are supplied with material of this kind which will satisfy their hunger not only for stories that appeal but also for a feeling of real achievement.

THE EDITORS

9 10 11 12 13 14 15 16 17 18 19 20 21 22 23 24 25   55 54 53 52 51 50 49 48